THE REVENGE AGENDA

Accidental Love

Book 3

SAXON JAMES

Content Warning

TW: sexual and physical assault

Author's Note

I hope you all enjoy The Revenge Agenda and adore both Rush and Hunter.

Writing diverse characters and ensuring people can feel seen with my books is a real passion of mine, especially when it comes to asexuality and people who are neurodiverse. Rush is my first character with *diagnosed* ADHD, but not the first I've written.

While I've written Rush as having ADHD, please know that this is only one experience and his character does not speak for everyone on the neurodivergent spectrum. There are many different ways to be human and his is only one of them.

I've utilized sensitivity readers and have worked hard to portray him as accurately as possible, so please remember that while his might not be *your* experience, it doesn't mean that others don't share his experiences so please keep discourse respectful.

Rush embraces his ADHD and sees it as a positive way of viewing the world, whereas I know that isn't the case for everyone. I also know that we're not all lucky enough to have a boss as levelheaded and accommodating as Ted. The one thing I specifically want to address is that while Rush struggles in his decisions whether to medicate or not, there are currently no evidence-based links between ADHD medications and a person's creativity. He is not anti-medication. He's still learning. Medication is always a valid option.

As with all of my books, The Revenge Agenda has been through a rigorous editing process, but ninja typos are thing! If you spot any, please don't use kindle's reporting feature as it can have author accounts flagged. If you're someone who likes to pass them on though, you're more than welcome to email: admin@saxonjamesauthor.com. This will ensure none of those pesky tweaks are missed with updates.

Thanks so much for reading!

Prologue

Rush

The office is silent, save only for the rapid tap of my fingers on the keyboard, the creak of my chair as it swings back and forth, and the hundred and one voices cluttering my head. I shouldn't even be working right now, but what would you know, I'm behind on everything, and the clawing in my chest is getting harder and harder to ignore the further behind I get.

So here I am, two days before Christmas, armed with a to-do list, a thermos of coffee, and every cell in my body begging me to stay on track.

I pick up my thermos and take a long gulp, mentally flicking through the Christmas gifts I've bought so far. I'm *sure* I've got everyone covered. I wrote a list. Checked it twice.

Fuck. What about Christian's husband? They're coming over for Christmas Eve, and how embarrassing if he shows up and I have *nothing*. Yeah, the guy's a millionaire, but it's the gesture. The feeling of inclusion …

My gaze catches on the coffee ring on my desk. Dammit. Last time I left a pattern of them behind, I walked in to find Eloise cleaning them for me. She has enough going on that she doesn't need that in her life again. I pull down my sleeve and wipe at it, but most of it has dried by now. Not surprising since I've been here … I'm scratching at the ring while I flip my phone over to check the time and—

Seven o'clock.

Like a Christmas tree lighting up in my mind, I jolt out of the seat. I'm fucking late.

Again.

He's going to goddamn kill me.

I grab my bag as I bolt from the office, motion-sensor lights in the ceiling flicking on as I pass them. Thank fucking god I packed my outfit before I left this morning because I can only imagine his face if I'd had to make a detour for that. It'd put me behind by *hours*. One of the good things about dating Ian is that he's as unpredictable as I am. I like that. Knowing that he forgets things—like my name or switching his phone on—and that he's as shy and anxious over meeting new people as I am. The one area where we differ, though, is that I'm notoriously always late, and he's a stickler for the time. It's like his life is planned down to minutes, and god forbid I overstay one of them.

But as someone with a laundry list's worth of "quirks," I'm not going to judge him for them.

I'm already half an hour late by the time I climb onto the cramped bus, but I'm hoping he can set his bitching aside so we can have a nice night together. He's away visiting family for the holidays and our one-year anniversary, so this is our only chance to see each other before then, and I have to remind that grumpy little gremlin in my chest that just because we've been together for so long doesn't mean he *had* to invite me to go with him. No. Family is a big step. And I'm

… well, it takes people a minute to warm up to me, and given this year my brain's been a scrambled mess since I stopped taking my meds, I can understand him wanting to take his time.

It's fine.

I just have to get organized.

Once I'm all caught up on work, I'll be able to make a schedule. Lists. Set time aside to design. Sew. Create.

What is that buzzing?

I can barely move between the commuters and people traveling home surrounded by shopping bags, but there's definitely a low hum I'm picking up on. Maybe a toy? Not a bee.

There's a tap on my shoulder. "Excuse me, but I think your bag is vibrating. You might have a call."

My … bag? But my phone's in my—

I pat my pocket, discovering my phone, in fact, isn't there. Not the back one either, which is odd because I sit on it so many times a day I'm going to end up with a phone-shaped imprint in my butt cheek … I frown, trying to picture the last time I had it. At the office? Did I pick it up? Shit. Maybe I didn't?

"Are you going to get it?" the woman behind me asks.

Get … it? Oh! The vibrating. So weird that I threw my phone in there, but I was in a hurry, and given I've found it in a Ziplock bag in the fridge before, I've proved it really can end up anywhere.

I lift my backpack and unzip it, plunging my hand inside to feel around the costume until …

My hand closes over something that is *definitely* not my phone.

But is *definitely* the thing causing the buzzing.

I scramble to find the button on the vibrating dildo and switch it off. Then I clear my throat and announce too loudly, "Must have hung up. Oh well!"

My whole face is burning, and I pray for the bus to drive faster. I want off already.

I crane my neck to look out the far window, trying to place how far away I am, when I catch sight of a two-story dark brick house with an elaborate white porch.

My shoulders slump. I've seen that building. Way too many times.

I hit the button, already exhausted over the thought of jogging back the two stops I've missed. I've also got my costume that I need to get changed into if I want to surprise him. At this point, I'm so late I shouldn't bother, but the thought of showing up in my work clothes, button-up damp with sweat stains over my panic at the time, makes me sad.

I want this to be special.

I want to surprise him.

Goddamn Ian deserves at least that.

He deserves a boyfriend who doesn't screw up every plan we have.

My mood is in danger of taking a dive when I shoulder my way past people to climb off the bus and into the cold night air. It freezes the anxious sweat at my hairline, and I take a long, deep breath of it, trying to ground myself so I can get through tonight.

First step is looking festive. Which means I need to find a place to change. Preferably close so I'm not running around the neighborhood in only a slutty outfit and an overcoat. I jog up the street, hoping for an alley or some bushes or—hey, I'd even take a kid's playhouse.

There's goddamn nothing, of course, and by the time I reach his street, I'm almost out of ideas. There are cars everywhere, a few of the houses lit up, probably with Christmas parties inside, and the last thing I want is someone looking out the window and seeing a strange man undressing in the dark.

I reach Ian's house, and the front living room light is on,

but the one around the side isn't, meaning the gap between the house and the fence is complete darkness.

Bingo.

This night isn't ruined, after all.

I glance around to make sure there's no one watching as I creep closer, then duck up the side. My heart is racing at the thought of a well-intending neighbor calling the police, so I move as fast as possible. I kick off my shoes, wriggle out of my pants, and scramble to get my buttons undone.

My balls have crept their way higher into my body to escape the cold, and I give the poor fuckers a pat, reminding them that soon Ian's mouth will be around them, and all of this will have been worth it.

The elf costume is a tight fit. Bright green, assless, with little gift boxes over my nipples that lift for a peek-a-boo effect, and a long candy cane pouch that I slip my dick into. My nipples are frozen and so stiff they're trying to escape the presents, but maybe he can warm those with his mouth too.

The thought of Ian opening the door and seeing me, the heat filling his gaze, his big arm sliding around my waist as he pulls me close and closes his mouth over my nipple, makes my cock stir.

Even in the cold, the little trooper is trying to rally.

And actually … it would look a lot more impressive if I'm hard. You can't suck on a floppy candy cane, can you?

I tug my overcoat on, then grab the dildo from my bag that I leave beside the house to grab later. Then I close my eyes, wrap my hand around my dick, and try to warm him up.

It doesn't take long. It never does with the prospect of being fucked by Ian. He's permanently horny, I swear, and he never misses an opportunity to take it out on my ass.

I'm hoping that with a whole night ahead of us, we can get the quick and dirty fuck out of the way bent over the couch by the door before we spend a long romantic night wrapped around each other.

My heavy exhale leaves a trail of white behind in the air.

It's going to be perfect.

I give my cock a few more tugs, making sure it looks irresistible, then go to check the time before remembering I don't have my phone on me.

There goes the idea of texting him to come to the door.

Oh well. I can work with this.

I'm probably only an hour late. That's nothing. Still plenty of time for us to be together.

I reach the front door, excited nerves bouncing around in my chest. Then I knock.

There's silence for a moment before I make out footsteps.

"Special delivery for Ian!" I call as the door's tugged open.

Light floods out onto the porch as I open my coat and watch Ian's eyes fly wide. His jaw actually drops, and *oh yeah, I'm getting it good tonight.*

"Sorry I'm late, baby," I rasp in my sexiest voice. "But I brought you a gift." I hold up the candy-striped dildo and hit the button to turn it on. "Which candy do you want to suck on first?"

But instead of his answer, a different voice cuts through the steady buzzing.

"What the *fuck* is going on?"

____

Chapter 1

____

Hunter

It takes me an embarrassingly long time to figure out what the hell is going on. On the one hand, my immediate thought is that Ian got us a pretty guy to play with for Christmas, but on the other—

"Hunter, who is that?" Mom hisses.

My entire family is here.

Pretty boy turns to take in the room, and his face goes from flirty to downright horrified. "I mixed up the days, didn't I?"

And that's when it hits me.

Really hits me.

"I … who are you?" Ian splutters. "Get away from my house, you creep."

He slams the front door, turning back to the room, ugly Christmas sweater blinking Rudolph's nose at us. "I'm so sorry. It used to be a safe street."

He fixes us with his twenty-thousand-dollar smile, but the

room doesn't shift. The tension only creeps higher and higher, tightening around me. I don't know if anyone else can feel it, but I'm choking on the dawning realization that man *knew* him. That man dressed up sexy and *knew* my guy. *Knew* where he lived, his name, called him *baby*.

I cross my arms over my chest, indignation boiling in my gut. "Who was that?"

Ian blinks at me like he's surprised I'm even asking. "I said I have no idea."

"He knew who you were."

"I'm in *real estate*. Everyone knows who I am."

My jaw tics. "That's how we're playing it, huh?"

"*Playing* it?"

"Just gonna pretend you don't know the half-naked man who showed up asking you to suck on his lollipop?"

"Actually, it was a candy cane," my sister, Audrey, says, sounding bored.

Ian waves her off. "If I had a dollar for every overeager, thirsty twink who showed his face around here, I'd be richer than I already am. I'm sorry you had to find out the hard way, but now you've moved here, I'll bet he won't be the only man overstepping boundaries."

Not … the only one? My heart clenches. "So how many are there?"

For the first time, my voice inches higher. I might be able to control my emotions most of the time, might be good at smothering down my anger, but this? This is testing me.

"Wait …" Ian looks around like he's trying to figure out if he's in on some kind of joke. "You don't actually think I knew that guy."

"That's exactly what I think, yeah."

Audrey lets out an amused snort. I shoot her a look to cut it out.

Then I ask a question I almost can't get out. "Are you cheating on me?"

"Baby …"

"Nope. That name is off the table."

He tries for a confident laugh that sounds weak. "You can't possibly think that."

"Well, I didn't until a random man showed up at the door expecting sex."

"You're pinning this on me? What am I supposed to do? Control every man in the neighborhood?"

"Not sticking your dick in any of them would be a good start."

Ian scoffs, throwing his hands up. "How much have you had to drink? You're being unreasonable."

"*Excuse* me," Dad cuts in. "You have some explaining to do."

"I've explained. I don't know who that man is. Do you really think I'd mess around with someone like *that* when I have Hunter?" Ian's words are coming faster. "Baby—"

"Don't."

"I love you. Only you. You have to believe me."

"I *have* to?"

"Oh, come on. We've been together for years. You moved here to be with me. We're *engaged*."

I look from Ian's pleading expression to my parents and sister. Dad looks ready to murder him, Mom's face is pinched like she might cry, and Audrey has gone back to her phone like my entire life isn't falling apart.

I just … I don't think I'm processing anything, mind flopping along like soggy toast.

I did move here. Three hours from where I grew up. I left my job, my friends, my family. For what? A man I thought was my future.

And where the rage and betrayal are struggling to come

alive, embarrassment rears up instead. *How the fuck was I so stupid?*

"How could you do this to me?"

"I haven't *done* anything. You're not listening!"

"Somebody's gaslighting," Audrey sings.

"That's not even a thing."

"Don't snap at my sister."

"Then tell her to keep out of it."

I snarl, struggling to keep everything pushed down. "Think of your answer carefully: have you cheated on me?"

"No."

"Right." I take off out of the house. The cold air hits me smack in the face, but I push through and jog down the steps on the front porch. My heart is hammering, and I'm struggling to hold on to my sanity as I think I really might be sick. This is the absolute last thing I want to be doing, but not having answers will kill me. Eat at me. Maybe he's telling the truth, and maybe he's lying. I have to find out either way.

I look up and down the dark street for the guy, hoping he hasn't gotten into his car and taken off. Loud cheers come from some Christmas party happening across the road, and it makes me want to throw something. I'd been so excited to live here. Like a real proper grown-up. Management job. Successful husband. Pretty street to raise a family.

And now all that's slipping away from me because of some *ho, ho, ho.*

My sense of humor is the only thing stopping me from completely losing my shit.

Movement down the block catches my eye, and as soon as I peg the coat, relief and nausea fill me. I jog down the pavement toward him, and when I'm a few feet away, he glances up, and I swear he looks as sick as I feel.

"Who the hell are you?"

"R-Rush."

"That's a stupid fucking name."

"Who are you?"

Hearing his pathetic voice has made this so much worse. I want to punch him. Shake him. Tell him exactly what I think of the type of person willing to sleep with a taken man.

"Are you sleeping with him?"

Rush's bottom lip trembles, and he sinks further into his coat.

"I'll take that as a yes."

"Are *you*?" he asks.

I'm taken aback by the actual fucking audacity. "Considering we've been together five years and just got engaged, I'd say that's a yes."

His mouth drops. "Engaged?"

"Sorry, sweetheart. Whatever he was telling you, he had no plans to leave me. You were his piece on the side."

My words aren't anywhere near as harsh as I want them to be, but Rush bursts into tears anyway. He's trembling all over, and at first, I think it's because he's been caught, but the more I eye the way he's hugging his coat around him, frosted breaths leaving sporadic bursts of white, legs and feet bare, I realize he must be freezing.

The last thing I want to feel for my fiancé's whore is sympathy, but it hits anyway.

"Why aren't you wearing clothes?" I grit out.

"I-I left my bag," he sobs. "I was waiting for you all to leave so I could go and get it."

"And fuck my future husband again?" I snap.

He sinks to the footpath, sobs shaking his body. Wow, Ian really knows how to pick them. This guy is falling apart and not even trying to hide it, when if anyone should be upset, it's *me*. *I'm* the one they fucked over. *I'm* the one they've been sneaking around on.

How dare this guy make me feel sorry for *him*?

My jaw clenches as his teeth audibly clack together. Was he really planning on standing out here and freezing because he didn't want to go back for his bag? Is pneumonia on his Christmas list?

"Jesus fuck," I mutter, shrugging out of my coat. Then I lean down and wrap it around his shoulders.

His sobs cut off, and when he looks up, the tears on his cheeks catch the light from above us. He blinks, eyes wide and vulnerable. "Th-thank you."

I hate everything about him.

"Don't." I storm back to the house, find his bag tucked around the side, and then head back down the street. He watches me the whole time, my coat pulled tight around him.

Once I'm close enough, I toss the bag at his feet. "Now, go home."

"There are no buses," he whispers.

"Call a ride. I don't care."

"I ... I forgot my phone."

Holy shit, now *I* might cry. I pinch the bridge of my nose as I really struggle to pull myself together. The fact Ian cheated on me hurts like a motherfucker, but knowing it was with *this* guy? *This* guy, who Darwinism should have caught up with a long time ago?

I should turn and head back inside. Let Ian take care of his side piece.

And yet, I pull out my phone anyway.

"Address?"

Rush blinks at me. "What?"

"What's your fucking address?"

He gives it, and I punch the destination into the app.

"Someone will be here in five."

Rush studies my face with unnervingly hazel eyes. "Why are you being so nice to me?"

"This isn't nice. I just don't want you to die. Which you will if you stay out here half-naked for the rest of the night."

He sighs and looks away, lip trembling again. "It was a surprise for our one-year anniversary."

"Your … what?" Dread passes over me. *"Anniversary? You've been fucking him for a year?"*

Rush's mouth drops, but I've all but forgotten about him as I storm back to the house. All those phone calls, all those messages, all those moments where he missed me and wanted me and couldn't wait for me to move here.

All.

Bullshit.

My jaw hurts so badly by the time I reach the house that I'm not sure I'm going to be able to get words out. I'm not so sure I won't punch him in the fucking face for all my family to witness. I'm not a violent guy, but turns out being betrayed and humiliated for an *entire year* will do that.

I throw open the front door and tug off my ring as I cross toward him. Then I flick it at his face.

"Wedding's off, asshole. Hope you and Rush have a fantastic anniversary."

Ian's mouth drops. "Whatever he told you, it's all a lie. He's been stalking me. Obsessed with me."

I laugh and pull out my phone, which is still open on the ride share app, showing the car pulling up out front.

I click out of it and type in 911.

"Call the police, then. File a report. We've got his address, right there."

Panic crosses Ian's face, and I know I've got him.

"That's what I thought." I turn to Audrey. "I'm staying with you tonight."

"I thought I'd outgrown sharing a bed with you."

"Please, wait," Ian snaps. "We need to talk. You can't leave."

I go to grab my coat before remembering I don't have it anymore. Well, fuck. It was an expensive one too.

"Can and will. We're done. I hope you have a merry fucking Christmas."

Then I turn and leave, my family following behind me.

Chapter 2

Rush

Tears keep dribbling down my cheeks the whole drive home. I've got one hand clenched tight around my backpack and the other stuffed inside the coat, trying to warm up.

My thoughts are flying. Zipping through my head is every moment with Ian, every word, every I love you, every shared vulnerability whispered in the dark. And sure, most of those vulnerabilities were mine, but he shared too, and now I have no clue whether the things he told me were real or a lie.

I guess it makes sense now why he called me *Hunter* that one time.

Pain shatters through my chest.

I'm lost, confused about what even is happening and how my perfect relationship could be ripped away so easily. But the bitterness is creeping in too. The reminder that his forgetfulness was *just like me*, that his *scatteredness*, his *quirks*, the reason he couldn't get a promotion …

"It's like we're made for each other, Rush. No one understands me like you do."

That. Fucker. I bet he doesn't have ADHD at all. I bet that's why he's always chronically on time for everything. I mean, the guy makes a plan for the day, and he … does it! No issues. No detours. No fun breaks. His socks are always matching and in the same place, for fuck's sake.

I should have seen right through him from the start.

I'd been so swept up in having someone who finally understood, on an actual level, not an *oh, I saw a video about that* level.

With a grunt, I curl forward, pressing my palm to my eye socket to try and hold back the tears. He doesn't deserve them, and maybe they're not even completely for him, but it *hurts.* The way my heart's burning shouldn't be normal, and hey, maybe I'll take a page out of my roommate Xander's book and be having a heart attack instead.

I laugh morbidly at the thought of being rushed to the hospital and having him turn up at my bed apologizing. It's embarrassing how much I want that. How much I need to see him. Talk to him. Ask him *why.*

The coat sitting on top of mine slips a little, and I tug it back up again. Which only makes me feel worse. It's a fucking nice coat. Soft. Warmer than mine. Makes sense since Hunter was hotter than me too. Taller. Bigger muscles. Squarer jaw.

He made me feel like a dumb kid.

And a horrible person. I'll never forget the torn-up look on his face.

Engaged?

The stupid tears hit again, and I wish this was one of those times I could quickly forget everything, but the sickly feeling infecting me is making it hard to move on. I feel like my whole chest has been opened up and I can't put it back together again.

The driver pulls up out the front of my house. "You okay?" he asks.

I nod numbly and stagger out of the car. I'm trying to pull it together, trying to mask the way I'm unraveling, but that ship has long since sailed because the second I step through the front door and spot my best friend and roommate Madden, I lose it.

I'm sobbing like I haven't in a long time.

"Whoa, Rush …" Madden closes the distance between us and pulls me into a hug. His bare shoulder is warm from the heat, and I bury my face into it, letting myself fall apart.

He holds me together until I'm done.

"Not that I don't love this impromptu snuggle session, but being dick out is usually my thing." As a nudist or naturalist or whatever the hell he wants to call it, he's right. He pulls back so he can study my face. "What happened?"

I'm torn on which thread to pick at first.

He lied. Cheated. On me? With me? Made me feel wonderful and then horrible. Called me names. Threw me out on the street. Made me face his fiancé. Freeze. No phone. No bag. No shoes.

I hiccup a sob. "He has a Hunter."

"A …" Madden shakes his head and then shouts, "Bertha, assemble!"

I jump. "Excuse me?"

"Trying something new."

"Interesting. Maybe try not to scare the shit out of me next time."

"What the truck was that?" Seven growls, thundering down the stairs.

"Rush needs us."

His footsteps pause, and I glance over at him. His red hair is a mess, and he's *also* shirtless, but unlike Madden, Seven's wearing black sweatpants riding low on his hips. "Whiskey time?" he asks.

I try not to pout. "I need to cry. And throw up. And then maybe cry some more."

"Jesus. Whiskey, it is."

Madden steers me over to the couch, and I collapse onto it. Molly and Xander join us, and Xander drops to his knees in front of me, crossing his arms over my thighs.

"Are you dying?"

"I wish I was."

"It doesn't feel nice, you know."

Seven whacks him gently over the back of the head when he reappears with a bottle of whiskey tucked under his arm and a large bag of candy in both hands. "You've never died."

"I almost have."

"Not almost. Not even close to almost."

Molly reaches over to smooth Xander's blue hair down. "Don't listen to him, baby. Your life is very dramatic."

Xander preens, and Madden clears his throat. "Can we get back to Rush now? Why the hell are you dressed like an elf?"

"It's Christmas."

"Yeah, but you don't see any of us in slutty festive wear."

"I've been called that enough tonight, thank you."

Silence ripples over them, which is a real feat, considering my roommates are never quiet. Seven opens the whiskey and has a long drink before handing the bottle to me, and I copy him, cringing as the liquid burns my throat.

Then I look at the floor and say the words that are all too familiar to me. "I'm such an idiot."

That earns me a swat to the skull. "Try again," Seven warns.

"My brain cells are limited enough as it is, thanks," I say, rubbing my head. "Why are you being mean?"

"Dude, you're sitting here dramatically falling apart, and I'm just waiting to find out who I gotta kill. What happened?"

"He … he cheated."

"That creep!" Molly flies to his feet. "Seven, get the car. Where does this guy live? I'll kill them both!"

I shake my head. "He cheated on me with his fiancé."

"Fiancé?"

I glance up at Xander's small voice and find him looking at me. I'm too vulnerable to meet his eyes, but the split second of sympathy is enough. "They threw me out. I was so excited for our anniversary, and we were supposed to spend the whole night together, but I must have mixed up the days, or he mixed up the days, and there were all these people there *staring*. I didn't have my phone, and it was cold, and—"

"Well, that explains why you didn't answer when I called," Madden says. "Stop for a second. Who threw you out?"

"Ian. And he said some nasty things."

"And who else was there?"

"Hunter. He gave me a coat and ordered me a car."

Seven and Madden exchange a look. "Who's Hunter?"

"Ian's fiancé."

"Huh." Madden laughs. "All I would have given you is a black eye."

"Yeah … that was strangely nice of him." Molly wrinkles his nose.

"He said he wanted me gone."

"Tell me you didn't try to stay?"

"Of course not. I went down the street. Then I remembered my bag, and so of course, I couldn't go back and get it in case they saw me, and so I was waiting for them to fall asleep, but it was so cold, and then Hunter was there with my things and making me warm and ordering me a ride."

"I promise you that if I ever found some hussy sniffing around Seven, I would not be compassionate. At all." Molly hesitates. "My default is to hate Hunter and hate Ian and ride out to defend your honor, but that actually sounds like a decent thing to do."

I dump the coat off me because unlike Molly, I'm more than capable of irrational hatred. It has nothing to do with him. And I appreciate what he did for me, but I'm going to be mad at him anyway. He was mad at *me*, so there's no reason for me to feel guilty either.

"It's Burberry." Xander smothers his face with it. "Gah, he smells so good. This is coming to bed with me tonight."

"Great. My boyfriend's fiancé smells good. I'm so glad."

Xander pulls a face and dumps the coat to the side. "Did I say good? I mean bad. Sooo bad. Dude has a serious case of BO."

I sigh because he really doesn't. I've been surrounded by that scent for the last half an hour. Ian gets to be surrounded by that scent for the rest of his life. Stretched out in his bed, sheets bunched around his waist while he scrolls through his phone. Just relaxed in that expensive cologne … "I already miss him."

I'm swamped in a group hug, like we used to do for Christian when he had his bad days. He's been home for a month now and hasn't needed a blanket burrito once, so apparently, getting married makes you an emotionally stable life form.

Unless you're Ian—then it makes you an epic douchebag who hurts people's hearts for no reason. I can see him and Hunter together, both of them so pretty and successful and stable. The way Hunter stared me down was unnervingly steady, like the only thing in his mind was me, and if Ian wants to be with someone like that, he can go nuts! Sounds boring, but okay.

"I bet they have pretty sex."

"We're not thinking about that," Madden says, nudging the bottle back my way.

"I bet *everyone* has pretty sex. Except me," Xander grumbles.

"What else am I supposed to think about?"

"What about your things?" Madden asks.

"What do you mean?"

"Well, you'll need to go get them. Do you feel up to that, or do you want one of us to go?"

I'm not following. "Get them ..."

"Unless you're planning on leaving them there?"

It takes an embarrassingly long time for it to sink in. I would need to pick up my stuff ... because he's not my boyfriend anymore. He probably never was. I can't go over there and yell at him and try to sort it out because he has an actual partner who he's committed to, and I was ... just another person to have sex with.

I clear my throat, gaze planted firmly in my lap. "He doesn't have anything of mine. He was always careful about that."

Neat freak, my ass. There was no compulsion to keep everything in order; he just didn't want Hunter to find anything of mine. All the traits and qualities and moments I thought we were really connecting ... lies.

All lies.

It's a battle in my head trying to sort them all out. Motivations are hard for me, and I've always been too trusting. If someone tells me something, I believe it. It's who I am.

It's exhausting to have my brain wired so differently from everyone else's. They all speak this language I'm still trying to learn, but even after twenty-eight years, I'm not fluent. I forget to be careful. Forget to interpret.

I'd felt safe with him.

I was just an easy target.

"I hate this guy so fucking much," Molly whispers.

I only wish I did too.

Chapter 3

Hunter

One month later

The need to run back to Portland hasn't completely left me. Trying to find a rental over the holiday period was icing on top of the shit sandwich that is Seattle, and bouncing between questionable-looking motels and hotels really put a damper on my first two weeks here.

Mom and Dad begged me to come home. Audrey even went so far as to tell me I could stay with her until I found another apartment, but if I have to hear her say, "Just because he's good for your hole, doesn't mean he's good for your soul," one more time, I'll probably smother her.

The fact is, moving home feels like failure.

I'm not ready to face all my friends and family and tell them that I moved all this way for some deadbeat. There's also the little voice in my heart hoping said deadbeat will come crawling back.

He tried. For about a week. Then it's been radio silence ever since.

It's not that I want to get back together with Ian—the trust is well and truly shattered—but it would be nice to know that I was worth something. Worth fighting for.

Not just the idiot who was easy to string along.

A spike of anger shoots through me as I climb into my car. What the hell was his plan? Did he really think he could keep fucking around behind my back and get away with it after I moved here? And how many others were there? Not having the answer to these questions is torturing me.

It's time to move on. Just let it go. I'm back at work today, and the salary and benefits this place is offering is a huge step up from the place I was working at in Portland, which was another reason I was reluctant to head home. Department head is something I've been aiming toward for years, but I was going to fossilize in my wait for something to come available. Insurance isn't the most exciting career path, but it pays the bills.

So I'm giving myself the fresh start I'd planned for … without the man.

It stings a lot like failure, but I'm trying not to let it bother me.

Who knows? Maybe there are other men in Seattle who I won't want to punch in the face. Given Ian and Rush are the only two I've met so far beyond servers and baristas and the trainers at the gym, it doesn't look promising, but at least I know there'll be plenty to fuck around with at least.

That might be all this city is good for, and I'll end up running back home in a year. Where the men in Portland really aren't that much better.

The morning commute is different from what I'm used to.

Still busy. Still frustrating, but the view out my window gives me something new to look at. Especially when I take a wrong turn that sends me ten minutes in the opposite direction before I can turn around again.

Luckily, I've given myself plenty of time because there's no way in hell I'm turning up late on my first day.

Or ever.

I turn up the radio as I drive, adjusting to the unfamiliar voices, and when the music kicks in, I try to channel the energy, try to get motivated and pumped up for the day. I'll meet my supervisor first and then my team. And sure, I have expectations and standards I want them to meet, but they're not unreasonable. Be on time. Meet deadlines. Hit goals. That's it. If they want to fuck around and chat and take personal days, that's all cool with me. So long as they do their jobs. My people are adults, and I'll treat them that way as long as they don't cause me headaches.

The traffic spits me out downtown, in a sleek glass building. We're on the third floor, which will mean no view of anything but more glass, but I'm oddly excited.

Checking in at the foyer, Ted meets me with a firm handshake and friendly smile. The morning is a blur of orientation and getting my access pass. A morning coffee break with the other department heads followed by a quick meeting and rundown. I'm turned around and have no idea which direction my office is in and where Ted sits, and even where my team are, but I don't care.

I love this.

The office is alive with energy, the hub of productivity giving me that deep feeling of purpose. It's the first time in over a month where I don't want to fall into bed and live there.

"Courtney," the woman next to me says, holding out her hand. She's close to my age, maybe a little older than thirty, and she's one of those people who looks like they're always smiling.

"Hunter."

"Welcome to the team," she says. "That's what I'm supposed to say, isn't it?"

"I'd say it's the standard scripting, given that's what everyone else has said to me."

"Not a very original bunch, are we?"

"Yeah, but there's something comforting about predictability." I spare a smile.

"How are you liking Seattle?"

That's not a question I have an answer for. "Still too new to know, I think."

"Well, get your man to take you to the Space Needle. It's very touristy, but—"

My heart sinks. "Ah, actually. We broke up."

Courtney does a double take. I expect everyone was told I moved here to be with my partner, and now I get to be the one to correct that story. "I'm so sorry."

"I'm not. Turns out he wasn't who I thought he was."

She clearly doesn't know what to say to that, and thankfully, she's saved from commenting by Ted.

"Want to come and meet your team?" he asks.

"Yes, of course."

I say goodbye to the other department heads and follow Ted out into the bullpen. It's got good energy here, which is a relief, and I hope like hell it's not as much of a dud as the rest of my experience in Seattle so far.

Ted pauses by a pod of four desks. "Team, this is Hunter Barrett. He's your new department head. Hunter, this is Eloise, Gates, Autumn, and—oh." Ted looks around. "I swear Carey was here a moment ago."

I glance over toward the empty desk that's cluttered with an assortment of drinks and paper.

"Lunch." Autumn almost shouts it. "He went on his break. He'll be back, uh, soon."

I quirk an amused eyebrow her way.

Ted laughs. "One thing you'll learn about Carey: he's a fantastic fellow, but he's never where you need him to be."

Great. Somehow, I can already tell that Carey and I are going to have issues.

Chapter 4

Rush

Well, my career is over. I've become rather fond of my "boring office job" as Christian calls it, and now I might as well pack up my desk and skip out the door. The desk that I'm currently huddled under, ass going numb.

Goodbye, Gates's smelly feet.

Goodbye, sensor lights that keep me company when everyone else has gone home.

Goodbye, Sandra and her wild weekend escapades.

I'll even miss that stupid spray thingy in the men's bathroom that scares the shit out of me every time it goes off.

The pointy toe of Autumn's shoe nudges me, and I swat her away. Then the second one comes at me. It's a full-on assault as she tries to drive me from my hiding place, and I karate chop her hideous flats.

No number of potential bruises or bloody noses are going to get me out of here.

Not with Hunter, *the Hunter*, standing just by me.

He talks again, and Autumn quickly stills.

"I'm so happy to be here. We'll have to organize some one-on-one time so I can get to know you all properly," he says in a ridiculously deep timbre. Of course he looks like Hercules and sounds like Zeus and smells like a goddamn cloud.

Probably fucks like whoever the god of sex is too.

"If no one has plans tonight though, I'd love to take you all out for after-work drinks."

Nope, nope, nope. I stifle my huff and struggle my phone from my pocket, trying to make sure I don't octopus all over the place and make a sound.

I open the Bertha Boys chat and type:

> SOS. The Hunter is here!

Responses come through immediately.

MOLLY:

> Where?

SEVEN:

> Need backup?

XANDER:

> You're being HUNTED?!

I didn't doubt for one single second that they'd be there for me.

I *did*, however, forget that my phone is not on silent.

With every message comes an obnoxiously loud *beep*.

"Ah!" I hurry to switch the sound off, drop my phone as it goes off again, and when I finally get a good grip, I power the whole thing down.

I'm panting, holding it to my chest as my eyes fall closed,

and I try to get my heart rate back under control. I work a menial job because I don't need any more excitement in my life and—

A harsh throat clearing makes my eyes fly open again.

To the sight of Hunter, leaning down and peering under my desk. He looks like I've slapped him, and I can't imagine my expression looks much better.

"*Rush?*"

"Umm … hello." I crawl out and pull myself up with all the dignity of a two-year-old learning to walk. Ted is standing behind Hunter, looking torn between asking what the hell I'm doing and laughing. Honestly, that's basically my default for dealing with life.

"So good to see you again," I manage weakly. But all I can see is a cold night and his darkened features and the feeling of absolute dread sweeping through me. The messages from Ian since then burn in my pocket.

They broke up.

He still wants me.

It was only ever *me*.

Yet Hunter looks at me like *I'm* the bad guy.

"Do you know each other?" Ted asks.

I go to say yes, but Hunter gets there first.

"Barely." His expression has slipped back into a tense mask.

"Well, this is Carey," Ted says, trying to get us out of this weirdness. "Carey, this is Hunter, your department head."

"Ah, yes. I got that."

Hunter's jaw tics. "If you're done playing hide-and-seek, maybe you could get to work cleaning up your cluttered desk."

Cluttered? I turn to look at my workstation, trying to see if anything is out of place. I've got the usual reminder Post-its around my screen, a bottle of water for hydration, half-finished coffee for brains, and emotional support peach iced tea for a boost. My "later" pile is in place, desk calendar tucked away under my keyboard, and noise-canceling headphones sitting right beside them.

Maybe that's the problem.

I should probably put them away when I'm not using them. So I do.

"Better?"

He scowls. "What about the trash? The food?" He points at my line of carefully placed M&Ms.

"They're my reminders."

"What?"

"I have ten jobs to do today," I explain patiently, like I haven't had to run this through with every second person in the office. "For each job, I eat an M&M. If there's still any left over when I'm done, it means I've forgotten something."

"Or you've forgotten to eat one."

I try to work out if he's joking. "They're chocolate. You don't forget to eat chocolate."

Hunter's eyes inch narrower. "Is this some kind of hazing of the new guy?"

"Rush is, uh, *eccentric*," Autumn cuts in.

I frown at her. "I'm not eccentric. *You're* eccentric."

"I'm not the one with a line of candy on my desk."

I give her a pointed look. "Exactly."

"Why can't you use a list?" Hunter asks. "Or anything that won't attract ants?"

"Do you know that ants are arguably one of the most intelligent insects? If I see one, I simply move it before it gets a chance to notify the rest of the worker ants. I always worry the poor things won't find their way back to the colony, but I figure the trash outside is as kind a place to put it as any." They're not going to worry about my M&Ms if they have a full food source available for them. The guilt kills me though. Could you imagine their mothers being all, "Anton went out to work and never came home"? Poor things. "Imagine if ants had little mini funerals? And little mini bow ties?" I snigger over the thought, making a mental note for Molly to draw something up for me later.

Hunter doesn't answer, and his long silence confirms my suspicions. Poor guy is neurotypical. I bet he's never looked up ants once in his life.

"Never mind," I say, sparing him the embarrassment for his lack of knowledge. "I'll get back to work, then, shall I?"

I drop into my chair and wake my computer up, inspecting the candies on my desk. There are only eight left. Which means I've done two jobs and have a suspicious feeling that I was about to complete one more. Or had I already completed it when I spotted Hunter and threw myself on the floor?

"I'll see you all tonight," Hunter says stiffly, and his abrupt voice behind me makes me jump. He stalks off, Ted following behind him, and I eye his suit, sure it's as fancy as the coat that Xander smuggled from me.

I lean over toward Autumn. "What's tonight?"

"Drinks. And you're coming because I know you never have plans, and if you do, you've already forgotten about them."

I sink into my chair. "I have Monopoly Monday—"

"It's Tuesday."

It *is*? I check the calendar on my computer, and it turns out she's right. Well, fuck. There goes that excuse.

"Well, I … there must be something …"

"What's going on with you? I'm sensing vibes."

That is *not* something I want to get into with her. "Bold of you to think I ever know what's going on."

Only this time, I do, and I'm totally lying, but what are my options? Tell her the guy I thought I was falling for was only using me to cheat on his fiancé? That the same guy has been messaging me nonstop and it's a real struggle not to reply? And his ex-fiancé is now currently my boss, who's probably going to make life difficult and tell the whole office that I slept with his ex?

I'll have to quit. And leave Seattle. I have no family, a shitty employment history, and no savings to my name. Dear fucking god, I'm going to wind up homeless. I don't even have a car to sleep in.

I've gotten myself into some tricky situations in my life, but this one really takes the cake.

I wonder if there's something in my contract to say I can be fired without notice if I'm a total, total ho bag?

Even unintentionally.

I'm still kicking myself that I didn't see the signs. That I got so swept up in Ian and our relationship and forgot to make myself focus and see it for what it was. I'm naive. Easy to take advantage of. Madden always worries about it, but I don't know how to be any other way. If someone tells me something, how am I supposed to *know* they're lying? How do people pick up on that?

I sigh, taking a sip of my cooled coffee, and follow it up with an M&M. I know for a fact I can't go to drinks tonight. I just can't. But telling everyone the real reason or making up an excuse is more effort than stopping by, having a quick drink, and then leaving again.

Though I am notorious for always forgetting about things, so it wouldn't be out of character for me to accidentally-on-purpose forget. Hell, I might *actually* forget. That would be convenient.

Though how I'm supposed to forget his judgmental gaze burning into me and the looming threat of having to face him every day, I'll never know.

If I go, it might be a chance to clear the air. Maybe I'll be able to pull him to the side and explain. Get him to stop hating me. Make it clear that I never knew.

Yes.

That's a plan.

Not one I feel great about, but we'll see what happens.

Would it be too dramatic to cut off my leg instead?

Chapter 5

Hunter

All day, I'm tempted to hand in my notice. This has to be a sign, right? Apparently, all the other ones since I got to Seattle weren't enough, so this is one last kick to get me out the door.

And I'm still not leaving.

I've got a stubborn streak in me a mile deep, and I can't shake the feeling that if I flee, Rush wins.

At least that's what I'm telling myself because it's easier to face than that tiny seed digging in behind my sternum, reminding me I can't get anything right. It's a lie. I know that. But it still hits deep.

I couldn't get that promotion.

I couldn't hold down my fiancé.

I can't even start the first day here off right with my team.

Instead, I look like an idiot who can't hold down a fucking conversation.

I'd always told myself I'd be a good boss. An easy one. I

wouldn't ride my employees and make them hate coming to work, but even after a few hours here, I'm the one who hates it.

Because my office looks out onto the bullpen, and I have a direct line of sight to Rush's desk. I either glance up directly toward him or put so much effort into not looking at him that an ache is building behind my eyeballs. Going back to the hotel and crawling under the covers seems like the perfect way to put an end to this nightmare, but I couldn't even get that right.

I *had* to invite them out for drinks.

Instead of canceling like any sane fucking person would do, I set up a group chat for my team on the work server and fire off an invite to have *a* drink after work while we get to know each other.

Then I try to remind myself that I'm *not* nervous as I plow through my remaining work for the day and forget the drinks are even happening.

Five thirty creeps up on me, and I purposely hang back as my team goes on ahead. I've reviewed their files, know that they're all meeting the majority of their goals. Apparently, Rush's candy trick must work for him … somehow.

I squash down the little nugget of guilt at how I spoke to him earlier and remind myself he's the kind of man who deserves it. He was my fiancé's man on the side for a year. A fucking year.

I reach for some of the embarrassed fury that comes so easily to me.

Did they snuggle in bed, laughing over how stupid I am?

Did Ian ever tell Rush he was better than me? *Is* he better than me?

Why the *hell* did he do it?

I groan, scuffling my hands through my hair, hating that my thoughts have cycled back to the same repetitive loop. This was supposed to be a fresh start, dammit.

All I need is to let the resentment go. Somehow, Rush has

the lowest mistake percentages on his paperwork, usually has everything in on time, and the customers love him. I need to be a professional about this. Detached. He's a different person at work, and I can hate him behind closed doors.

Releasing a long breath, I pull on my jacket, fix my hair in my phone camera, then head to the bar down the block.

Ted told me Urban Dive is a busy place in the afternoons because people from all the local businesses meet up there before heading home. If we're doing one drink, then surely I can cut things off in half an hour; there's no reason for us to be there all night. I'm their boss, not their friend, after all. I want to break the ice and make sure we're all comfortable with each other before I have to come in and manage them.

Ted was right about the bar. It's full of people in suits when I step inside and probably feels busier than it is because it's so small. It's fully wood, with greenery and hanging string bulbs over the bar area, so many voices mixing together I can't make out the music coming from the speakers.

It takes me a minute to spot Gates and Autumn hugging a small table near the bar.

Come on, Hunter. You're good with people. You only need to make it through half an hour.

I glance around again as I cross toward them and spot Eloise at the bar. She's alone, and even as I search, I don't spot any more familiar faces.

The knot in my gut lessens.

It looks like Rush chose not to come.

It makes it easier to breathe and smile when I reach my team at the same time as Eloise does. She hands over a beer with a shrug. "I took a wild guess."

"Any beer works after a long day, thank you. Though, as the boss, I should be treating all of you."

Gates laughs. "Think of it as a welcome gift."

"And you can get the next round," Autumn adds.

Next … round? I open my mouth to let them know I can't stay long when I'm cut off from answering by someone colliding with my back. I stumble forward, knocking into the table and sending drinks sloshing over the sides of the glasses. Somehow, my beer stays in my hand … and also all down the front of me.

"Fuck." I shake my free hand out and turn to find Rush standing there, mouth hanging open and hands in the air.

"I'm so sorry," he rasps.

Autumn giggles. "Believe it or not, this isn't the first time that's happened." She reaches over and pulls Rush to the table. "Maybe if you were on time and concentrating, you wouldn't always get yourself into these messes."

The shock slips from Rush's face as he scowls. "I maintain society's obsession with time is unhealthy."

I set my drink down as they bicker and swipe at the front of my shirt. Thankfully, it looks as though I wasn't covered in as much as I thought I was, and while the wet spot over my stomach is uncomfortable, that's the worst of it.

"Well, we tried to give you a good welcome," Eloise says. She's wearing dark red lipstick, black-framed glasses, and is absolutely stunning, considering she has four kids. Aren't kids supposed to, I dunno, turn you into a haggard, sleep-deprived troll? Clearly, I have a lot of experience.

"Just an accident," I say tightly, willing myself to believe it. I might not like Rush, but even someone like him wouldn't do that on purpose. At least that's what I want to believe.

"Tell us about you, boss," Gates says. "Who's our fearless leader?"

"No one special." I manage a smile. "As Ted said, I'm Hunter Barrett. I was first in line for a promotion in Portland with WCX that was never coming. So when this position came up, I applied, interviewed, and …" I pick up my beer again and take a sip.

"Didn't you move here to be with your partner?" Autumn asks.

My molars almost crack, and it takes all my willpower not to throw a glare Rush's way. "It didn't work out."

"Oh, I'm so sorry," she says, and it sounds genuine, at least. But then she keeps talking. "Though, you never know. Rush and his boyfriend just broke up, but someone wants someone baaack ..." Autumn nudges him in a teasing way, and it takes me an embarrassingly long time to put together what she means.

"No, he doesn't!" Rush hurries to say.

Autumn snorts. "*Please.* I saw Ian blowing up your phone today. He wants you bad."

Ian.

Messaging Rush.

When that *fuckface* broke all contact between us.

Huh. Well. I guess it goes to show that he didn't want me that much after all.

Did they even break up? Or was it all a lie they're telling people so it doesn't look like Ian has jumped into another relationship again so soon?

So he doesn't look like an asshole.

A cheater.

Will he propose to Rush too?

Fuck this. I thought I could do it, but I can't.

I down the rest of my beer and slam it too hard on the table. "I need the bathroom."

Then, while I'm there, I'll work out a fucking exit plan from this nightmare. I'm tempted to text Ted with my resignation because I don't see how I'm supposed to live through this. Switch off. Knowing Rush and Ian are still in contact and I've been tossed aside like the trash.

I rub the ache in my sternum with my knuckles as I walk, trying to massage it away. It's not even him I'm all that upset about. After how he betrayed me, I have no interest in returning to that. It's the rejection. The being made to feel worthless after investing years into this person who wasn't who I thought he was.

It just. Isn't. Fair.

The hall to the bathrooms is narrow and dark, thankfully empty, but as I reach the men's room door, my name is called.

"H-Hunter?"

I recognize his voice immediately, and I don't think. Just turn, grab his shirt, and pin him to the wall. Maybe I shouldn't have drunk that beer so quickly on an empty stomach because the alcohol has gone to my head, and all I can do is glare at Rush through watery eyes.

"What the fuck do you want?"

His hand closes over the one I have bunched in his shirt, and instead of shock, he blinks up at me like he's concerned about me. "I just wanted to talk."

"Why the hell would you think I want to talk to you?"

"To clear the air?"

"Clear the air? You slept with my fucking fiancé."

"And you were nice to me after that."

"Nice?" I almost laugh.

"Plus, you're my boss now. We have to get along. Please don't tell everyone what happened—I don't want to end up homeless and racing cops across state lines because I had to steal Madden's car to live in."

I stare at him and the way he's so fucking earnest. "Don't worry about that because I'm quitting."

"Why?"

"Because I can't stand to be around you. Especially knowing you're still … still—" My voice breaks, and I suck down a sharp breath to cover it.

Rush's free hand rests on my shoulder. "I'm really sorry."

My gaze shoots to his wide green one because that's the last thing I expect him to say. "What?"

"I'm not sleeping with him. I haven't texted him back since that night."

"And he's *still* texting you?"

Rush nods. "I assumed he was doing the same with you."

I huff and release him, shoving away to the other side of the hall. "Well, he hasn't been. Congratulations, you fucking won."

"I don't think either of us won. That was a pretty shitty thing he did."

"You telling me you're not going to go running back to him?"

"Why, would you?"

"Of course not!"

"Then why would you think I would?"

That derails my anger for a moment. "Ah, because …"

Rush gives me a sad smile. "You kinda hate me, don't you?"

"You can take the 'kinda' out of that sentence."

"But *why*?"

I gape at him. "You were having sex with the man I loved. Jesus, are you fucking kidding me?"

"I get it, I had really bad RSD for a couple of days afterward. Thankfully it doesn't last long anymore because my friends are the best support network." He pauses while I wonder what RSD is. "If it helps, I don't think we were the only ones."

My gut drops through the floor. "If it *helps*? How the fuck does that help me?"

"Well, I felt terrible, but then my friends did some super-stealthy deep dives into him, and we think there were at least two other guys."

"Two …" That asshole was sleeping with *three* other men? I'm nauseous all over again, and I'm suddenly really fucking happy that I'm right by the bathrooms. "I think you need to go. And for the record, one, two … a hundred others … you should still feel terrible. What you did to me is something I'd never do to anyone. That's an absolute dirt move, and I don't know how you can even face me after ruining my entire life."

Rush throws up his hands. "You're not listening. I didn't ruin your life—I saved it! You could have married that guy and been stuck with a cheater for the rest of your life. We're not the issue. Those other guys aren't the issue. Ian was. So you're welcome."

All the smothered anger comes flaring back to life. *I'm fucking welcome?*

"Let me get this straight. You want me to thank you. For fucking my fiancé?"

Rush waves his hand. "Technically, he fucked me"—I let out a strangled moan—"but no, that's not the point. The point is he was an asshole, and now you're free of him."

"An asshole who's still messaging *you*," I grit out.

"You're not taking this well."

"Is there any other possible way for me to take it?"

"I don't know. I don't understand all these emotions. It's black-and-white to me, but apparently, you're having a freak-out over it, and you won't tell me what to do. Do you want a hug?"

"Not from you."

"But you do want one?" He hooks a thumb back over his shoulder. "I can get Eloise. She gives the best mom hugs."

I release a long exhale through my nose and draw up to full height. "This conversation is officially the biggest waste of my time today. And I caught you hiding under a desk."

"I panicked."

"I could tell," I say mockingly. "Tell the others I've left."

But before I've taken a step, Rush grabs my arms to stop

me from passing him. "Why do you hate me so much? To be clear, that's not rhetorical. What's the actual real reason?"

"I already told you."

"Because I slept with him?" For fuck's sake, Rush has the audacity to sound hurt. "But I can't help that," he whines.

"Some advice for you? Don't go around sleeping with taken men, and then you won't find yourself in this mess."

I shrug out of his hold and walk away until I hear him faintly say, "I didn't *know*."

And there it is. The thing I've been refusing to acknowledge this whole time. Maybe Rush was as much of a victim as I was. But if he was, then I can't hate him. And I really need to hate him.

Because otherwise, I'll be back to hating myself.

Before I can let myself answer, I keep walking, right out of the bar. I'll make my excuses to the team tomorrow.

Chapter 6

Rush

I read back over my email for the millionth time, making sure I've caught all those ninja typos and unfinished sentences.

Hunter,

Reasons why you shouldn't quit.

What happened with Ian was not your fault.

You've already moved all this way.

My team, quite frankly, cannot go through another manager because of me.

I don't want you to be out of a job because of me.

Ted will hound me over the weirdness between us and I'm too weak not to tell him. I don't want to tell him. I need an ally.

A coffee cart comes to the office on Thursdays and I'll even show you the perfect potted plant to sneak tea into when October rolls around and

Autumn embraces her "fall aesthetic" which comes with the most undrinkable collection of what I'm pretty sure is expensive dirt.

I'll return your coat.

I'll get your coat dry cleaned before I return it, because I'm about ninety percent sure there'll be cum on it.

We will never speak of the incident ever again.

I'll even come into work early for you.

Okay, that last one was probably a lie, but I really will try.

I think you'd be a good boss even though I have absolutely no basis for that hunch.

We can team up and get revenge on Ian.

Let me know if you are amenable to any of the above.

Your (unknowing) partner in crime,

Rush

I'VE BARELY PUT my phone down after hitting Send when an email comes right back to me.

RUSH,

How the hell are any of those things points to make me STAY? If anything, it's like you're trying to shove me out the door. And don't email me outside of work hours.

Hunter Barrett

OKAY, so apparently, none of my suggestions appealed to him.

HUNTER BARRETT,

Just to check: that's a no to the coat?

Rush

. . .

RUSH,

Of course I want my coat back, but not after hearing what's happened to it. Cum, Rush? Really?
Hunter Barrett

HUNTER BARRETT,

Okay, now I'm confused. I've sat here for the last hour torn between respecting your boundaries to not email you before nine and answering your question. Which would you prefer I do?
Rush
P.S. The cum is unconfirmed, and you don't need to worry: it's not mine.

RUSH,

How is it possible that every time you attempt to make something clearer, you make it a thousand times more confusing?
HB

HB,

I'm still not sure whether I'm supposed to reply.
Rush

RUSH,

Please tell me you didn't sit there for another hour wondering? It's past midnight!
H
P.S. YES you can reply

H,

Thank you for being clear. Firstly, I didn't actually realize the time, but I'm awake and you're awake, so does it really matter? Second, when I got home in your coat, my roommate, Xander, stole it. He probably didn't think I'd ever see you again, to be fair, and I thought the same. Plus, your coat smelled really good. Though, I suppose that was just you, because when you held me up against the wall tonight, you smelled the same way. So because you smelled good, he stole it, and I assume he's been jerking off in it, because why else would he steal it, and also he's a virgin who's always horny, but can't get over his medical anxiety to actually find someone he wants to sleep with. I assumed he slept with Seven, but they both claim they never have. If I'd known you were going to be my boss, I would have made sure when Xander stole it that I stole it right back. But I will now.

And I'll make sure it's clean.

Rush

*R*USH,

It's too late for this conversation.

H

I STARE DOWN at the email, debating whether I'm supposed to ask when a more appropriate time is or if that's him putting an end to the conversation. It's so frustrating when people aren't clear.

To stop myself from spending another hour obsessing, I toss my phone on my bed and head down the hall toward Madden's bedroom. It's dark inside, but when I push the door open and knock on the wood, he lets out a deep grunt.

"Oh good, you're awake."

"Wasn't." The light flicks on suddenly, and I blink at the brightness shining my way from his phone.

"Ouch."

"So sorry to hurt your poor eyes at one in the morning when you're sneaking into my room."

I throw myself onto the side of his bed and mutter, "What's with everyone being so obsessed with the time tonight?"

"This morning."

"Good point."

Madden's bed is one of the comfiest in the house. I love lying here, love that it feels familiar and smells nice, and his sheets are some kind of billion thread count that feel amazing on my skin, but I'd always be too worried about sliding off if I slept in here.

"You came in here for a reason," Madden says.

"Did I?" I suppose I must have since it makes logical sense. From his sheets, to the door, to my room, to my phone … "Ah. Hunter is quitting."

"The Hunter?"

"The Hunter who is now my boss Hunter who was previously the Other Guy Hunter, yes."

"Why does that have you up and stressy?"

"I'm not stressy."

Madden nudges me with his foot. "You're still. That means you're stressy."

Huh. He's right. "So what do I do?"

"About?"

"The Hunter quitting."

"Why do you care if he quits?"

While I know from the outside that Hunter leaving sounds like a win for me, it really isn't. Sure, it'll be nice to keep my job and my home and my friends, but logically, there's no reason for him to go, and it's one of those things my brain has latched onto and is convinced it's stupid—because it is, objectively, really stupid—and now I can't let it go.

"I emailed him a list."

"A list of what?"

"A list of reasons he should stay."

Madden takes a moment to process. "In the nicest way possible, why the fuck would you do that?"

I remind myself to be patient with him. "A list of reasons to stay is generally a list created with the intent of making someone, well, *stay*."

"I'm not talking about literally. I mean, what part of that sparkly brain of yours thought that emailing your mortal enemy at one on a work night was a smart thing to do?"

"Technically, it was at ten. Then he replied and told me not to reply, but he asked a question, and the whole thing was a confusing mess. I worry he might not be the best communicator, which isn't a good quality for a boss."

"Right. So what part of that sparkly brain of yours thought that emailing your mortal enemy for *three hours* on a work night was a smart thing to do?"

"Well, if I left it for tomorrow, I might have forgotten."

"That sounds like a good thing to me."

Okay, *now* I'm getting exasperated. "But then how would he have gotten my list?"

"Rush, he doesn't need your list. If he wants to quit, he'll quit."

"But then he won't have a job. And he'll have to move home—does he even want to move home, Madden?"

"If he does or doesn't, that damn sure isn't any of your business." He stifles a yawn. "Are you going to be able to let this go, or do I need to get up?"

"I'm unsure right now."

Madden laughs and throws his pillow at me. "That's a no. Come on, let's go heckle."

"Hmm … it's been a while since we heckled."

Madden throws off the covers and climbs out of bed, white ass pale in the moonlight streaming through the window.

Madden never wears clothes at home, only wears them out

when absolutely necessary, and while I wish I had that confidence, I also really love clothes. Experimenting with fabrics that feel good and don't make you sweat or itch or be suffocated by the material is fun.

It's why I started designing. Not professionally—I couldn't make it through my degree and am still strained by the debt the few courses I took left behind—but turning my passion into a career sounds way too stressful to me.

Christian did. Xander did too. I've never asked Molly if design is something he loves, but his job seems to make him happy. For me, I need the freedom to create, to be able to walk away from something that isn't working and feel no pressure to go back before I'm ready. Knowing the clothes will be there, in six months' time, exactly how I left them, is comforting.

"When you do wear clothes," I ask Madden as I follow him down the stairs, "is there a material you prefer? I know you don't like anything restrictive, but what about linen? Or are you a cotton man?"

"I'm an elastic gym shorts man, and that basically makes up my wardrobe."

There's nothing I hate worse than elastic pressing into my skin, but to each his own.

"You know what I don't get," Madden throws back over his shoulder. "Didn't your ex-dickweed realize Hunter was going for a job at the same place as you? Why would he let that happen?"

"You're asking *me* to understand why someone did something?" I've already tried to make sense of that and only been able to come to two theories: either he was cockier about cheating than I thought, or, more likely, I never actually mentioned *where* I worked. I'm sure I might have talked about insurance at some point though? Maybe? Actually, I don't think I did that either.

"Okay, taking bets," Madden says. "Who is it going to be tonight, and what are they pimping?"

"Used car salesman Kent, and he'll be offloading …" It's been a while since we've seen mops. Or window cleaners. Last time was a saucepan set. "I'm going with tools."

"Might want to get more specific there, champ. Tools is a broad category."

"Fine. A, uh, multitool. It has a main purpose but has a way of measuring as well."

"Ohhh, good one. I'm going to go with fine china."

Dammit, we haven't seen fine china in a while. "Who will it be?"

"Forty-year-old virgin."

The guy's nicknamed that not because he looks like a virgin but because he looks like Steve Carrell. "Nah, they'll have Nana Bette or Miss Trunchbull on that."

"We'll see …"

Madden collapses onto his armchair, and I flop back onto the couch that's been here for who knows how long. It's mid-century, at a guess, and the owners left it behind with a bunch of other furniture for us. I'll never be able to thank Rylan and Kai enough for renting us this place for as cheap as they do.

Not only that, but it brought us Bertha Boys together, and these guys are more of a family to me than my own blood. I don't know where I'd be without them.

"Ready?" he asks.

"Shoot."

Madden picks up the remote and clicks on the TV before flicking over to the infomercial channel. When it comes on screen, we both watch blankly for a moment.

"Well, that's not fancy plates," Madden says.

The man and woman on screen are modeling what looks like bright blue plastic flip-flops with bristles all over them.

"One size fits all," the man says as the grinning woman slips her feet inside.

"Well, that's a new one," Madden says dumbly.

I'm with him though. Not only does the product look ridiculous, but the woman is rubbing her feet in and out like she's doing feet porn.

"Two dollars on her next word being 'wow.'"

"I'll take that bet."

We both wait, letting the man talk, until … *Wow, my feet feel so smooth.*

Madden cries out, and I high-five myself.

"Easy call."

"Fine. Double or nothing, split screen of before and afters in three … two …"

He doesn't continue. "I'm waiting."

"One and a half … and … a quarter?"

"What exactly are we counting here because it's not secon—"

"Now!"

The split screen pops up, and he shouts the word a moment later. "You're good at this," I tease, handing the eight dollars over.

Madden cracks his knuckles, looking cocky. "It's a skill."

"Or cheating."

"Definitely what I said."

We're up for the next half an hour heckling the hell out of the salespeople and the product and mocking the usual lines they use. *Before Easy Feet, I was so insecure every time my friends and family commented on my feet …*

"Oh no, poor little model has friends and family. How sad for her."

Madden laughs. "I'm impressed they *talk* to her."

"And now that she has Easy Feet," I say in a mock presenter voice. "They can say they love her unconditionally since they're not hung up on a tiny cosmetic flaw. The miracle!"

Madden tucks his hands behind his head and sighs. "We have grown bitter, my friend."

"Have we?"

"Well, I have. You've always been like this."

I tilt my head to the side. "I don't feel bitter."

"Is it a feeling or a mindset?"

"Definitely a feeling."

"Then maybe bitter isn't the right word."

I scoff. "Well, don't listen to me. I'm not good with feelings. Either they're too much or not there at all."

Madden hums and rubs his knuckles against his chest. "Maybe it's better that way."

I already know exactly who he's talking about. Even for someone as oblivious as me, the pining comes through loud and clear.

"Penn?" I check since it's been a while since we've talked about Madden's crush on his best friend.

"Eh, nothing new there."

"I'm sorry," I say because what else is there to say? Penn's a great friend, but he's straight. Madden knew that when he went and fell for him, but while I think it's helpful to point that out, I've learned from experience people don't want to be faced with logic. Especially when feelings are involved.

Madden falls asleep not long after a few more bets, but I still can't get my thoughts to switch off. Madden's heartache. His ill-placed crush. Choosing the worst person to fall for. Hunter and I did too, only in our cases, we had no way of knowing.

Does he feel like Madden does? I know he's mad at me for what happened, but I can't figure out why. We both are in the same position; if anything, we should be allies.

I open my phone and scroll back through my messages with him, gaze catching on a detail I'd forgotten.

The coat.

Shit.

Better do it now before I forget again.

I creep upstairs and into Xander's bedroom, searching by the light of my phone until I find it folded in the bottom of his closet.

Xander grunts in his sleep. "Whatever you're doing, Rush," he says dreamily, "close the door on the way out."

That I can do.

And I've remembered the coat.

And I made ten bucks off Madden tonight.

Look at Rush, winning all around.

Chapter 7

Hunter

I thought that when I logged into my work email this morning, I'd find an email from Rush waiting. But there wasn't. Which is obviously a good thing, even if I'm curious over what he would have said.

The emails last night feel like a dream, but as I read back over them, it becomes very clear, very quickly, that they actually happened, and I think Rush was completely serious.

I lean back in my chair, eyeing the resignation letter left open on my screen. I'd been a second away from emailing it through to Ted last night when Rush's email came through, and then after the strangest exchange, I'd fallen asleep and forgotten about it.

Kinda easy to do when Rush was the only person on my mind.

Rush, and how much I actively want to hate him, even if he's making it difficult.

Speaking of … nine rolls past with still no sign of him. Autumn, Gates, and Eloise are all at their pod, Gates punching away at his computer while Autumn and Eloise laugh at something over coffee. The glass office wall separates me from the bullpen, and while I've been gunning for an office like this for years, it also makes me feel … cut off.

Which won't matter if I resign.

Though if Rush doesn't get here soon, he'll be out of a job, and then I won't have anything to worry about.

Before I can follow that thought too far, I check my reflection in my laptop screen to make sure my hair is still meticulously styled after I'm sure I've run my hands through it a billion times already. Then I haul ass out of my office and head toward my team.

"Good morning," I say, forcing myself to sound confident.

"Hunter." Eloise greets me with a kind smile. "You disappeared last night."

Not my most professional moment. "Yes, I wasn't feeling the best. I think the stress of the move and a new job got to me."

"Poor thing." Autumn's hands are clutched around her mug, and I get a flash of Rush's emails and wonder if her drink tastes like dirt. "You should have said. We didn't have to catch up last night."

"Well, one of the things about me is that I like to keep my commitments." My gaze strays to the obviously empty desk. "Unlike some people, it appears."

"Who, Rush? He's always late."

My gaze flies back to Autumn. "Always? And it's allowed?"

"Rush is … umm … forgetful."

I take a measured breath. "Unfortunately, being forgetful isn't reason enough to not meet the requirements of your role."

Autumn shrinks in on herself.

Shit.

Gates snickers. "Talk to Ted. He loves Carey—that kid can get away with anything."

I check the time and find Rush is already half an hour late. "I think I'll do that."

Ted is on the opposite side of this floor to me, in a bank of offices the managers work out of. As a supervisor, I need to be accessible to my team at all times. Ted's role is more hands-off than mine.

His door is open when I get there, which I take to mean he's free, so I knock lightly on the frame.

"Morning, Hunter. What can I do for you?"

"I wanted to talk to you about R—Carey, actually."

Ted grins like he already knew. He waves a hand toward the seat across from himself, so I step inside, close the door behind me, and take it. "What's the problem?"

"He's late, and the team tells me that's normal for him."

"Correct."

I'm surprised that he straight up admitted it. "I'm unsure how to word this politely, so I'm just going to ask: is being late acceptable here?"

"Carey does his work."

"How is that possible when he's not here?"

"Do you only work between the hours of nine and nine thirty?"

"That's not the point."

"Then what is the point?" The patient smile he gives me makes me feel like I've walked into a trap. And that he's had this conversation before.

"I get the feeling that whatever I say next, you've already got an answer for."

He leans forward. "I'd assume so. Look, when it comes to Carey, I'm … protective. Your role has had a higher than usual amount of turnover in the last few years, for a number of reasons, but one of the sticking points that keeps coming up is

Carey. He's a wonderful man. Very friendly. He has systems in place for doing his job, and he has amazing rapport with his customers. I'd love to see you find a single other person out there who has notes as detailed on their clients as he does. But with all of his positives, there are also negatives for a traditional workplace. He's never on time. He works odd hours. He gets distracted and distracts people around him, and his to-do list gets wildly out of control before he'll randomly decide today's the day to get it all done."

"That's a lot of negatives," I point out.

"And it's your job to manage them."

"I'd like to request a performance plan to help him fix his lateness."

Ted shrugs. "Go for it, but it won't work."

"Why?"

"It's been tried before, it failed before, and I still refused to fire him. Wanna know why?"

"I'm on the edge of my seat."

"Carey has ADHD. It's ableist to expect him to be anyone other than who he is."

Well, fuck. I didn't know that, and I like to pride myself on being a pretty cluey guy. Ted is right. That changes things. I'm not sure yet exactly how, but if I do stay with this job, I'll be figuring it out. Of course Rush is the one I'm going to have to devote some of my focus to. Of *course* this is one more reason for me to be thinking about the last guy I want to think about.

Of course.

Because that's the shitshow my life is at the moment.

"If I relax the start time for him, then I need to relax it for my whole team. It's unfair otherwise."

Ted smiles. "That could be one way to handle it. I didn't hire you to supervise a neurotypical team, Hunter. I hired you to supervise a team. Of people. And all those people are different. I'll give you the same spiel I've given the other people before you: your only job is to ensure your team hit their goals. However they do that is up to you."

That's way more freedom than I've ever been given before. Jobs come with a list. A set structure you need to do to get through the day and go home. Anything outside of that and you need permission from higher-ups. It's been drilled into me from bussing tables during high school to the two jobs I held down while in college to my position at WCX. Corporations have structure, and people get hella pissed when you fuck with that structure.

"Just to be clear," I say, sitting forward a little as the freedom goes to my head. "My team, my rules?"

"Don't break any safety guidelines, meet your KPIs. That's it."

"Okay." A million ideas are already flying through my head as I stand. "Okay."

"And no firing Carey." Ted rubs at his forehead. "I'm done with hearing people complain about that man."

"Got it. Thanks for the chat, boss."

My mind is whirling when I leave his office as I try to figure out what the hell I got myself into. Quitting still isn't off the table, but it's looking a whole lot less likely now I've been given that kind of direction.

That direction being that I *don't* have direction.

Anything.

At all.

But before I get carried away with my ideas, I need to talk to my team. If I'm going to make changes, if I'm going to shake things up in a *good* way, I need to make sure it will be welcome. Do any of them want to start late? Start early? I won't know until I actually ask them.

I'm about to turn the corner to my office when I glance toward the elevator that's dinged. The doors open, and Rush runs out. The wavy, sun-bleached curls that normally sit on top of his head are a windblown mess, his tan cheeks are pink, and his backpack is hanging off one shoulder. He's also clutching a pot of what looks like colorful rocks.

I try to smile, but it feels stiff. "Rush."

"You're here!" He throws his hands up like he's actually … happy to see me? And somehow, the pot stays hovering in midair.

"What in the—"

"Oh." Rush laughs, the kind of easy laugh that makes his chin thinner and a tiny dimple appear in his right cheek. "I fastened my belt around it so I wouldn't put it down on the bus and forget." Then from what seems like nowhere, he pulls out a large coffee. "Just have to drop this off. I'll meet you in your office. Sound good? Okay, bye."

And without so much as a sorry for being late, Rush hurries across the office, sidestepping people and throwing out hellos in the most chaotic way I've ever seen someone exist. I can't pull my eyes away until he disappears from sight.

I have no idea what that was, but I guess I'm going to find out.

The rest of my team are on calls when I get back, diligently doing their job, and I remember my time in those cubicles. It was … tedious. Answering the same questions, helping fill out the same applications, the same claims, talking insurance all day long.

If I still want to quit, I'll be going back to that existence.

If I stay … I have the opportunity to make it better. For them and for me.

But staying means having to face Rush. Having to face the reminder of all that hurt.

Can I really go through that every day?

Chapter 8

Rush

After dropping off Ted's coffee like I do every day, I hurry over to Hunter's office. I know I'm late. I know he's going to ream me for it. Hopefully we can get that part over and done with so I can get on with my day. It's one of the things I hate most about this constant turnover, always having to have the same conversations, like Groundhog Day.

The movie. Not the date in February.

So far as I know, that doesn't repeat on itself, though I suppose if it did, we wouldn't actually know about it.

I'm still sweaty and frantic when I reach Hunter's door. It's open, so I head inside, unstrap my belt, and drop the pot onto his desk.

"Ta-da!"

Hunter stares at my gift. "What … what is it?"

"A plant. I know my list was a lot and maybe didn't help, so I asked myself what sorts of things help people feel settled. Pets were a good idea, but I didn't think you'd be too happy about me bringing a puppy into the office, so I got you a plant instead. If you have something to look after, you'll have to keep coming back." Though I probably should have taken Madden up on his offer to grab something from work instead of panicking and buying—

"These are *plants*? They look like … like …"

"Asses?"

His wide, dark eyes shoot up my way. "*Yes*. Are these things real?"

"The lady at the shop told me they are. Google supported her story. They're li … lithops. I think. But they all look that way, and there are a bunch of different colors, and apparently, when they're ready, the two segments spread apart, and a flower grows from the middle."

Hunter chokes on a laugh, and I think it's the first time I've seen anything other than a scowl on his face. It gives me hope that maybe this plan isn't completely doomed. "You're telling me that I'm going to have a pot of rock-looking, ass-shaped plants on my desk that are going to sprout their own floral butt plug?"

"Technically, just a flower. Did you *want* a floral butt plug?"

He ignores the question. Too personal? "What in the hell made you buy these? Is this your subtle way of calling me an ass?"

My face falls. "What? No. Never. I mentioned the puppy to Madden, who suggested a plant, and when I dropped your coat off at the dry cleaner's this morning—which I shocked even myself by remembering to do—I spotted a little plant shop and thought I'd grab a succulent. But she didn't have any of those little flower-looking succulents. And actually, I don't think she was a very good plant lady because there were a whole lot of huge trees and flower bouquets but no succulents? Does she not want to make money? I've seen enough social media pages to know that those things are where people are at for aesthetic reasons. So she showed me those, and I thought they were kinda weird and fun, and I was already running so late that I panicked and bought them. Not because they're mini asses."

Hunter sighs, but it's through a smile. "Can you sit?"

I all but collapse into the chair he points at.

"I'm sorry," he says.

"What?"

"I …" He rubs his mouth. His hands are huge. His mouth is big too. "This whole situation has been a headfuck, honestly. I blamed you because I had to blame someone, and even though I don't care about him, it still hurts. Being rejected and betrayed like that isn't something I'm going to get over in a hurry. What I'm trying to say is that I'm glad you've moved on from it. I probably won't be able to, but I will do everything I can to keep things professional. Like you said it … it wasn't either of our faults." The anxiety twisting tighter in my gut finally loosens. "We will keep things professional." He clears his throat and nudges the plant my way. "And you can keep your gift."

"Does this mean you're going to stay?"

He starts like my question catches him by surprise. "I've been going back and forth on it all morning." He absently spins the pot in a circle on his desk. "And I think I'm going to."

"It was my emails, wasn't it?"

He snorts, and even it sounds amused. "No, it definitely wasn't. I'm not even sure I followed half of them. Tell me you weren't serious about my coat?"

"Oh, no, I was. But it's okay because I was wrong. No cum in sight when I dropped it off this morning."

"Well. Good."

"Was that sarcasm? You sound disappointed."

"I'm relieved, just still struggling to believe I'm having this conversation."

I wave my hand his way. "You'll get used to the feeling. Now, are you going to yell at me for being late? I don't really know why wasting more time to do that is beneficial, but you might as well do it while I'm here."

Hunter studies me, dark eyes running over my face to my chest and back up again. "Actually, no. But I was planning to have one-on-one meetings with you all, so we might as well get yours done now."

"Oh, good. That's much more logical."

He smirks as he wakes up his computer. "I'm glad you think so."

"You are?"

"It's an expression. But since you asked, no. I don't actually care."

"That's fair. I haven't done anything yet to earn you caring about my opinion."

Something about that makes Hunter frown. He glances over at me and then quickly back at his computer. "Why did you take the time to email me last night?"

"Because you were upset, and you weren't thinking clearly. I thought maybe I could help."

"But why you?"

I lean forward, planting my elbows on the desk, open belt rattling with the movement. "I'm assuming that no one else knows what went down, and I felt sad for you that you moved here and had to go through that. It wasn't okay. I don't know if you have any friends or family here, but I wanted you to know that I can be a friendly face, and you can hold it against me all you like and not believe me when I say I didn't know, but I was upset too. I went through the same thing you did, basically. If anyone gets it, I do."

"Yeah … you mentioned something like that," he mutters. "Revenge, huh?"

I nod, smile spreading over my face. "He'd deserve it."

"Can't disagree there."

"See? We already have something in common! You're going to warm to me yet."

"Don't get ahead of yourself."

But it's too late because I already am. Hunter's one of those guys who looks put together. The kind who intimidates me, the kind I know I'll never be. He's way too mature and would probably run scared from my friends after a minute in their presence. That kind of adultishness always catches my interest. Ted is like that too.

I can't help wondering whether it's all an act or they really do have their shit together.

"Why are you staring at me?" he asks like he doesn't want to ask.

"You're very clean."

He chokes on a laugh. "What?"

I wave a hand over him. "You've shaved, your hair is parted neatly, I'm pretty sure you wax your eyebrows and have some kind of skincare routine, and I can't see a single wrinkle on your clothes."

When he talks again, it's a deep rumble, and I find Hunter's voice unexpectedly soothing. "And those things make me clean?"

"Make you look clean. I have no idea about your hygiene. I can confirm I'm a regular showerer and brush my teeth every morning and night even though …" I point to my hair. "I am not someone who ever looks clean and put together as much as I might try."

One of his dark eyebrows rises a fraction. "Do you actually try?"

"On occasion. I have been known to try. But then I never end up looking the way you do, so at some point, I realized it was wasted effort and my time was better spent elsewhere."

"Like picking out rude plants for your new boss?"

The teasing in his tone lights me up inside. "You're joking around."

"Am not."

"That was definitely joking."

He huffs and turns back to his computer. "Favorite thing about working here?" he asks stiffly.

"Making my boss like me."

His fingers still on his keyboard. "Rush …"

"Do you not want an honest answer?"

I'm ninety percent sure he's trying not to laugh as he drags his big hand through his neat black hair. "Least favorite thing about working here?"

"My boss not liking me."

Hunter groans and drops his head forward onto his desk. "I'm trying really hard to be professional here."

"Might want to work on that. Looks more exasperated to me."

"Can't imagine why that would be …"

"Generally, when someone looks exasperated, it means they are exasperated."

Hunter swings his seat back around so he can pin me with a look. "I think I have everything I need from you."

"Well, that was painless."

"Not the word I'd use."

Whatever word he'd use doesn't matter because it's over. I convinced him to stay, and I didn't get torn a new asshole for being an hour late. That's what I call a successful morning.

I'm up and almost out the door when Hunter calls out. "Forgetting something?"

I wouldn't be at all surprised if I am, but I've got my bag, my phone, dropped off Ted's coffee … "Oh! My belt." I drop my backpack onto the ground and hurry to do it up. "Thanks for that. We might have started some uncomfortable office rumors."

Hunter's eyes are locked onto my bag, scowl back in place. "Not hiding any more *elf* costumes in there, are you?"

"I can't believe my boss has seen me with my bits out."

"Definitely not what I was focused on that night."

I go to take a step when Hunter stops me again.

"*Rush.*" He nudges the pot on his desk. "I'm not keeping this."

My jaw drops. "Well, *I* can't take it."

"Why not?"

"That thing is way too pornographic for the bullpen. If people find out my boss gave me booty plants, they might start asking questions."

He actually face-palms.

I take that as my cue to run.

Chapter 9

Hunter

Rush's desk is in my direct line of sight. I don't think that's an accident.

While I'm sure it was great for everyone who came before me, for me, it's a fucking nightmare. Every time I glance up from my desk, I see him—or don't see him, more often than not. Rush makes me exhausted just looking at him. He's either pulled someone into a conversation, is up pacing around while he talks on his phone, sitting backward in his desk chair with posture that is anything but ergonomic, or disappears across the office altogether.

He's so distracting that at this rate, *I'm* going to be the one who doesn't get through his work.

I make a concentrated effort not to watch.

Autumn knocks on the door. "Were you ready for me?"

"Sure am." I point to the chair. "I wanted to catch up with everyone. Hopefully get your thoughts on a few things."

"Like what?" she asks curiously, pulling out the chair that Rush was draped over earlier.

"Work. How are you liking it here?"

Her angular face twitches. "It's … good."

"You're not being tested. I assume you don't hate it since you're still here, but if there's anything that'd make you enjoy it more, I'm all ears."

"Really?" Autumn visibly perks up. "Well … I mean …"

"Just say it."

"It would be cool to decorate for the holidays."

"Which ones?"

"Any? All?" Autumn thinks for a moment. "I really love Halloween. I dress up every year, but no one else does, so then I end up feeling like an idiot. All I want is to get excited and hand out candy, but people look at me like I'm nuts. Really puts a damper on things."

"Well, I'm not making any promises, obviously, but I like that idea." Especially because things like that are a good way to get the team involved. Maybe even have a few teams come together. Boost morale. "Anything else?"

"It would be fun to raise money for charities too. Have some in-house initiatives. Like a bake sale …" The more Autumn talks, the more she lights up, and I find I'm smiling as well. She's younger than everyone else here, only early twenties, but it's clear she's excited to have been asked. People like Autumn are what every team needs.

"You have good ideas."

"I spend a lot of time watching videos online," she says matter-of-factly.

"Good to know where I'm going wrong."

"We all have our strengths, boss man."

The nickname thrills me. "You've been through a few different supervisors, right? Why do you think that is?"

Autumn laughs, star-shaped earrings swaying around her

neck. "Rush. He's a hot mess, but I love him to bits. Sweetest heart. Weirdest brain. I know he's not easy to manage, but the last guy tried to force him to get medicated or be fired. I don't think I need to explain to you why pushing that on someone wasn't a good call."

There's something in her tone that makes me curious. "Is that you relaying information … or warning me?"

"Take it how you want to take it. We're all a bit weird, and I like it. I'd never tell Eloise her obsessive need to check in on the babysitter is psycho or that Gates doesn't need to answer every call with *well, isn't it my favorite client?* even though it makes me want to stab pins into my eyes."

"Noted."

"Good."

I hesitate. "Does he really answer *every* call like that?"

"For at least the two years I've been working here. Need anything else?"

I shake my head. "Email me if you think of anything."

She leaves, and on a whim, I pick up my phone and call through to Gates to ask him to come in for a chat.

"*Well, if it isn't my favorite boss.*"

It takes all my willpower to bite back a laugh.

Yeah. Maybe this job isn't the worst thing I could be doing.

▭

EVEN AFTER STAYING BACK LATE to work and stopping by the bar for a drink, I'm home earlier than I'd like. And I'm playing fast and loose with the word *home*. Living out of a suitcase in a sub-par hotel room that's making me hemorrhage money isn't what I'd pictured when I'd envisioned living in Seattle.

Ian was.

His house was.

The first time I'd seen it, our future together played out so clearly in my mind. The neat, suburban street. The tidy house. The kids playing in the front yard.

Him fucking any and all manner of men in our bed.

I huff and strip off to shower, hoping to get the thoughts out of my head. Rush said there were others. I'd gotten that impression from Ian, too, but was trying to ignore it.

Were there so many others that my own fucking fiancé has already forgotten my existence?

I scrub myself so hard that by the time I step out of the shower, dripping all over the tile, my skin is red raw. Against my own better judgment, I can't stop from obsessing over the messages he's been sending Rush. Does Ian miss *him?* If he's got others, why would he be so persistent in getting in touch with Rush?

Sure, the guy's hot as hell, but so are many, many others.

That can't be the only draw card here. Or maybe it is and Ian was *that* shallow.

I dry off, scrubbing my hair until it stands up all over the place, and the second my skincare routine flits through my mind, I push it right back out again. I'm not *that* put together, Rush, thank you very much.

It actually makes me laugh that he somehow thinks that about me. The whole hotel room behind me is visible in the mirror. Basic white sheets, chipboard closet, small TV on the wall. It matches the *barely holding it together* guy that's renting it. Even though I'm smiling, I look wrecked. My hair is a mess, my cheeks are splotching from scrubbing, and my eyes are so bloodshot red they make the brown look muddier than usual.

I'm starting to understand why Ian wasn't worried about losing me.

On a whim, I pick up my phone and open my emails, and my thumb hovers over the one to Rush. It's just one question. All I need is a quick answer to get over my curiosity. Then, I can go back to moving on.

I click on our emails and type before I lose the nerve.

RUSH,

I know I said sorry earlier, but it's hit me that I didn't actually say sorry for manhandling you in the bar. So, uh, sorry about that too. Hearing that Ian was still messaging you hit me right in the ego because I was only worth two messages then radio silence. Guess you're the kind of guy men will put in the effort for. Guess I'm not.

But as I sit here, trying to move on with my life, those messages keep playing in my head. What the hell could he possibly be saying a month later? How could he really think you'll crack and text back when you said you haven't so far? What's his end game? And even as I write all that, I realize it's none of my business.

But when I say I struggle with seeing you at work, those types of thoughts are the reason why. I think I'll always compare us and wonder where I was lacking.

So that's my brain dump for today, I guess it's my turn to be sending the inappropriate emails. I know I should delete this, but I can't bring myself to. I want you to understand.

Hunter

THE MORE I reread what I sent, the more my confidence gurgles away, blood leaving my head like it's been sucked down a drain. Inappropriate probably doesn't cover that email—especially since I'm writing it buck naked. Good thing he doesn't know that part.

"Fuck …" I moan around a laugh. Who's Mr. Put-Together now?

There are still way too many hours until bed, and I know from experience there isn't even any mindless TV for another few hours. I've walked the neighborhood to the point all the cement sidewalks and brick buildings are memorized, and I'm in danger of sitting here and zoning out until it's late enough to order room service again.

What a life.

It's not until half an hour and multiple refreshes of my email later that I realize something.

With a sigh, I open my emails again,

Rush,

Disregard what I said about business hours. You caught me at a bad time.

Hunter

Like I've said the magic word, he emails back within minutes.

Hunter,

Thank you for apologizing. Again. It was unnecessary but appreciated. As for being the kind of guy people put in the effort for, I only wish that was true. I'm the kind of guy who's easy to take advantage of—hence why I never worked out there was something odd about a guy who'd have his phone off for days at a time. I realize now that's shady because my friends made me a red flags for dumb-dumbs guide, it's on a poster board hanging in my bedroom.

The messages might not be your business, but I'm happy to share the ones I've actually read, which wasn't many. The first few were about missing me and trying to get me back. Then there were a few dick pics and some threats about losing him forever. One on our anniversary, another at midnight on NYE. Molly cut me off cold turkey with the messages and frequently checks that I haven't opened them before he goes through and deletes them himself. I don't know what the most recent ones have said and I'm not curious enough to check.

As for where you're at, I understand. I get it. I'm also curious why you're emailing me at eight at night when you've had all day to talk to me. But I think that's one of those things you're not supposed to ask people.

Rush

P.S. Thank you for clarifying the time thing. I was about to save this to send tomorrow but that makes things much clearer.

Does Rush realize that I have no clue who any of the people he talks about are? That's … three? four? people he's mentioned now. Are they friends? Family? I flop back onto the bed and cover my face with my hands. I'm not sure why his casual mention of all these seemingly supportive people is hitting me so hard. I have my parents. My sister. Friends I've known for years.

Friends who haven't called to check up on me.

The loneliness tries to take hold again, but this time, I grab my phone and reread Rush's email, settling on the very last paragraph.

Rush,

What am I doing emailing you at eight at night? Giving in to thoughts that were too loud to ignore. I might not be as mature and well-adjusted as you think.

Hunter

Hunter,

Loud thoughts are kind of my thing. Try purple music or coloring or researching ants. I also have a list of podcasts I can recommend the first few episodes of, but I'm currently on a taco hunt so I'll have to get those to you later.

Rush

. . .

AND LIKE EVERY time I email him, my head is left spinning. A taco hunt? Only the first few episodes? Resigned to another night spent alone, I open my music app, search up purple music, and hit Play.

Apparently, "music" was a loose term.

I'm about to turn it off when I decide to give it a bit longer.

Then I open Google, smile trembling my lips, and type in one word.

Ants.

What has my life come to?

Chapter 10

Rush

There is a misplaced pot on my desk.

I know it's misplaced the second I catch sight of it, because I didn't leave it there, and as I get closer, it becomes clear it's the one I gave Hunter yesterday. At least twenty colorful butts stare back at me.

Sticking out of the soil on the side is a sign with a cute ant drawn on it.

I pick it up and read: *I thought it was import-ant to return this.*

My snort is so loud I struggle to stifle it.

Autumn glances up from her desk. "What have you got over there?"

"A connection."

Her eyes widen. "Wanna connect a little quieter?"

"You wouldn't understand."

"I literally never do." She answers a call, shooting me a

you're strange but I love you smile, and I throw back an *I think you're even stranger but I love you too* one in return.

Then, I turn back to the ant in question. Because there's only one person this could be from … I think. From what I can recall, I haven't mentioned ants to anyone else, and it would be an odd coincidence this would appear the day after I told him to look them up.

Plus, you know, the pot *was* in Hunter's office.

Look at that. It only took one day for me to upgrade us from animosity to colleagues to trading puns.

Everyone knows puns signal true friendship.

Puns, plural, because this gift was for him, and I'll be sending it right back.

"Would you answer that ringing?" Cranky Gates snaps, looking pointedly over the partition at my phone. It might be the last thing I want to do, but it's better to get it over with than have Gates grumbling under his breath all day—that kind of muttering can't be good for his throat.

Unfortunately, after that call, more come through, and I jump from job to job, updating portfolios and filing claims and renewing coverage for the next year.

The others leave for lunch, but I swallow my sandwich at my desk and keep moving. It's one of those days where I don't stop for a moment, and it isn't until late afternoon that I realize I'm so frazzled because I forgot to write my to-do list and that the butt-pot is still on my desk.

I lean back in my chair, craning my neck toward Hunter's office, and find it empty.

Bingo.

Perfect time to strike.

My ant is decidedly less cute than his, more anatomically accurate, and I impress myself with the cranky face and hands-on-thorax pose.

Why are you trying to ANTagonize me? All I'm feeling is disappoint-mANT that you didn't appreciate my gift.

Then, with super-sneaky stealth mode, I duck into his office and plonk it on his table. I'm tempted to take his pen so he can't write back, but I'm way too curious to know what he's going to say.

I jump when my phone vibrates in my pocket.

I fish it out, and as soon as I see the "Ian" on the screen, my good mood plummets. Objectively, I'm done with the guy, but there's still that tiny nugget in my chest that is convinced I loved him at one point. I don't miss him, but I do miss the happiness I felt over having a boyfriend.

Or at least when I *thought* I had a boyfriend.

"That him?"

I almost jump for dear life at Hunter's deep voice, and I whirl around and find him leaning confidently in the doorway. He can talk all he likes about not being mature or whatever, but he intimidates me. He did on the night we met as well. How one person can be so sexily *himself* isn't something I can process.

"You enjoying sneaking up on people and scaring the shit out of them?"

A tiny smirk. "You're in my office."

Huh? I glance around and confirm that, yes, apparently I am. Ian's message still has me thrown, and it's taking a second to ground myself.

"I can't help but notice you didn't answer the question," he says, "so I'm going to take that for a yes."

"It's not a yes. I just can't figure out what answer to give you."

"That's up to you."

"I'm not very good at making the right choices, so sometimes it's nice for people to tell me what their expectations are, and then I can decide if I want to meet them or not."

Hunter's dark eyebrows flex together as he studies me for a moment. "Okay, then … I guess I was sort of hoping you'd confirm or deny my guess."

"And how would you feel if I confirmed it?"

"Gutted." His smile is stiff. "And relieved if you denied it, though judging by your face, that isn't going to happen."

"I can block his number."

Hunter studies me, completely unreadable. "Do you want to block his number?"

"It's complicated, because I do, but messaging him became a habit, and breaking habits isn't something I do easily. I don't want to message him, but taking away the option to makes me all panicky and weird."

"Okay."

There's something in his tone I don't like. Something that makes me shift as I try to read on his face what people mean when they won't say it. "Does that annoy you?"

"I … I'm not going to tell you what to do."

"You're my boss. That's literally your job."

"Not when it comes to your personal life, it isn't."

That would make things so much easier though. To have a personal life wizard who could follow me around and point out where I'm going wrong and when I'm running late and reminding me to eat and exercise and reach out to people.

"Actually, why *isn't* that a job?"

Hunter doesn't immediately answer. "What?"

"A life wizard."

"Do you mean a life coach?"

"No, I mean a wizard. Because if they could do all *that*, it would be magical." Not having to be yelled at for being late ever again? Not having friends get cranky with me for not reaching out in months? Not going all day without realizing that I forgot to eat? Yeah, I'd pay for that. With the money that I don't have.

But hey, it looks like I'm not getting fired, so maybe I can save for it?

I open my phone to leave myself a note when I glimpse the preview from Ian.

Can you please just—

Damn, that's an unfortunate place to leave off. There could be way too many endings to that sentence.

Can you please just talk to me?

Can you please just jump off a cliff?

Both versions are wildly different in tone, and I snigger at the thought of Molly seeing him write something mean. He'd tell Xander, and then I'd have to call my vicious little attack dog off. I can only imagine the nasty things he'd say to Ian if he got the chance.

"That good, huh?"

I glance up, surprised to find Hunter still watching me.

"Ah …" I stuff my phone away. "Nope. Everything is fine here."

"Right." The bastard actually rolls his eyes at me. "Do me a favor: if things do restart between the two of you, I don't want to hear about it."

I almost growl. "I've told you that's not happening. We can't keep going over this. I understand we're not close and we don't know each other, but we've exchanged puns, for crying out loud! I don't do that with just *anyone.* Mostly because people don't really like puns, but I figure that has to at least mean we're friendly. And friends don't lie to other friends."

"Friends lie to each other all the time."

I wrinkle up my face. "What kind of friends do you have?"

"Ah, the usual kind."

If those are the types of people Hunter has been relying on his whole life, no wonder he's gotten cynical. But that's okay. Maybe he *does* need to meet my friends. Shake things up a little.

Hunter rubs a big hand over his face. "I think the reason I can't move on is because he feels like he's getting away with it, you know? There were no consequences except losing me, and judging by his reaction to that, it wasn't much of a loss. So while I'm moping in a hotel room every night, he's—"

"A hotel room?"

He waves his hand like it's not important, but how long has he been staying there? Hotels are nice for a holiday, but not long term. What if there are bedbugs? Or people having noisy sex in the room right next to you? "My point is—"

"I *said* we could team up for revenge. I wasn't joking about that."

The look that crosses his face is almost comical. I definitely can't read it. "What, you want to egg his house or something?"

I shrug. "Not my area of expertise, but some of my roommates are very petty. They'd have some random ideas."

"Your roommates?"

"Uh-huh."

"Is this coat-cum Xander one of your roommates?"

"Sure is."

"And you want to go to them for help?"

"Why not?"

Hunter watches me, and I watch him, and both of us just stand there watching each other.

I wait for him to catch up.

He doesn't.

"So … revenge? Yes or no?"

"It seems … drastic."

"More drastic than fucking a bunch of guys behind your fiancé's back?"

Hunter's jaw tenses as pure anger crosses his face. It reminds me of the night we met, when he looked like a titan about to go on a rampage. "Good point."

"Anyway, you let me know. I need to go answer my phone before Gates spits his false teeth at me."

"He has false teeth?"

"Doesn't everyone over the age of forty?"

"Not even close." The tension in Hunter's face makes me realize I don't actually know how old he is.

"Wait. Are *you* over forty?"

Hunter almost falls off the doorframe as he chokes. "I'm thirty-one, asshole."

"Ah. So almost."

He throws his hands up. "Go answer your phone."

"Is it ringing?"

Hunter huffs, takes me by the arm, and tugs me out of his room. I'm not prepared when his dark eyes meet mine, and I forget to look away, forget what he said or if I should be coming or going. Those eyes crease slightly at the corners for the second before he closes his door between us.

I have to physically shake myself free from whatever *that* was.

By the time I get back to my desk, grin taking over my face, I drop back into my chair and cross my hands behind my head. I wait for the phone to stop ringing before I pull the little plug from the back and relax into the luxury of stillness.

The office isn't a good place when I'm feeling overstimulated, and today has been an absolute mess, so I grab my noise-canceling headphones from the drawer and lean right back in my chair, trying to see into Hunter's office.

Our eyes instantly meet, and he shakes his head my way before turning to his computer.

The interoffice chat window pops open on my screen.

HUNTER:

Now I know what you meant about "exchanging" puns

ME:

Did you consult a dictionary?

HUNTER:

I just didn't assume you'd be enough of a cocky shit to play boomerang with this stupid plant.

ME:

You really are breaking my heart. I put a lot of thought into that gift.

HUNTER:

Nice try, but you already told me you bought it on a whim.

ME:

It's hard to guilt trip people when you don't remember what you've said half of the time.

HUNTER:

That doesn't sound like a bad quality to me.

ME:

Yeah because now you get to use it against me. Enjoy the gift. It's yours.

HUNTER:

It's distracting.

ME:

It's a plant! What's the problem?

HUNTER:

The problem is that I'm an ass man ;)

I stare at the words, waiting for them to rearrange into his real reply. But they don't change. Just keep staring back at me. Taunting me. Because ... that was a joke. He's joking with me. Intimidating Hunter suddenly isn't so intimidating.

And I have an *incredible* ass.

Chapter 11

Hunter

I'm not sure which part of my brain knocked loose when I agreed to do this, but I can't get out of the car. It's a quiet street, Victorian home hidden behind a bunch of wild trees, with Rush and his roommates all waiting for me to show up.

I'm sure this crosses some kind of fraternization rules at work.

Then again, probably every one of our emails do too.

We exchanged more last night, and even though objectively I know I need to put an end to them, every time I close my phone and resist replying, I can't stop thinking about it. I must be lonelier than I thought, and emailing Rush helps keep that emptiness away.

Maybe it's one of those situations where people who go through shared trauma together bond. I'm not sure that seeing my fiancé's side piece half-naked at our door could be considered traumatic, but it wasn't pleasant.

Is shared unpleasantries a thing?

Whatever it is, there's something there when I think of Rush that goes beyond him being one of the people I'm supposed to manage.

A face pops up in the window that's visible between the trees, and I realize I've been spotted. I can't even leave and pretend that I got lost and couldn't find the place.

I leave my car and walk up the long front path, apprehension settling over my shoulders. What will Rush's friends think? What's he told them about me? Am I the asshole in this situation? Or do they think it's weird that his supervisor is stopping by for a casual visit to plot revenge against *our* ex?

Fuck it, I'm here now.

I'll fake confidence to get me through this, and if they all hate me, I know how to show myself the door. I haven't done anything wrong, but I know from firsthand experience that means fuck all when you're hell-bent on finding someone to blame.

I blamed Rush; there's no reason to think his friends won't blame me.

Yet that doesn't sit right with me. Some small part of me actually wants these men to like me. I have absolutely no one in Seattle, and I don't want to put off the first people I meet.

My hands are tucked deep into my pockets as I climb the front stairs. A plaque reading *Big-Boned Bertha* sits by the glossy white front door, and as I'm convincing myself to knock, the door flies open.

A small guy with blue hair is all I manage to catch sight of before he throws himself into my arms.

"I'm so, so sorry! Ian is a horrible person who can go to hell for what he did to you both, and if I ever see him, I'll rip his balls out through his throat and then teabag him with them." The guy's arms squeeze tighter around me as I wriggle my hands free from my pockets and set them gently on his back. I have no idea what's happening here, but I don't hate it.

Then he sniffs, right by my collar. And again. "You smell just as good in real life."

Ah. I pull back a little. "Xander?"

His whole face lights up. "Rush has talked about me?"

And maybe it's evil and not the way to make friends, but I can't stop myself from teasing. "He said you liked my coat."

Xander eases himself away from me. "So that's where it went."

"I'm glad you appreciated my, uh, taste." And when I realize what I've said, I hurry to add, "In clothes!"

Xander laughs and grabs my hand, tugging me inside. I'm caught off guard by all the physical contact. It's not bad. Just different. "*You're* Rush's boss, then?"

"Technically, yes."

"Technically?"

"I've just started at the company, and given how Rush and I met … I don't … I don't feel that dynamic."

Xander bats his eyes up at me. "I'd let you be the boss of me any day."

That stuns me stupid.

"Let him go, Z," a large man with dark red hair says as he steps into the hall. Xander pouts and drops my hand, and they have some kind of exchange through looks before Xander crosses his arms and heads into the room the redhead came from.

"Sorry about him."

"He was fine."

Redhead disappears, too, just as there are thunderous footsteps overhead, followed by what sounds like someone falling down the stairs.

And when I retrace my steps to investigate—it *was* someone falling down the stairs.

"Jesus, Rush!"

He blinks up at me from where he's splayed on his back on the bottom few steps. His shirt is on inside out and back to front, and he's got both legs in one side of his sweats. "Ah … hey …"

I duck down to help him sit. "Are you okay? You didn't hit your head or anything, did you?"

I feel around his hair, but Rush catches my wrists and pulls them away. "I'm fine. Probably bruised in multiple places, but it happens. I'm not even the clumsy one around here." He laughs as he releases me and reaches for his pants.

All I can do is watch as he pulls one leg out, revealing miles of hairy thigh and a cozy bulge beneath his briefs, before he stuffs his leg back in the right side and the view disappears again.

I clear my throat and drag my gaze to the wall. "Any reason why you're half-dressed?"

"I lost track of the time and heard you down here. I'm told it's polite to make introductions, but given you're already inside, I take it you've at least met someone. Unless you let yourself in, which is kind of rude, but okay with me."

"I met Xander."

"Oh no. Did he try to have sex with you?"

My mouth drops as I try to figure out what to say to that. "He said I smelled good, but that was as creepy as it got."

"Oh good, he's learning manners. Let's go."

"Where?"

"The living room is where we have our important meetings."

"And this is an important meeting?"

"Of course." He gives me one of his bright smiles.

And this is exactly why I find it so hard to ignore him and act like he's any other employee. I really had no hope when it came to him. Not when he's so … pure. Happy. Pretty fucking naive. It's becoming clear to me how Ian had such an easy time of stringing him along and why Rush didn't notice he was being played.

With me in another city and Rush distracted and unfocused, we were perfect prey. I wonder what he looked for in those other men.

I shake it off before my mood can take a nosedive. Plotting revenge requires anger, not sadness. But before we can step into the room, Rush pauses, turning slightly and setting his fingertips on my chest. The touch is so unexpected it takes me a moment to realize he's said something.

"What?"

"Just checking you're still okay with this? It's sort of weird, having you here. And I don't want you to judge my friends once it's over because things might get strange, but please give them a chance. They all have big hearts." Rush's voice is sort of scratchy but so sincere, his hazel eyes dancing in the dim light of the hall.

"Wait. You think I'm going to judge *them*?"

"Obviously. We're not like you."

Like me. Fucking hell. I want to headbutt the wall to prove to him I'm not as in control as he thinks. "All morning, I've been freaking out thinking they're going to judge me."

"Really?"

"Yeah. I want them to like me, obviously."

"But why? You might never have to see them after today."

That's the question, isn't it? Why do I care what this bunch of random men think? I'm comfortable in social settings most of the time, but since moving here, my confidence has taken a real hit. Being the guy with a stable job and a stable relationship helped create this perfect family guy persona, and without that, I think I'm having an identity crisis.

I'm standing in a house with my employee who fucked my ex, for fuck's sake.

My hands slide through my perfectly styled hair, and I ignore the urge to fix it again.

"Can we get this over with?"

Rush laughs and tugs a chunk of hair that's fallen over my forehead. "Careful, you'll start to look like me."

He turns and leads the way, giving me a second to run my eyes over him. From his chaotic blond curls on the top of his head to his tanned, lean form and … Jesus. Rush has an ass. An ass that's on full display in those sweatpants.

Yeah. I'm never going to look like him.

"Everyone," he says, and we step into the living room. "This is The Hunter. Hunter, this is everyone."

He's not joking about everyone. There are another six men watching us.

There's a round of hellos as I lift my eyebrows Rush's way. "*The* Hunter? What, I have mythical status or something?"

"I know you're joking, but you really do. I think you're underestimating how much I talk about you."

Considering until the last few days, Rush wouldn't have had anything positive to talk about, that doesn't fill me with confidence. "Okay, but to clear things up, I've apologized to him for being a dick."

"You were mean to Rush?" Redhead snarls.

"Down, Seven," a guy with brown curls and big eyes says, resting a hand on Seven's leg. "I'm sure The Hunter has a perfectly reasonable explanation for why he was a dick to someone like Rush."

"Look, I was angry about what happened and how I found out. It was misplaced, but the night we met, I was a bit of an asshole."

Seven frowns. "Didn't you order him a ride?"

"And give him your coat?" Xander adds evilly.

"Yes, but I was a dick while I did it."

They exchange looks, and Rush laughs. "I told you that you were being kind."

"I … that wasn't …"

A blond man with a British accent pipes up. "Regardless of how you felt, you made sure Rush was okay. That signals a decent person in my books."

I'm not used to praise, especially not from strangers. He can see it that way all he wants. I'd been mad at Rush for making me feel sorry for him and wanted nothing more in that moment than to make him go away. Preferably forever.

That doesn't sound like the type of thing you'd tell someone's friends.

"Either way," I say, taking the seat next to the one Rush has fallen into. "I've moved on. Kinda. And that's why we're here."

Seven gives a scary-looking smile. "Revenge."

"Yes. That."

Rush hugs one knee to his chest and slings the other over the armrest, angling him closer to me. "Okay, who's got ideas on how we do it?"

Xander's hand shoots into the air. "Isn't it obvious? To get revenge on him for fucking you both over … you need to fuck each other."

Chapter 12

Rush

Fuck each other? Well, that's one avenue I hadn't considered. Shocking, given how hot Hunter is, but I guess with how we met, thinking about him and sex in the same context wasn't something my brain was into.

Fucking him wouldn't be a hardship though. Especially now he doesn't seem to hate me, that will definitely make things easier.

"But how will that work?" I ask. "It's only revenge if he knows about it."

"Film yourselves," Christian suggests.

"Only if you're comfortable with that," Seven rushes to say. "Don't do anything you'll regret."

I wave a hand toward Hunter. "Would *you* regret sleeping with this man?"

"I wouldn't," Madden adds. "Would you?"

"Well, I guess we do work together, which could cause some issues."

Hunter jerks around to look at me. "That's the only issue you have with this plan?"

Is there another one? I screw my face up as I think it over. I suppose there's always the chance Ian won't care, but with how much he still messages me, it'd probably get him in the ego at least a little. He was *engaged* to Hunter and stringing me along for a year; if he just wanted sex with any old person, he wouldn't have gone to those lengths. Thank fuck we used protection, is all I can say. Oh. Maybe that's it.

"I have condoms if that's what you're worried about."

"Condoms …" He looks a second away from laughing, but he pushes it down again. "They're talking about us having sex. Together."

"I know. I'm following."

"You …" His eyes sweep over me before coming to rest on mine. "You'd sleep with me?"

"Have you looked in the mirror lately? You can't be that surprised."

"No, it's … it's not …"

"You mean the awkwardness? I thought we were past that. We're friends, aren't we?"

"I don't think I'd go that far."

"But—"

He sets his big hand on the knee I'm hugging, and I go almost cross-eyed looking at it. Having those hands on me? Yes, please. And I should probably stop thinking about *that*, given I thought it would be a smart move to wear sweats today.

"Any other ideas?" Hunter asks. "Ones that don't involve pimping ourselves out."

Xander snarls. "My idea would have worked."

"Of course it would have," Madden says. Thankfully, he

followed the rules about wearing clothes when guests come over, even if he's only in loose shorts that, from a certain angle, I'd probably be able to glimpse brain. "But if The Hunter doesn't want to fuck our boy, that's his call. If you ask me, he's missing out, but—"

I don't catch the end of what Madden said, just fixate on the part about Hunter not wanting to fuck me. Am I not hot enough? Doesn't he think I can suck a cock like no one's business? Ian cheated with me for a reason, dammit.

"Excuse me," I snap. "I am a fucking scream in bed."

The room goes oddly quiet as Madden cuts off.

Hunter's lips twitch. "What?"

"I'm *just* saying, there's no one you could fake fuck better than me."

"Fake fuck?"

"Well, *actually* fuck, but for fake reasons."

He stares at me for a moment, something he does a lot. Apparently, Hunter takes time to think instead of blurting out whatever's on his brain. "I'm not going to fuck someone for revenge."

Xander sniggers. "Didn't say you wouldn't fuck Rush though, did you?"

"Can we move on?" Hunter asks through a sigh.

"Hold on a moment," Émile says. At least with his accent, he sounds fancier than the rest of us, so hopefully, Hunter will listen to his advice. "Poorly executed, but I think Xander's right. Ian sounds like a narcissist. Rush was his plaything, and in his mind, he was getting one up on Hunter by keeping Rush as a pet. Honestly, he probably felt inadequate compared to Hunter, as most of us would do next to a six-foot-two king, so in his mind, this was proving to himself that he was desirable. Rush is his. Tied into his virility as a man. Knowing that you took his plaything would be a devastating blow. And, let's face it, fun for the both of you."

"I *just* said—" Hunter starts, but Émile cuts him off.

"I'm not saying to have sex. I don't think you need to go that far. But what about kissing? Or even pretend kissing. You only need one photo to send him. It can be closed-mouthed and everything."

Hunter turns to me, grim look on his face. "I thought you said they'd have good ideas."

"No, I'm sure I said they'd have random ideas. And so far, this is exceeding all my expectations."

"And mine. Does anyone have anything that doesn't involve Rush and me sharing bodily fluids?"

The silence is deafening.

"Maybe we *should* egg his house." What else do we have at this point?

Hunter groans, burying his hands in his hair again and messing it up even more. I like it. The contrast between buttoned-up work Hunter and this T-shirt-and-jeans-wearing Hunter. It's mildly disappointing that he didn't want to have sex because I wouldn't have been opposed to exploring those tree-trunk thighs with my tongue.

But it's just as well. We still have to work together.

My friends throw out some more ideas, and Molly takes notes as they talk. I try to act interested and involved, but some of the things they throw out there are college-level pranks, and I can't see Hunter being interested in any of that.

We wanted revenge.

We have a good plan.

But if Hunter doesn't want me, I'll let it go; sexual attraction isn't something you can force.

What feels like a second later, he stretches his hands out over his head. "Well, thank you. I think we've got some good ideas to go over."

"Wait, you're going already?"

He turns to me with a small smile. "We've been here for an hour."

"*Have* we?"

The smile widens. "Time flies when you're plotting revenge."

And that might be the case, but I'm not ready for him to go yet. All morning, I'd gotten worked up in my head about my friends and him and how it would all mesh together, but now he's here … it's pissing me off we didn't get a moment alone. Well, other than that moment where he found me ass up on the stairs, and I don't really count half-naked embarrassments as part of our relationship. Even if that's what started us in the first place.

"Are you leaving because you're done with this conversation or because you have plans?"

Hunter eyes me curiously. "Why? What did you have in mind?"

Nothing, actually. All I know is that I don't want Hunter to go. It's Saturday morning, we're not back at work until Monday, and the emails are all fun and great, but I'm getting a kick out of talking to his actual face instead of my screen, and I want some more of that.

We could hunt down Kismet the cat and see if Hunter has any more luck getting the furball to love him than the rest of us. Or we could do naked yoga with Madden. Go out for lunch? I gnaw on my bottom lip as I flick through ideas and dismiss them just as quickly.

Then I think of my atelier. It's nothing fancy, and he'll probably be confused, but it's something I know a lot about and will give us talking points. Just us. Maybe help him thaw to me a little more.

"You like clothes."

His gaze travels the room before landing on me again. "Well, yes …"

"Follow me." I jump out of my chair and feel Hunter follow me. "Thanks for all the help, guys!"

"Do you want your list?" Molly asks, holding it up, and I pluck it from his grip as I pass. This will come in handy when I want to burn something later. TPing Ian's house? Sending a baseball-bat-sized dildo to his office? Fuck me. The asshole would probably use it to spite us.

We climb the stairs and follow the hallways deep into the house until we reach the room at the back that I've set up as my atelier. It's got soaring ceilings and high windows that filter in the afternoon light, sending everything a burned rose color. The room is like a deep inhale after being in a musty closet for too long. I love it.

"What's this?" Hunter's deep voice shivers through the quiet space.

"My safe place."

"Safe?"

I approach my workstation and run my hands over the fabric I left lying there. "I like to hide here sometimes. When my thoughts get too much. Or the world gets too busy. It's quiet, and the others know that when I'm in here, I need space. We all have our coping mechanisms. Christian and his blanket burritos, Seven and his late-night internet holes."

"I don't know what either of those things mean."

"You don't have to. But we do. All of us. They're my family, and I really hope you don't hate them because I love them more than words, even if I don't understand them all the time."

"It's cool that you have that."

"Yeah?"

Hunter nods, hands in his pockets, strolling closer to look at the suit I half abandoned that's pinned to a bust. "None of my friends have contacted me since I moved here."

"Have you contacted them?"

"They're not the ones who went through hell."

"Maybe they don't know what to say to you."

He stays quiet, and I replay the question to work out if I've said the wrong thing. He keeps his thoughts to himself, which only makes mine louder. Faster. Racing through all the possibilities of what could be going on behind those dark, intense eyes.

Was this all a mistake? Should I have never mentioned the revenge and dragged him here and got my friends in on it? Does he think it's weird that I need a place to get away? That I make clothes?

"Why isn't it finished?" he asks, running his finger along the edge of the suit.

"I got distracted."

His eyes crease as he holds back his smile. "Of course you did. Do you finish anything?"

"Believe it or not, I do. When Christian got married, I took a week off work, didn't sleep, and made us all suits and a dress for Elle on super-short notice. They looked fucking awesome."

He turns to me. "I sort of love that you mention all these people and assume I know who you're talking about."

"Huh. Sorry."

"No, I'm being serious."

I consider him for a moment. "You can talk to me."

"Isn't that what we're doing?"

"No, I mean …" What *do* I mean? "You said your friends haven't called. Well, I might not know what to say either, but if you need to talk to someone, you can fumble through it with me."

"Thanks," he says on a whisper.

"Give me your phone. I'll put my number in, and then you don't have to use work emails anymore."

Hunter hands his over and watches as I punch in the numbers. When I'm done, I hold it out and look up at him, surprised that we're standing closer than I thought. His gaze roams over my face, hovering on my lips before flicking up to my eyes again. It's hard to meet his steady gaze. Hard to keep contact and wonder what he sees.

"You would really sleep with me for revenge?"

I take a moment, trying to figure out what kind of answer he's looking for from me. "I … I wouldn't with just anyone. Like, I hook up sometimes, but it's not my favorite thing. You, well, we're friends. Or at least I consider us friends. And I don't like that Ian hurt you. I don't like that he hurt me either, obviously, but if Émile's right and we can get back at him …" I shrug, forcing myself to meet his eye. "It would be worth it. And you're really hot, so it's not like I wouldn't enjoy it in the process."

He doesn't laugh like I thought he might. "What about after?"

"Well, I won't kick you out of bed if that's what you're worried about."

His expression tightens. "Wouldn't it be awkward?"

"Isn't that up to us? Besides, you said you wouldn't do it, so this whole discussion is pointless, isn't it?"

"True." He takes a long, measured breath. "I didn't say I wouldn't kiss you though."

Well, that shocks the hell out of me. "Really?"

His lips twitch. "I didn't say I would either."

"Well, I'm here for it."

"How would we do it? You know. If we did."

I glance over at the sewing machine on my workstation. "We'd prop your phone up there."

Hunter hesitates, then takes the phone I'm still holding and takes a step away. He flicks it over to video and positions his phone so I'm in the frame. "Like this?"

I nod, not sure exactly what's happening, but the excitement in my gut tells me to go with it. "Then we'd turn it on. And you'd kiss me."

"I'd kiss you?"

"Yeah … it'd look better like that. I think."

Hunter's frozen for five seconds … ten … and then his finger flicks out to jab at the big red button, and when he swings back around toward me, all the earlier amusement is gone. He stalks closer, one hand closes over my waist, and he grips the back of my neck with the other. He tugs me against him, chests meeting, thighs bumping, and as I draw a sharp breath, his mouth slams down over mine.

Hunter commands the kiss like he commands a room, in control, taking the lead, rearranging my scrambled mind, and leaving me reeling. His teeth clamp down on my bottom lip, and the second I grunt in pain, the second my lips part, his tongue pushes its way inside. I grip onto his shoulders, trying to match his passion, trying to remember what we're doing this for, but losing the battle as my need overrides my brainpower.

The distance between us disappears, both of us pressing tighter together, chasing the passion of the kiss and the sizzling chemistry building in my gut.

The possessive way Hunter's holding me has lust burning up my veins, and my cock is reacting eagerly. Insistently. I'm a horny mess as I grind it into his hip, and the delicious groan he lets out spurs me on.

Hunter's hand leaves my waist and drops to my ass, grabbing a painful handful. His fingers dig in, and I wrench from his mouth with a throaty moan.

"Fuck," he grunts, mouth dipping to lick his way along my neck. My legs are useless, a jelly mess, unable to hold my weight anymore.

I'm shaking against him as his teeth dig into the dip where my neck meets my shoulder. Cock aching, I pant as I try to catch my breath.

His hand tightens on my ass, squeezing, kneading before he releases it like he's been zapped. Hunter's lips disappear from my neck, breathing as labored as mine. "I think … I think we've got it."

"Got it?"

"The shot. To send Ian."

"Oh. Right. The shot. Yes."

He pulls back a fraction so he can see my face. "Is that still okay?"

"Of course, that's what we did this for. The whole reason. Revenge. Ha. We sure showed him."

Hunter studies me for a moment. His thumb swipes my cheek in a way that doesn't at all help the situation in my pants. "Should I not have done that?"

I shake off my haze. "I will never regret a kiss like that."

____

Chapter 13

____

Hunter

Well, I didn't wake up this morning expecting to be in this kind of ethical dilemma, but here I am. The first time I rewatched my kiss with Rush, I was sort of blown away by it. The fiftieth time? Yeah, I'd had to jerk off by that point.

I was completely unprepared for how hot a kiss it would be.

I'd expected awkward. Forced. It's why I'd launched right into it before I could stop myself, but with the way Rush immediately let go, went to putty under my hands, rubbing himself sluttily against my leg ...

My head drops back because that image is goddamn sinful, and I really don't have it in me to get off again, especially since I need to be able to go to work Monday and look Rush in the eyes.

There's also the matter of the video. And Ian. Who I'm supposed to be sending the video to.

It's what Rush wanted, but now that I've seen it, I don't want to share that moment.

Does that then make me an asshole for kissing Rush under false pretenses?

Or am I allowed to suddenly find boundaries I didn't know I had?

And like everything in my life lately, I've managed to turn kissing a hot man into a clusterfuck. Maybe I should have slept with him. A quick, impersonal hookup. Filmed it. Sent it. Moved on.

I don't usually kiss my hookups, and maybe that's the difference?

Or maybe it's because everything with Rush is already so complicated that no matter what we did, it was always going to get messy. It's still strange to me how easily he admitted he found me hot and would sleep with me. The honesty was clear, and while I'd been more cagey in my interest, I can't deny it's there. The second Xander had suggested we fuck, my mind immediately ran away with the idea, and now that we've kissed, it's only making me crave more.

It's probably a good thing Rush wasn't Ian's idea of a gift to share because now that I've tasted him, I'm craving him. Would once have been enough? I'm almost understanding why Ian did what he did; the only difference between us is that I never would have cheated, no matter how desperately I wanted someone.

My horny high dissolves.

As attracted to him as I am, even if Ian and I had slept with him together, that would have been it for me. When I'm in a relationship, I'm committed. I'd never cross those lines, emotionally, mentally, or physically.

Ian is a filthy fucking reminder that not everyone feels that way.

Does Rush?

It's not a gamble I can take. Not after what happened.

I need to put that attraction aside, delete the video, and resist the urge to keep emailing him.

I don't delete the video, but I do make it the rest of the day without reaching out.

Sunday isn't so easy. I'm antsy, and work isn't holding my attention. It takes next to no time to duck down to the store down the street so I can stock the small fridge and cupboard in my room, and so, keeping my fingers crossed to the universe, I pull up house listings.

Some cute apartments, a few houses I already know are out of my price range, and … wait. I pause on a two-bedroom home that looks fucking perfect.

It's pale yellow, has a tidy front porch, hardwood floors, and a bay window at the back that overlooks the green yard. The kitchen and bathroom have seen better days, which is probably why the price is what it is.

From the small map, it looks easy driving distance to the office as well.

My heart is thundering in my rib cage as I fill out the interest form and ask when I can see the house. I need it. I can't—for my bank balance and my own goddamn mental state—miss out on another place. Just looking at the photos already feels like home.

It's only a few minutes later that I get a reply:

I'm sorry Mr. Barrett, this home has already been rented.

What the *fuck*?

I almost throw my phone. Today. It was listed to-goddamn-day. How many real estate agents are working on the weekend, let alone *renting* a fucking house with zero goddamn notice. Did those people even look at the property? Or did they just sign a check?

The long, loud growl that erupts from me is feral.

I can't keep doing this. I can't.

I've made the decision to stay at work, to keep chipping away at building a life in Seattle, and I'm buffered from every angle. How many more signs am I supposed to be hit over the head with before I give up? Jesus. Even the kiss with Rush is going to make things weird. Am I better off heading home? At least my parents won't be charging me a hundred and fifty bucks a night rent.

Even thinking that makes my stomach curl.

Rent.

Parents.

Moving home.

I'm trying so fucking hard to stand on my own two feet. That's what's most frustrating about all this. Am I really that unlucky? Or is there something so fundamentally wrong with me that I can't see where I keep screwing up?

I'm burning to talk to someone. To not feel so isolated.

My parents will only baby me, and while I'd love their support right now, what I need is tough love. Someone to remind me to keep going.

So I open Audrey's number and hit Call.

"Brother," she says as soon as she answers.

"Sister."

"Do you need something, or are you just bored?"

I snigger. "Bit of both?"

Audrey laughs, and there's a muffled conversation in the background before she's back. "Okay, shoot."

"I think I'm failing."

"So don't."

"Wow. That easy, huh?"

"I don't see why not."

"While I love the sentiment, I'm going to need some help with the execution. I'm still in the hotel, I can't find anywhere to live, and I kissed one of my employees. Who happens to be the same man Ian cheated on me with."

There's a long silence. "Was it a good kiss?"

"That's the only reason I'm even mentioning it."

"Okay, so go with that."

I groan. "This isn't the part we're supposed to be focusing on."

"We can only focus on one thing at a time?"

"That's all I can handle." I scrub my hand through my hair. "I think if I find a place, everything else won't seem so bad. I'll actually be able to settle."

"Then find a place."

"I'm trying, but every time I send an enquiry through, the house is already gone or way too expensive for me."

"Borrow money from Mom and Dad."

I clench my jaw. Audrey's never had issues with asking for help, so maybe that's why she's running her own small business and has made a decent dent in her mortgage. But Audrey's always been very black-and-white, very literal in her way of thinking. If there's an easy and logical way to do something, that's the route she'll choose.

She'd never move to Seattle, ditch her fiancé, live out of a suitcase, and then set fire to the one good thing she has going for her.

If Ian had been *her* fiancé, he probably would have ended up on the street.

"Next plan?"

She sighs. "I dunno, Hunt. Why are you making things hard on yourself?"

"I'm not. I'm trying to do this on my own. Is that really a bad thing?"

"Of course it is."

"What steps would you take?"

"Move home."

It's getting very hard to keep my cool. "And if that wasn't an option?"

I can tell Audrey is already growing bored of this conversation. "Let's say I *had* to stay in Seattle for whatever reason. I'd either ask my boss for a signing bonus to make the first month's lease, *or* I'd walk into every real estate agency in the city asking what they have coming up and making it clear I have money ready to pay. Then I'd fuck my employee."

I scoff. "You would not."

"Okay, no I wouldn't. But you will, so I figured I might as well give you the go-ahead."

My face is burning. "I'm not going to fuck my employee."

"Well, fuck somebody. I always think more clearly after sex, and with the hot mess you currently are, I figure it can only help."

"Still weird to be talking to my baby sister about this."

"I pretend to be a virgin for Dad's sake. Please don't make me have to do it with you too."

"Yeah, sure, you have sex, I get it. So I find a place and go hook up. That's your advice?"

"Yep, though I'm struggling to see why you need that advice at all when it's so obvious."

Damn, she makes me want to shake her sometimes. "You're ignoring the part where finding a place isn't in my control. I can do all those things and still come up empty."

"Or you could do them and succeed. Have you asked around the office? People knowing people. That's how everyone gets ahead."

"Except then they'll know I'm living in a hotel."

"And there's your problem. You've always been too proud. You can either be proud or get a roof over your head; wanting both is just greedy."

"Right."

"Hey … you know I love you. Whatever you choose."

"Yeah, love you too."

"All you have to remember is don't fail."

We hang up, and I don't feel any better than I did before the call.

Don't fail …

It's motivating to think of it as simple as Audrey sees it, but I'm a realist. If life really was that simple, I'd be winning at it already.

Maybe I should have called my parents. Audrey gave me the dose of calm I needed, but I really could have used some comfort too, and Mom would have doled it out in spades … right before demanding I come back home where she can look after me.

I could reach out to one of my friends, but they're the kind to blow off my concerns and make a joke to try and get me feeling better.

You can talk to me.

I huff, pissed off with myself, because I *know* who I really want to reach out to. I know the person I wanted to call when I was calling Audrey.

The thing is, I'm pretty sure Rush wouldn't be able to help me at all. He'd go off on tangents and bring up random facts and talk about people I've never met … but it would be distracting, if nothing else. And it sounds dumb as fuck, but I like hearing his voice. Like talking to him.

I should be protecting myself better than this, but I'm an idiot, apparently.

My interest in Rush isn't going to help house me though, and at the end of the day, I can't put my job—the one stable thing in my life—on the line because of one kiss.

Rush will have to take a back seat in my mind. My fucking libido can take the week off.

Just like my pride, apparently, because I'm going to have to swallow it all and talk to people about my living situation, then hope like hell they can help out.

If they can't … I don't know what I'll do.

Don't fail.

Way easier said than done.

Chapter 14

Rush

The pot is back on my desk. I probably should be annoyed, but it's amusing at this stage.

There's a note like last time, and his ant illustration is pointing at me and wearing a bow tie. It's adorable.

Why are you so defiANT?

I smile and tuck the note into my desk drawer, then scramble to dig through my bag and find my notepad. My ant is slightly cuter than the one I drew the other day, and I add a halo above this one's head.

I prefer the term compassionANT.

I'm about to reach for the sticky tape and attach my drawing to the pot when I notice the dispenser is missing from the outline I drew on my desk. Each of my items have pseudo-chalk drawing outlines to keep them in line, like my own stationery crime scene. Now, Miss Peacock is missing from the office block with my tape.

Or something like that.

I open my mouth to ask Autumn if she knows where the fucking thing is when Eloise steals her attention first.

"Did you hear poor Hunter is practically homeless?"

My head shoots up. Apparently, the way to get my focus these days is to mention Hunter. "He's *what*?"

Her lips quirk as she looks me over in concern. "I know. I couldn't believe it. Hannah from accounts said this morning that he was asking around about places. And you know we have that suite out the back of our place, but we literally just rented it. I feel terrible."

"Yeah, uh-huh, okay. Homeless—can we go back to that?"

"He's staying in a hotel, Rush. It's horrible."

I rub the coarse stubble on my jaw. "I think he mentioned something about that, actually."

"He *did*? How long has he been staying there?"

"How am I supposed to know that? If he was moving in with his ex and that didn't work out, then probably since they split?" Well over a month ago. "Why doesn't he rent a place?"

"Keeps getting knocked back," she says miserably.

Autumn swings her chair around to face me. "Don't you have a bunch of spare bedrooms?"

"No. The four bedrooms that aren't currently bedrooms are being used for other things."

"What other things?"

"Xander's paint room, my atelier, Molly and Seven's office, and then the junk room."

"Why can't he have the junk room?" she asks.

"Because it's for junk."

Autumn sniggers. "I knew you were going to say that."

"Then why did you ask?" I snap.

Eloise's eyes are wide. "You can take the junk *out* of the room and it's no longer a junk room, Carey. He could stay with you."

She's looking at me like I'm an idiot, and I'm not confident that I'm not giving her the same look right back.

"But then where would we put our junk?"

"I dunno, the trash?"

The *trash*? I splutter over my words. "And what if we need something from the junk room that's no longer a junk room and we can't access it because we've thrown it away and it's now at the dump?"

"If it's in the junk room and you haven't used it, then chances are you'll never need to."

"But in my hypothetical scenario, I *do* need to, and now I can't."

"Then buy it again," Eloise says, and I'm sure she only refrains from adding *dum-dum* to the end of that sentence out of respect for the workplace.

"But if I buy it again, then I have it again, only in this scenario, I now have no junk room to store it in, which means I have to throw it out again, and now *two* things I can't use are at the dump." I shake my head sadly. "Honestly, Eloise, it's easy enough to suggest a man gives up his junk room, but you haven't thought this through at all."

Her mouth hangs open. "I'm going to make a coffee."

I snatch my to-go cup off my desk and hold it out to her. "Pretty please."

She takes it with a deep sigh, and if that's how she's already feeling at ten in the morning, it's going to be a long day for her. Maybe I'll order her some flowers to perk her up. I grab my phone, but as I go to attach the headset, my eyes land on the missing body—er, tape.

"Did you take my tape?" I ask Autumn.

She glances up from where she's just answered a call, and as she greets them, she holds hers up to me.

Eh, it'll do.

I tear off some tape, then attach it to my image so I can *finally* attach the image to the pot.

And of course, now that whole ordeal is over, Hunter is back at his desk.

Oh well. What's he going to do? Throw me and P.L. Ant out on our asses? I don't think so.

We shoulder open his half-closed door, and I let myself inside. "Morning!"

His lips twitch. And considering it's been three whole days of not seeing him or that lip twitch, it immediately lights me up inside.

"Rush."

"Hunter."

"Carey."

I hold up the pot. "P.L. Ant. I named him."

His gaze drops to the pot. "You named him?"

"Of course. We're basically in a custody battle right now—he needs *some* sense of belonging."

Hunter licks his lips, but his eyes are full of amusement. "Are you going to want to see the plant in a bow tie as well?"

"That could be the best idea you've ever had."

He hums. "How about flexible work arrangements for a good idea."

"I think I'm still a fan of the bow tie thing."

He laughs and points to the chair. "Sit your ass down."

I fold into the chair, hugging our pot to my midsection. "Okay, tell me your idea."

"You can't show up on time to save your life, so now you don't have to."

His words take a second to process. "I'm listening."

"You—and the team—get to set your own hours. As long as they're between seven and nine and you complete your set hours and assigned work. You can clock on and off to keep track."

"You're shitting me."

"I'm not." The smug smile he gives me is well deserved. "But it's going to require communication between you four and me. Think you can manage that?"

"Hey, I never have a problem with communication," I pretend-grumble. "Everyone else has a problem communicating with me."

"And yet, we manage."

I think back over our conversations. Since we resolved the tension between us, I don't think Hunter's gotten snappy with me once. I also can't remember getting snappy with him.

That's a bit cute of us.

"Why are people saying you're homeless?"

"They're *what*?"

"Saying you're homeless. Didn't we *just* say we don't have communication issues?"

"I know what you said, but who the hell is saying that?"

"Eloise. Who heard it from Hannah in accounts. They all sound worried about you, but you told me you're in a hotel, aren't you?"

"I am."

"Then why are they making out like you don't have somewhere to live?"

Hunter goes to run his hand through his hair but catches himself in time. He redirects to rubbing the back of his neck instead. His bicep moves under his tight shirt, and I have to bite my lip painfully to stop from saying anything. Hunter is a goddamn snack.

And my boss. Can't forget that part.

"This is why I didn't want to say anything."

"About?"

"I'm having trouble finding a place to rent. It's not a big deal, but I thought I'd ask around to see if anyone knew anyone. That's all."

I laugh, considering Ian is in real estate. "Kinda sucks that the one person who could have helped you is the whole reason you need to find a place to begin with."

Hunter's gaze sharpens. "I'm not calling him."

"I never said you should."

"Fuck." This time, he gives in and burrows his fingers into his hair. His voice is rough when he talks again. "He might be my only chance though."

"Are you really that desperate?"

"I can't keep living out of a hotel, Rush."

I deflate, mind stuck on my junk room and the fact he probably needs it more than Madden needs to store his multiple late-night purchases. Where I'm going to put everything, I have no goddamn clue, and it's giving me the ick to even offer this without a plan, but I … I can't *not*.

"We have a spare room," I say. "You can move in with me and my friends, but head's up, until you tell him not to, Xander will creep into your bed for snuggles at night. It's harmless, and he's sweet, but he always wakes up with a boner, so it's best to let him know up front and save you both the embarrassment. Unless you like being knob-nudged as a wake-up call, in which case, that's a guarantee. Don't worry about the junk. I'll … we'll …"

"That's very kind of you to offer, but it's a solid no. After …" He exhales stiffly. "I can't live in the same house as you."

"Scared you'll kiss me again?"

His eyes shoot to the door. "I'd prefer if no one in the office found out about that."

"Good idea."

"Have you told anyone?"

"No. Not even Madden."

"All right. Good."

My lips twist to the side. "What did Ian say?"

"About a house?"

"About the kiss."

"Oh." Hunter looks away suddenly, twisting his chair toward his computer screen. "I didn't … I couldn't send him the video."

"Ah. Not hot enough?"

He swallows loudly. "Yeah. Exactly."

"We can try again."

"Probably better we don't." He glances back over, dark, intense eyes sweeping over me. "It's crossing lines, and truthfully, I don't want to be kissing you and thinking about him. I don't want to think about him at all, and when it comes to you, that's basically a guarantee."

I shrug. "If you're kissing me right, you shouldn't be thinking about anything." When I was kissing him, Ian was the last thing on my mind.

Just Hunter.

And how goddamn sexy he is.

"But not sending the video was probably smart because now you can call him and get his help finding somewhere to live."

He covers his face with big hands and groans into them. "I really don't want to."

"Then keep living in the hotel."

"I *can't*."

"Then call him."

"Rush …"

I throw up the hand not holding P.L. Ant to me. "I really don't know what I'm supposed to say here. There, there? Does that work?"

"It doesn't work, but it's just occurred to me that you'd get along great with my sister."

"I dunno. I'm usually a flop with family members."

"You wouldn't be with her. Trust me."

I'll let him be confident about that. It's not like I ever *will* meet her, so neither of us can be proved right or wrong.

"She told me not to fail," Hunter says softly.

"Why does she think you would?"

"Because I do at just about everything."

I tilt my head to the side. "You got a promotion. You're stepping out on your own in a brand-new city. You've been here for like a week, and you're trying to work with our team instead of against it. All my friends love you. And you have a plant baby with me. What part of that is failing?"

Hunter barks a laugh. "The part where I still don't have anywhere to live."

"Okay, so call Ian. We can both agree he at least owes you this. Then, once you've found a place, you'll never speak with him again, and you'll have a home, and I can go back to admiring the hell out of you because you won't be doubting yourself anymore."

"Yeah, but you're forgetting the part where I have to actually talk to him."

"Of course I didn't forget that. I told you to call him."

"Yes, but … it's going to hurt."

Ohh … it's not the actual talking to him that Hunter's dreading. It's the feelings the conversation might bring. "Want me to stay?"

"I … shouldn't rely on you for every little thing."

"Says who?"

"It's not right, Rush."

I huff and plonk P.L. Ant onto his desk, then sit back in my chair with my arms crossed. "Let me make this easy for you. You have a call to make, and I'm not planning on going anywhere. We've got you."

"We?"

I nod to the pot. "We."

Hunter's lips do that sexy-as-fuck twitch again, and then he picks up his phone. He searches for a moment before clicking on the screen and lifting the phone to his ear. A second later, he changes his mind and switches it over to speaker instead.

It rings so long I think it's going to cut out, but just as I've given up hope for an answer, Ian's smooth voice comes down the line. "Hello?" He sounds irritated as hell.

"Ian."

"Yes?"

I hold back a snarl because doesn't he realize he's supposed to say Hunter's name back? It's like a game.

Hunter gives me a warning look, and I hurry to zip my lips.

"I wouldn't be making this call if I wasn't desperate."

There's a pause. "Okay …"

"I need help finding a place to live. I've been bouncing between hotels since you screwed me over."

"And why are you calling me?"

I remind myself not to get involved.

"Because you're a real estate agent, and I need somewhere to live." Hunter's voice is getting tense. "After what you did to me, the least you could do is help."

"Did to *you*? You left me. So what I was getting some ass on the side? You lived in another fucking city. I have needs. That was all ending when you moved here. That man was just a hole, but you didn't even give me the decency of a chance to explain. Fuck you."

And while I'm one hundred percent over Ian, I'm stuck on what he said about me. A hole? After a year together, after falling for the man and planning out my life with him … that's really all he thought about me?

"How dare you," Hunter says, and I glance up at the dangerous tone in his voice. His eyes are right on me, and it makes me feel small. Vulnerable. "A hole? *Needs*? You're pathetic. An absolute fucking moron. Enjoy the midlife crisis. When you end up alone one day, you'll have no one to blame but yourself."

"Yeah, but at least I'm not homeless. And judging by your records in front of me, you've been blacklisted by every agency in Seattle. Have a nice life, babe. Try not to miss me too badly."

He hangs up, and the silence left in the wake of that phone call is deafening.

Instead of cursing him out like I expect Hunter to, he clears his throat and asks, "You okay?"

"Umm … yeah. Just … I wasn't expecting that."

"Me either. And we both know he's wrong. He clearly doesn't think that when he's been messaging you nonstop."

"Right. Yeah." Still not sure that makes me feel any better. The problem is, Ian isn't the first guy to treat me like shit, and I get the gut-sinking feeling he won't be the last. I want love. I want a boyfriend who's as crazy about me as I am about them. Who doesn't try to make me into someone I'm not or love me *despite* my "quirks." I don't have quirks. I'm just myself. Will it ever be enough?

"*Carey.*"

I jerk up to meet his eyes.

His smile is soft as he reaches for the pot and pulls it toward him. "Our baby doesn't like seeing you upset."

Something lights up behind my rib cage. "Sorry."

"Don't be. The only one who should be sorry, as usual, is Ian."

"Yeah, that was …" I puff out a breath. "Are *you* okay? It kinda sounds like—"

"He's put the word out not to rent me a place? Yeah. At least now I know why I was having the worst luck."

"What are you going to do?"

He crosses his arms over his desk, and for a moment, he looks invincible. "Not fail. That asshole lit a fire under my ass. I'm not leaving Seattle. I don't care how long it takes me."

____

Chapter 15

____

Hunter

"Are you sure you want to do this?" I ask, leaning over Rush's phone with him. I'd told myself I wouldn't leave work with him, told myself we'd have some distance, but here we are, at Urban Dive, with the text message thread with Ian between us.

"It's probably worth a try. For me and you. I have nothing to lose at this point." Rush has the sweetest furrow over his brow as he punches out a message.

I read from beside him. "Sorry I haven't texted back. I've needed time."

"Think that's enough?" he asks.

"Yeah, you don't want to come on too strong."

Rush sighs and drops his phone on the table before reaching for his beer. "I hate this."

"You don't have to do it. Stringing him along won't be fun."

"I need him to admit what he did. Then, once I have the evidence, we show his boss, and he can suck eggs for once."

I grin his way. "You're a real little supervillain, aren't you?"

"I think Rush sounds like more of a superhero name."

"What would your superpower be? Speed?"

"Are you kidding?" Rush flexes a mouthwateringly round bicep. "Strength. I could bench-press a building and still be looking for more."

I pat his hand, trying not to seem condescending about it. "Sure you could." Apparently, my tone didn't get the message.

He gasps, feigning offense. "Arm wrestle. Now."

I eye him, wondering if he's serious. "I didn't realize this was going to turn into a pissing contest."

"It's not." He cocks his head. "We're arm wrestling."

It's hard to tell if this is one of those times he's being literal or if he's fucking with me. The only thing that gives him away is the slightest curl to the corner of his mouth. He sets his elbow on the table, stare on his hand, and while this feels stupid and juvenile, I might as well play along.

"Fine." I prop my arm up and wrap my hand around his. "On three?"

"Wait. Are we going to put a wager on it?"

"A wager?"

"Yes. I think there should be some kind of reward for the winner."

"I thought your reward was proving to me how strong you are." I smirk. "Now you're begging to spoil me."

"Getting ahead of yourself, aren't you?"

Little does Rush know, I'm confident. My suits might cover most of it, but I've always looked after myself, and since moving into the hotels, I have an easily accessible gym I get to use every morning.

Rush's biceps might look tasty as hell, but they've got nothing on mine.

But what do I want to win?

"So what do you want?" he asks, echoing my thoughts.

My gaze slides over his face and comes to a rest on his mouth. There's one thing I want. One thing that's been on my mind since it last happened, but kissing Rush isn't something I'll do as the result of a bet. "No idea."

"If I win, I want you to have custody of P.L. Ant for the entire week."

My laugh is unexpected. "*That's* what you want?"

"It will make me feel appreciated." He pouts.

"You are so full of shit."

This time, it's Rush's turn to laugh, but before we can start, his message tone goes off.

The amusement dies from both our faces as he checks the screen.

"Is it him?" I ask.

"Sure is." His jaw tightens as he swipes open the phone. He reads out loud. "*I know, baby, but all I wanted was a chance to explain.*"

After how cold Ian was to me, I can't say it doesn't hurt to hear his kindness toward Rush. Even if it's fake.

"What, do you have beer-flavored cum or something?" I mutter darkly.

"Wouldn't you like to know?" He winks, and while it's cute and gives me a thrill because, yeah, actually, I would, it doesn't help to cut through the crappy feelings.

"I think I'm going to need another drink for this." I stand from the table, but Rush immediately sets his hand over mine.

"Are you upset?"

"Just … frustrated."

"Should I not have suggested this?"

I flip my hand over to catch his and give it a squeeze before letting go again. "No, it was a good idea. I need somewhere to live, after all, and the thought of getting that *and* getting him in trouble is amazing. It's just … harder than I thought."

"Because you love him?"

I snort. "No. That's why it's harder than I thought. I don't love him. I don't miss him. So I really didn't think it would bother me at all."

"I'm sorry."

His confused, stilted tone makes me smile. "Not a situation where you need to apologize, but thank you for trying to connect with me."

I'm not sure of the look that crosses Rush's face because I leave to grab us both another drink and try not to picture taking his hand again.

When I get back, Rush has finished his first drink and immediately turns to the second. "You know, it's almost like you're trying to get me drunk."

"And why would I want to do that?" If anything, I'd prefer to let myself get a little tipsy, to the point where I stop censoring my words and wants. To where I'd let myself ask Rush if he liked the kiss as much as I did. If he wanted to do it again.

"So I'll put out."

I almost choke on my gulp of beer. "You really think I'm the type of guy who'll take advantage of you like that?"

"Nah, but drunk, sloppy sex is fun."

My dick perks with interest. "Only if both parties are willing while they're sober."

"I already told you I'd have sex with you," he points out like he's making a comment about the weather. "But you never said the same, so I understand your point. The drunk thing was a joke anyway, but I'm more than happy for you to cover the drinks all night."

I knock his knee with mine under the table. "Ah, but that sounds suspiciously like a date."

"Does it? I thought most people split bills these days. Something about the patriarchy."

"Not with me. If I ask someone on a date, I cover it all."

"Very chivalrous of you."

"Nah, not that. I figure if I'm the one doing the asking, then it's on me. If the other person asks, I'm more flexible." Then, pushing my luck, I add, "I guess I'm a giver."

"That's a very good quality to have."

"In all areas of life."

Rush's eyes flick up to mine and away again before he shifts in his seat. "So, since *I* asked you out for a drink, does that mean I should pay?"

"This isn't a date, Rush." We've somehow leaned a fraction closer to each other. "But the drinks are on me."

"Well, that—"

Only I don't get to find out what "that" is because his phone goes off again. It sets my teeth on edge, but this time, it isn't because of whatever potential message is there. It's because it interrupted … whatever that was between us.

"What does it say?" I ask stiffly.

"I told him that I wasn't sure I was ready to hear it, and he asked me to give him a chance."

"A chance to screw you over again."

"Probably. But thankfully, I have a secret weapon this time." He glances up with one of his rare moments of eye contact. "You."

I light up inside. "Me?"

"Yep. I'm only going to message him while you're with me. Then you can help. It'll be the reality check we both need."

My need to touch him makes me lean over and tap him on the shoulder. "Teamwork, huh?"

"Exactly."

"Think our plan will work?"

Rush considers my question for a moment. "It's a long shot.

He has to think that I've had no contact with you since that night if he's going to get loose-lipped about the whole thing, and the variable here is that neither of us knows if he knows that we work together."

"Did you ever tell him where you work?"

"Who knows? He knew I was in insurance, and that's about it. When we talked, it …" Rush's cheeks pinken, but he pulls his shoulders straighter and continues. "It was more about sex. How much he missed me. The things he wanted to do to me."

Every word pisses me off. "Right."

"It's becoming clearer that he really did think of me the way he said. A hole."

"Fuck that." I take Rush's phone from him. "If he didn't want to get to know you better, that's on him. He has issues. Not you."

"I would agree with you if it wasn't for one thing."

"Which is?"

"That it's a common theme in my relationships."

Rush might sound matter-of-fact about it, but my pulse rate keeps skyrocketing. All these men, getting to do things with him that I can't stop thinking about, and all they did was take him for granted.

"I might suggest dinner," he says.

I frown and try to pick what might have gotten us to this subject change. "Dinner?"

"Yes." Rush takes his phone back. "He can explain over dinner—that he will pay for—and I will try to get information about you out of him. Ohh, maybe I'll act all worried that you'll see us together—that's a legitimate concern for a side hole to have, right?"

"Stop calling yourself that."

"It's how he sees me."

"But it's not how either of *us* sees you." I pinch his side until he looks my way. "I'm serious. That's enough of that."

"Okay. Yeah, you're right."

I'm not sure I believe him though. I watch his face the whole time he types out a message to Ian asking if they can get together to talk, not liking this plan at all. The response is immediate, a date and time for a restaurant downtown tomorrow night.

I'm uneasy as fuck, but it isn't my place to mention that. Rush isn't my guy to protect, and the wires getting crossed in my brain at the moment are too much. He's my employee first and foremost, but I'm struggling to keep that focus with everything else going on. The cheating and abandonment, feeling close to Rush after this fucked-up experience, then closer still after we kissed. Plus, he's a good person.

I really tried to hate him.

And now, I might be falling for him a little bit.

Fuck me, I'm pathetic.

There's no way I can bounce from one long-term relationship that ended badly straight into another one, let alone with the man my ex cheated on me with.

But Rush never said anything about a relationship.

Just sex.

No-strings-attached sex.

And as I watch him take a long sip of his beer, admiring the bob of his Adam's apple as he swallows, my mind fills with filthy images of the two of us.

I can't act on the soft feelings I'm growing for him, but I *can* act on his offer.

An offer that I'm starting to think I'm way too weak to resist.

Chapter 16

Rush

Two drinks turn into four … then five. I can hold my alcohol, but I like the way everything takes on a tingly, happy haze. Especially Hunter. The worry that was blanketing his forehead is gone, and he's back to himself again. All black, neatly parted hair, and square jaw, and confident thoughts. He's the kind of guy who belongs in the world. He might not feel that way right now, but it won't take him long. Not someone like him. The world was made for men like him.

And my legs will spread for men like him pretty fucking easily, especially five beers in.

He's looser too. I can tell in his easy smiles and eyes as sparkly as my brain.

It doesn't happen a lot outside of my Bertha roommates, but I'm comfortable with him. He doesn't make me do mental gymnastics to follow what he's saying or question me pointlessly and waste both our time by making me justify what I want to talk about and why.

I'm a reasonably extroverted person, but some people make conversations hard. For no good reason. It's nice to find someone I can talk to and have it be easy.

Our stools have snuck closer to each other too, each drink helping shrink that distance between us until my knee is resting against his thigh, and neither of us is making a big deal out of it.

I pretend not to notice, and I really hope he's pretending too.

"We never did manage that arm wrestle," he says.

I struggle to remember back past beer number four. The teasing and challenge seem unimportant now. I throw a smirk back his way. "You want to measure dicks again?"

"Technically, I don't think we did to begin with."

"Bet mine is bigger."

Hunter chokes on his laugh. It's a sound I'm coming to enjoy because it means he likes what I've said but doesn't want to like it. "Are we still talking about a hypothetical test of masculinity?"

"Definitely not. I'm talking about actual dicks."

Hunter swipes his tongue over his bottom lip, eyes creasing in the corners. "I've seen your candy cane and can confirm you are *definitely* bigger than me."

My jaw drops. "You said you didn't see anything."

"I said I wasn't focused on it." His eyes shine with mischief. "I lied."

"Wow. Woooow. And here I was, thinking our relationship was built on mutual trust and revenge."

"Technically, we haven't gotten any revenge yet. Might as well throw the trust out of the window too."

I cross my arms and huff. "That's because you said our kiss wasn't hot enough. It was perfectly hot, thank you very much.

In fact … maybe since you're an epic liar, I don't believe you. I demand to watch it instead."

Hunter glances around the bar. "Right here?"

"Yes."

"Now?"

"Obviously now because otherwise I run the risk of forgetting, and the more I think about it, the more I really, really want to see it."

He laughs, and I like that it's lighter than usual. "I don't want everyone witnessing that."

"Why? Think it'll cause a spontaneous orgy?"

"Anyone ever told you your voice has no volume control?"

"Frequently at work. I ignore them."

"Shocking." He drags his lip between his teeth. "I'll show you. But not here."

"Then where? The hall to the bathroom? Want to relive where you shoved me against the door?"

Hunter's expression twitches. "No. My car's in the parking lot if you want to go there."

"You're not planning on driving home, are you?"

"No, Mom."

I cock my head, trying to figure out if he's accidentally used the wrong name or if that's sarcasm I'm detecting. Because I can't tell, I decide to fuck with him instead. "You have a Mommy kink?"

"Rush!" Hunter slaps his hand over my mouth as he glances around us. When he turns back to me, his face is hovering inches from mine, eyes shining with … something. Something that makes me feel good. "I can't take you anywhere, can I?"

If my mouth wasn't sealed, I'd point out that he absolutely could take me to the bedroom, and I wouldn't even fight him on it.

I lick his palm instead.

It doesn't make him move his hand. All I'm rewarded with is a stern look my dick is struggling to ignore.

"You done here?" he asks, voice taking on a delicious rasp.

I can only nod.

When he releases me, I'm out of my seat and halfway to the door before I get a chance to blink. I know what I'm hoping will happen in that car of his, but I can never be sure I've read the signs right.

If it turns out this video is as hot as that kiss felt, things might escalate. If it's as embarrassing as Hunter made out, I can say goodbyyyye, sexual tension.

My fingers and dick are both crossed, hoping my instincts are spot-on.

I pause a few steps into the parking lot, realizing I have no clue what he drives. We didn't leave work together, because that's what movies tell you to do when you're having an illicit, well, *revengeship* in our case, but it's all the same. Hunter is taking his time approaching, and I can't help the long sigh that comes from me.

"You're ruining this."

"Ruining what?"

"The buildup."

His eyes narrow a little. "The buildup … to our on-screen debut."

And hopefully other things. "Exactly. The video. Of us kissing. And evidence it has happened."

"I don't need evidence."

My evil side comes out to play. "Why? Think about it often, do you? Relive it as you're falling asleep? Or maybe when you're in the shower? Ever think about me with your dick in your hand?"

"For fuck's sake, Rush, you can't say that shit to your boss."

I wrinkle my nose. "You don't act like a boss to me. But if you like, I can call you *sir*."

I can't tell if his groan is a good kind or a bad kind. Until he sets his hand on my hip, dragging me closer to a silver car, and whispers right by my ear, "The first time I ever laid eyes on you, before I'd worked out what was happening, I'd thought you were there for Ian and me to play with. And I knew exactly which candy cane I wanted to suck on."

Ah. Want sizzles through my core as I turn my face until we're so close I'm looking at him almost cross-eyed. "Someone have a sweet tooth?"

Hunter's smile is slow and predatory and ignites the small, broken pieces of me alight. Being looked at like that is my weakness; it's maybe the reason I get myself into so much trouble with men, but one I-need-to-touch-you look is all it takes for me to give them my full permission.

Self-worth? Who needs it.

I have my issues. We all do.

But when it's *Hunter* looking at me like that, the need is more overpowering than I've ever experienced.

He chuckles. "Getting in the car?"

"The car ..."

"To watch the video."

I'd rather reenact it instead. But I climb in the car, being a good boy and not humping Hunter's leg. It's a close call though.

The second the door closes behind me, I'm cocooned in his scent. I breathe deeply, relaxing into how it settles all of my senses, wanting to ask what he uses, but knowing he'll give me a brand instead of listing all the ingredients and scents, so I let it go. It was getting loud and buzzy inside, but the dark and quiet here are too much of a swing because now my thoughts are getting loud.

"Here." He passes me his phone. The smooth timbre of his voice is nice against my skin. Like a feeling rather than a sound.

I take the phone and click Play.

It's me, awkwardly hovering, before Hunter steps into the frame. The man is fast, viper-focused, and from the second our mouths touch, it goes from possible snuff film to straight-up porn. Well, if porn had clothes and no naked parts.

My dick reacts to the image, focusing less on myself and more on the way Hunter is fucking dominating that thing. His hand on my ass, his body curling over mine, the way he's clutching me like he refuses to let me go.

And when on-screen Hunter moves onto my neck, I can feel it. The tingles vibrating along the sensitive skin. The hum of my blood as my heartbeat rises, sending extra supplies to my rock-hard cock.

It ends, and the silence that falls rings in my eardrums, sets my skin on edge.

There's no way Hunter doesn't think that kiss was hot enough unless he's the kinda guy into, I dunno, choking or something.

So did he just not want to send it?

Or is it something else? Embarrassed to be seen with me or worried it means he'll never win Ian back. The intrusive thoughts are all wrong and unwelcome, but that doesn't stop them from coming. From racing through my mind with convincing finality.

"See?" He clears his throat. "Not hot at all. Nothing. Definitely not something we can send." There's a heavy pause. "Couldn't really expect much else, considering it was our first try."

First try. I'm staring at my lap as I say, "I'm sure the second attempt would be much hotter."

"You might be onto something. But if you're pretending like you don't know me, we can't exactly send it to Ian anyway, right?"

He's right. Footage like that will mean never getting him to cough up a confession about getting Hunter's name blacklisted. But …

"It never hurts to have a backup plan."

"I do like to be prepared. Organized. Ready for anything."

"Then it makes sense. To make sure we have this to fall back on."

Hunter's large body leans over the center console. "It would mean kissing again."

Anticipation is heavy on my tongue. "Until we get it right. Can't expect to nail it the second turn. Maybe not even the third."

When I force myself to look up at him, Hunter's pupils have blown out. "I'm no stranger to hard work."

I tap the side of the console he's leaning on. "Not much room for activities."

"Back seat?"

I don't bother to answer, just throw open my door, jump out, and tumble into the back. Hunter climbs in after me, and I'm expecting more of the same untethered need, but he hesitates. Not enough for me to check in with him but enough that he catches my eyes before I can look away. Fingertips gentle on my cheek, for a second, two, then he closes them firmly over my jaw and yanks it down. As soon as my mouth opens, he pushes his tongue inside.

For a second attempt, we're nailing this thing.

It's squishy, and my leg is cramped up, but then Hunter shifts, free hand finding my thigh and hitching my knee over his lap. His satisfied hum is hot on my tongue.

I'll practice all damn night if I have to.

Chapter 17

Hunter

I wish I could tell myself that this isn't what I'd hoped would happen. That I could make out like I'm some good guy who only wanted to chat and be platonic and this is all a total accident.

But the second I suggested we head out to my car, this is exactly where I'd hoped we'd end up.

Maybe I'm heading to hell. But if I am, Rush is headed right there with me.

A backup plan.

If he wants to pretend that's what this is, I'm happy to play along. Especially with him half on top of me, moaning into my mouth. I can't stop touching him. Feeling him. Kissing him. Our tongues are a twisted mess, trading need between us, trying to get the upper hand when we're both pretty well fucking on top. I map out the hard planes of his back and cup his throat and stroke his jaw, marveling in the scratch of his stubble against the pad of my thumb.

My cock is aching at the proximity. At how close it is to Rush's. At the sound of his heavy breathing meeting mine and growing louder by the second.

I want to do so much more than kiss.

It's torture.

Tasting parts of him and knowing the rest is off-limits. Touching safely, when all I want is to drive my hand into his pants and stroke him until he comes. To see his mouthwatering body succumb to pleasure.

The urge to satisfy him is clinging to me. A storm welling in my chest. The same chest Rush is shamelessly groping as he shifts and ruts his cock into my leg.

"You trying to tell me something?" *Say yes, and I'll give it to you. Gladly.*

He thrusts against my thigh again. "Only that my cock is hard and has apparently taken a liking to you."

"Well … I said no to revenge fucking, but …" I bite his bottom lip. "I don't remember ever saying hand jobs were off the table."

Rush doesn't give me time to doubt myself, just grabs my jaw and kisses me hungrily. His hands drop to hurry along my buttons, popping each one before moving on to the next, and when they reach the top of my pants, that button falls victim to him too.

As much as I want him to touch me, I also want to touch him just as badly, so before he can pull me out, I knock his hand away.

"You … you sure?" Rush asks. "You don't want me to take care of you first?"

"Seeing you fall apart and knowing it's all for me is the only thing I care about." I open his work pants with both hands, peeling them back to find his glorious cock waiting for me. He's got a wet spot on his cotton briefs, and I'm filled with sheer elation as I free his shaft and remember that I not only get to touch *that* cock, but that cock belongs to Rush.

I spit into my hand and wrap it around him, giving him a solid stroke.

"Oh, okay. Yes. Like that. Perfect."

It's hard not to laugh at how adorable he is, so before I can give in to the urge, I kiss him again. My free hand grips his waist, holding him to me, guiding his hips into a sexy rhythm as he fucks my fist. I wish I could take my time, watch and taste, enjoy the thick length taking pleasure from my hand. His balls are still tucked away too, and his body is hidden from view, and all of this could be so much more, but what I have now will be enough. Will keep me going. Will probably be too much when we're both back at work and I have to pretend that I don't want him as much as I do.

Future Hunter is going to hate me.

Current Hunter has a handful of Rush's dick and has said "fuck it" to all the consequences.

Rush's deep grunts send shivers down my spine, the sounds and scent of sex building around us. My car windows are fogged up, Rush is clinging to my shoulders to steady himself, and those beautiful fucking lips are grinning as he gives himself over to me.

I break my mouth from his, lips dipping to his ear. "I want your cum, and I want it now. Flood my fist with it. Then I'm going to use your load to jerk off, knowing that you gave it to me to touch myself. That you wanted to make me feel good. You want to make me feel good, don't you, Rush?"

"Yes. Good. So good."

My thumb circles his tip with each firm stroke, collecting the precum and desperate for more. Loving that I'm making him feel good. That I'm getting Rush off. I want to give him release, that brief moment in time where the aching, mind-spinning lust splinters and blankets him with incredible relief.

"Almost there?"

"So close."

"Faster." I tighten my grip on his hip. "Take what you need." My only regret is that I can't cup his balls, knowing I'm about to take what's in them for myself. "You want me to come, Rush?"

"Yes. So much."

"Then give me something to jack off with."

He shudders, fingers biting into my shoulders. "My cum. You want my cum."

"Just yours. That's all I need to feel good."

He cries out, body spasming, cock throbbing out his sheer relief right into my hand. I catch every drop, milk him through it, wait for him to slump against me.

"Now you can take me out," I tell him.

Rush hurries to dive in after my cock, and the second he pulls me out, he leans forward to wrap his lips around it. There isn't much room to do it in here, but Rush's mouth is fucking magic. A warm kiss, wrapping my length in the kind of tingles that make me beg for it to be over with while also begging it to last forever.

He pulls off with a *pop* and a crooked smile. "Not a great angle, sorry."

"I disagree." My eyes run over his body. "It's a great angle for me."

I wrap my messy hand around my dick and beat it like it's my day job. The cum is sticky, a slick glide of *thwick thwick* with every pass. Rush might be bigger than me, but I know how to use my cock, and if he was bouncing on it right now, I'd have him screaming.

But this is enough, I remind myself. This is perfect. So hot and arousing. Using Rush's cum like this, smearing it into my aching skin, it's unlocking a possessiveness I haven't felt before.

"Take off your shirt."

He hurries to part the buttons and open the front, leaving his tie hanging loosely between his tight nipples, his soft dick still hanging out of the front of his pants. His hair is a tangled mess from my fists and his cheeks red and flushed while he works to bring his breathing back down.

I fuck into my fist, ass lifting from the seat, finishing line in sight. Rush offers to help once more; I assure him I've got this. Would I love to have Rush's hands on me? God fucking damn, I would. Is it smart with all the things going on in my head? Hell no. There's a difference between self-preservation and being self-destructive, and apparently, I'm toeing the line, flirting with the cravings and bringing on more.

My fist quickens. Breathing deepens. Every ab muscle tightened into sharp relief.

Rush bites my earlobe and tugs until I grunt in pain. "All I can picture is straddling your waist and using my cum as lube while I sink down onto your cock."

My dick explodes, unexpected and sudden, rolling waves of my orgasm taking me by surprise. I sink into the high of it, letting it peak and then ebb before I work to bring my vision back into focus.

The first thing I see is Rush's smug expression.

"Like a bit of dirty talk, do you?"

"I'm definitely not complaining if you want to let it out now and then."

He laughs and leans in to kiss me. This time is softer than before, a gentle meeting of mouths as his tongue caresses mine like a thank-you.

By the time he's finished, he's all jelly-limbed as he melts into the seat beside me.

"Are you okay?"

"Best practice session I ever had."

"Yeah, me too."

He sits up suddenly, steadying his head with his hand like he's had a head rush. "The video!"

"What?"

"We didn't film it."

"Were we supposed to?"

He pins me with an incredulous look. "That's the whole reason we're practicing. We don't have a backup plan if we don't even have evidence of it. What are we supposed to do? Text him with story time?"

"Rush, it's okay."

"Of course it isn't. I don't think you understand."

"Understand what?"

"That if we didn't film it, it means we … kissed. Just kissed. No revenge, no evidence, no getting back at Ian."

I want to point out that obviously it wasn't *just* a kiss. That I hadn't realized that I was supposed to be filming. That I don't want to do any of this for Ian—it's all because I want to. But if this is all just revenge to him, how do I give him those thoughts without him feeling totally fucking betrayed?

"I guess it slipped my mind," I say instead.

"We'll remember for next time."

"Next time?" I can't pretend I don't perk up at that. I'd thought that was it, but apparently, Rush is seriously all in with this game. Discomfort sits heavy behind my ribs.

"Isn't that why you practice? To be prepared for the main event?" Based on his tone, Rush is completely unaffected by what happened between us, like it was no more than a business transaction. If that doesn't boost my confidence, nothing will.

"That felt like a main event to me."

"Oh, don't get me wrong, the sex was mind-blowing, but our end game here is kissing. So that's the main event, which is what we should be practicing. Unless, of course, you want to send him a homemade porno, then we can practice that all you need."

Of course that's what he means. Fuck, I'm an idiot. Rush didn't mean next time as in more sex. He meant next time we're kissing. I'm getting ahead of myself. A thought flitters past that maybe that's what happened with Ian, but I instantly dismiss it.

While I might understand how Rush is so tempting, while I get why you'd want to go there multiple times and hear the sounds he makes as he comes over and over and over, I'll still never forgive it.

The world is full of hot, nice people; that doesn't mean you get to cheat to experience them all.

"Okay," I say. "We practice the kiss again."

"Exactly."

"And leave each other's cocks alone."

"Why don't we play that one by ear?"

He actually makes me laugh. "But without a camera, it's just fucking. That's it," I echo him.

"True, but I wasn't lying before."

I'm not following. "About what?"

His hazel eyes spark as he leans in. "I really *do* want to sit on your cock."

"You're going to get me in trouble."

"Why?"

"Because one day I won't be able to keep saying no to you."

He nudges my cheek with his nose, then gives my cock a soft squeeze. "Remind me of when you *were* able to?"

"Fuck you."

"I *just* told you I'm open to it."

"That's not what I meant."

"Stop promising me a good time and taking it back!"

I growl and drag him into my lap, kissing him to shut him

up. And only for that reason. Only. "You've been a pain in my side ever since I met you. This doesn't mean you win. I was weak and horny." I'm lying through my ass, and we both know it.

"So you're saying I just have to wait until you're weak and horny again?"

"Is that any way to speak to your boss?"

"Maybe not." He nuzzles me. "But seems appropriate for my ex-boyfriend's fiancé."

I groan. "Please don't remind me that *he* had sex with you."

It kills me that Ian got to have Rush in all those ways. The jealousy from the cheating is quickly being replaced by the jealousy of him getting to have Rush first.

Rush pouts. "But *I* have to remember. How is that fair?" Then, he grabs my jaw and tilts it up toward him, lips hovering over mine. "Maybe when you're weak and horny next … you can help me take the memories away."

Chapter 18

Rush

Going from a night with Hunter to a night of sitting in a restaurant waiting on Ian doesn't feel like it should be allowed. Firstly, I'm early. In what universe that could ever possibly happen while Ian is running late, I'll never know, but all I can think of is the time I've spent with Hunter and how viciously I want to make things right for him.

I need to play this cool. Take emotions out. And hope like hell that Molly never finds out about this because he might be made of sunshine, but Seven's not, and Molly would be all too happy to sic him on me.

I'm not convinced that explaining this is for a good, perfectly reasonable, completely vengeful reason would be enough to protect me.

But I'm here anyway.

Because Hunter deserves it. And Ian deserves to eat mud.

Ooops, better get those thoughts off my face.

I'm a second away from assuming he's stood me up when he walks in, looking as expensively breathtaking as always. I'd been impressed by him in the same way I'm impressed by Hunter. Men like that own the world. They're comfortable in it because they know it's for them. But now that I *do* know Hunter, I can recognize the differences between them.

Hunter is confident.

Ian is cocky.

He doesn't impress me anymore.

His speckled green eyes fall on me as he approaches, and I remind myself to be timid. Sad. I have to consciously rearrange my face, but thankfully, I have a lot of experience when it comes to mimicking emotions and actually showing it. I feel things deeply. Inside. Those things don't often explode from me on the surface, so to make people more comfortable, I put effort into displaying what they want to see.

And what Ian wants to see is a hurt little lamb who misses him.

I miss him like my umbilical cord.

"Rush," he says softly as he reaches me. He pulls his chair out with a scrape that scratches my brain, and I tuck my hands under the table, ready to prick my palm with my nail if I need to.

"Hey …"

"I'm so glad you met up with me. Fuck, I've missed you. So much."

"Ah, okay …" I toss my salad of a brain for a proper response. "I mean, I've missed you. Obviously. I'm … hurt. Confused."

"I know, baby, I know." He holds his hand out over the table and opens it, waiting for me to slot mine into the space. I know what I'm supposed to do, but it's giving me images of touching moldy cheese, and I can't give him what he wants.

"I think … I need an explanation."

His sigh is short and impatient. "It was a mess. I've been a mess for a long time. You *saved* me, Rush."

My eyes dart up to his, but I can't hold them long enough to pick if he's being genuine. "What do you mean?"

"I didn't tell you I was engaged. I know that. It was—it *is*—my biggest regret." Ian holds up his hand to call over a waiter and orders us both a drink. "It's a hard story, and it's taken me time to come to terms with things."

"What things?"

He pulls his hands back and crosses his arms over the table. "You really want to hear this?"

"Yes."

"Okay, but it's not pretty. My ex—Hunter—I met him at a conference. He was holidaying in the same hotel I was staying at. We hit it off, and it was like a fairy tale. He was sweet and attentive and kind. A fox in bed. We didn't get to see each other much because of different cities, but we were both determined to make it work." He lets out a humorless laugh. "Well, *he* was. I didn't notice, but he started to get controlling. Wanted to know where I was and where I was going. Who I was with. Called every day and would get shitty if I was out or still working. Then he drove up randomly to see me one day—and you know how I hate being caught by surprise—but I couldn't tell him to leave. He organized a romantic dinner and proposed. I didn't want to say yes, but I felt stuck. It was in fucking public, Rush. The whole restaurant was staring at us. When I tried to talk to him about it later, he brushed it off, told me I was overreacting. I'm not proud of it, but he had a hold on me. I'd let him control too much, and I didn't know how to get out."

The more Ian talks, the more he paints a picture of a Hunter I don't know, the more confused I get. Hunter isn't like that, and I know he's saying all of these things to make himself look better, but … does he actually believe them? I can't pick up on any doubt. I'm not sensing a lie. I really wish I was better at these things because while I can mask and mimic my way through a situation, the hard part is getting a read on it to begin with. Here would be a good moment to sympathize though.

"That sounds horrible."

"It was. I'd thought that was my life now, that I had to go along and hope things would get better. And then I met you."

Suspicion prickles in my chest. "What about me?"

"You *freed* me. You came into my life and showed me someone genuine. Someone who cared and loved. Someone who I thought Hunter was before his true self came out."

It's a real struggle not to defend Hunter.

"I tried so hard not to fall for you, but I did. Rush, you were my *everything*. I tried to stay away. Then I told myself I'd only slip once, but you had a spell on me. You made it impossible to resist you. Every time you called or messaged. Every time I saw your face."

The passion in his tone should probably be convincing me, but I'm oddly detached from it all. Does he really think that's what happened? Our memories of the events are very different, and yes, I acknowledge my memory isn't the most reliable, but I was *sure* it was him pursuing me. He'd show up places he knew I'd be. He'd call and beg to see me. He'd guilt me if it had been days without seeing him, and I'd always been happy to meet because I was in love. Or at least, I thought I was.

It's hard to believe it now though.

"I knew you were my future," he whispers. "I knew I couldn't let you go. I was planning to break up with him after Christmas—we hadn't even talked about him moving in with me. He showed up with his family one day and said he was staying. I panicked."

It's plausible. Almost believable. People say there are always two stories and the truth is somewhere in the middle. In this case, there's three of us. I know Hunter and I see things differently, but there's truth in both of our memories. Is there truth in Ian's as well? I scratch at my palm.

"Why didn't you ever tell me?"

"I was embarrassed. Almost scared of him. It made me feel weak. I never wanted to be that way in front of you."

"Thank you for telling me that."

He straightens. "You don't believe me."

"I didn't say that."

"You don't need to, Rush. I know you."

I shake my head, wanting him to believe me. "I'm conflicted," I say, throwing out the first word I can think of. "Upset. It was a real shock, and I've felt terrible ever since." Fuck, can I list any more emotions?

"I know. And I hate that I did that to you. If I could go back, I would have ended things with him as soon as I fell for you."

"Okay …"

"Please take me back."

I glance up in surprise, not having expected him to come right out and ask. He's always been guarded and careful about what he says, but I guess when you're not hiding a relationship, you don't have anything to be careful about anymore.

"I need you, baby." He holds out his hand again, and I drive my thumbnail into my palm. I have to take it. I *have* to.

I can't.

Hoping I can distract him, I change tack. "I'm scared he'll see us together," I whisper, sending a silent apology to Hunter for what I'm about to say. "That night … he threatened me. Told me if he ever saw us together that he'd …" What do bad guys usually say in this scenario? "Hurt me." It's a pathetic attempt, but Ian eats it right up.

"I will never, ever let anything happen to you." He shifts his chair around until it's beside me. "Look at me, baby."

I do. Meet his eyes. For two seconds ... three ... before I physically can't anymore.

"I will protect you."

"But *how*?"

"However I have to." His hand sneaks onto my thigh as he leans in. "I fucking love you so much, baby. I'll do anything for you." His hand slips between my legs. "Missed you. Missed this."

My skin is crawling. I force myself not to pull away. My dick has never been so soft.

"You can't protect me from him," I say. "He said he'll be watching."

Ian chuckles. "I'd like to see him try."

"What do you mean?"

"Let's just say his time in Seattle is coming to an end."

"Why?"

"There's a, umm ..." He holds back a laugh. "Housing shortage, babe. Trust me." His smarmy voice is rubbing me all wrong. "I can guarantee he won't be hanging around if he can't find somewhere to live."

"You can't know that. That he won't."

He winks. "I'm very, very good at what I do."

"Yes, but how can *you* affect anything?"

Ian doesn't answer right away. "All I need is your trust. Can't you do that for me?"

I push away from him and the table, hoping it looks natural and not like I can't stand his hand on me anymore. He's clearly not going to give me more than that.

"I can't risk it. He scares me. I want to be with you too, but unless you can give me solid proof he won't interfere, I just can't."

I hesitate, hoping he'll come clean, but he keeps his mouth shut.

So I turn and storm from the restaurant, hoping like hell he takes the bait eventually. And until then, I need to get as far from him as possible.

Chapter 19

Hunter

Rush isn't at work. He hasn't called in, and even though he normally strolls in sometime around midmorning, it's now after lunch, and I'm getting worried.

I check my emails for the millionth time, and there's nothing there. No messages either.

If it wasn't for him meeting up with Ian, I'd blow it off as him having a sick day and forgetting to call, but last night, I couldn't stop thinking about them at dinner. It dominated my thoughts this morning as well. I've even left P.L. Ant on his desk with a note saying *if you need a confidANT*. It had felt cute at the time, a casual way to let him know I'm happy to talk about it—need to, actually—but it doesn't help if he's not here.

I pace my office again, wondering whether calling him is overbearing. I don't want him to feel like he needs to report in to me over every little thing, but fuck me, I'm curious. And worried.

Somehow, I need to force myself to concentrate on the work in front of me, but my eyes won't stop flicking over to where Rush normally sits.

Losing the battle to sit still, I get up and pace into the bullpen. The rest of my team are busy on calls, and I wait for Gates to end his.

"Heard from Carey today?"

He snorts. "He'll probably wander in at three, thinking it's nine."

"I'm sure he knows how to tell the time," I say tensely.

Gates just smiles and answers the next call. Autumn ends hers next.

"Know where Carey is?"

Her wide eyes immediately fly to his empty desk. "Ah, doctor's appointment!"

"Really?"

"Yeah, he mentioned it yesterday. Inflamed, uh, lar…ynx?"

"You're a terrible liar."

"No, I swear."

I chuckle so she knows I'm not mad. "You're also very loyal. I'm just worried that he's not here yet."

She slumps, and her lips pinch. "I don't think he's ever been later than this before. I take it he hasn't called in sick?"

"He hasn't in a long time, so it's about time that he did," Eloise says, adding to the conversation. "That man has always been too worried about losing his job to look after himself. He deserves the occasional day off." The way she looks at me is like she's daring me to argue.

"Couldn't agree more."

But talking to them has only made me more worried. Rush has never had a sick day? He's too worried about losing his job? Yeah, that kills me.

Instead of returning to my office, I beeline for Ted's. Thankfully, he's in and isn't a dick when I do something I'd never dream about doing during my trial period. "I'm so sorry to do this to you, but do you mind if I head off early today? I don't feel great."

"Yeah, of course. Everything okay?"

"I'll be fine. Just a stomach flu."

"Okay, rest up, and I'll see you tomorrow."

"Will do." And I say that with total confidence because I'm a fucking liar. A terrible boss, too, if you think about it. I'm letting my personal shit get in the way of work. How the hell did I score this promotion?

I say goodbye to my team and let them know they can catch me on email if they need anything, and then I head out. Instead of driving home, I go in the opposite direction to Rush's house.

It occurs to me once I'm almost there that I hadn't wanted to overstep and call him, but here I am, showing up at his place uninvited. For all I know, he's not there. Maybe he has company. Maybe Ian told him a bunch of horrible things about me and got in his head.

I have no clue what I'm about to show up to, but by the time I've pulled up out the front, I've convinced myself this is the right move.

I'm not as intimidated as the last time I walked down the long path, but my breath still catches right before I knock on the front door. I'm expecting Xander again, but the man who answers is much more imposing. Seven. Well over six feet, solid build, heavily tattooed and pierced, with red hair and an expression that always makes him look suspicious.

"The Hunter."

"Just Hunter."

"What do you want?" He leans with one hand casually gripping the door. I try not to let it bother me that he didn't immediately invite me in.

"I came to see Rush."

"Does he know you're coming?"

"Nope." I leave it at that. Just stare at him, and he stares at me, like we're both waiting for the other to break.

"Hey, Seven, who's—" A cute brown-haired man ducks under his arm, and it takes me a moment to remember his name is Molly. "Hunter!"

I smile, relaxing that he at least seems a lot more friendly. "Hey. Rush home?"

Molly cocks his head, echoing his boyfriend's body language in a spooky way. "He know you're coming over?"

Jesus fuck.

I could lie and say yes, then make out like Rush forgot, but I'm not an asshole. "He doesn't, but he wasn't at work, so I wanted to check he's okay."

"Couldn't pick up the phone?"

I narrow my eyes, gaze swinging from Molly to Seven and back again. "What's going on?"

"Nothing's going on."

I cock an eyebrow, and this time, I mimic their stance. "Then why are you being so rude?"

"It's not rude to ask if someone is expecting you."

"No, but it is rude to not tell the person they have a visitor."

We're in a standoff, Seven looking unimpressed, Molly looking torn, and me *hopefully* looking like I have the upper hand when I'm definitely not sure I do.

Finally, Seven takes a step back, tips his head, and roars, "Rush! Visitor!" His eyes hold a challenge when they turn back to me. "There. I told him."

Taking a chance, I roll my eyes and step past them, and thankfully, neither of them tries to stop me. The house is as warm and settling as it was the first time I was here, and it might be old and large, but it's got a cozy feel to it. I can see why Rush loves the place.

"Unless you want me opening every door on the top floor, you might want to show me which one his bedroom is," I call back as I climb the staircase.

Molly bounds up ahead of me. "Since you're twisting my arm and everything ..." He doesn't sound too offended, so I keep on faking confidence and following him.

Molly stops outside a random door. "This is his room, but he's not in here."

It's possible Molly is lying, but I take a guess. "Atelier?"

"Ah ..."

"That's a yes." I grin and head in that direction, passing Seven as he approaches. Just before I turn the corner, I hear Molly whisper, "My heart will shrivel up and die if those two don't fall in love."

Love is getting way too far ahead of ourselves, but I'm not going to tell him that. The fact he thinks that at all gives me a boost, even if I didn't stick around to hear Seven's answer. I get the feeling that guy doesn't like me all that much, but then, I'm not so sure he likes anyone.

The atelier door is closed, so I give it a light tap, and when I don't get an answer, I crack the door a little. "Rush?"

"Who's there?"

"Hunter. Can I come in?"

He doesn't immediately answer. "Hunter?"

I almost laugh. "From work?"

"No, no, I know Hunter." The door yanks open. "Why is Hunter here?"

"You didn't show up to work today." I study him, looking for signs that he's sick or unhappy. Neither is immediately obvious, but there's definitely something going on.

"Work? What time is it?"

"Two."

"a.m.?" His voice sounds vague and detached.

I snigger and glance up at the sunlight streaming through the windows. Rush follows, squinting toward the brightness.

"Huh." He meanders over to the workstations and sifts through swaths of fabric, ribbon, and plastic containers of what sounds like pins.

"What are you doing?"

"My phone was here somewhere."

"Want me to call it?"

"Why would you do that? I don't have it on me."

I laugh and hit Call on his number anyway.

The ringtone blasts through the room, making him jump and grab his pocket. "Found it."

"What a relief."

He pulls it out and checks the time. "It's two fifteen."

"It is."

"I thought it was still nighttime."

"Must have been a bright moon."

He mutters something before turning back to his work. An entire countertop is littered with paper, and when I creep forward, I make out different suit designs. Some have been scribbled out, others have been overexaggerated, and others are stick figures, but as Rush scratches his pencil roughly over the paper, I take a moment to watch him.

He's moving fast, carelessly, lips forming silent words, and face fixed in concentration.

"Everything okay?"

"Working," he says.

"But not at work?"

No response. Instead, he growls, scrunches up the paper, and grabs another one from a stack. His T-shirt has coffee splotches down the front of it, his curls are fluffed up and frizzy, and he's got one leg of his sweats rolled up and fluffy socks on his feet. And he's apparently forgotten I'm even in the room.

"Are you mad at me?"

He shakes his head, lifting it to blink at me a few times. "What?"

"Did I do something wrong?"

His forehead flexes, face doing this cute twitch thing. "I'm not following."

"You're ignoring me."

"Not ignoring." He trails off, turning back to his design. "Working. Lots of work. Must do."

Considering I literally have never seen him focus so hard on anything in his life, I'm not really sure what's going on here. I've seen Rush at work. This is *not* Rush at work.

"Should I go?"

Still no answer. Beginning to feel very unwanted here.

"Right. Well. Just wanted to make sure you're okay." Though I'm not sure I can call this *okay*.

I back toward the door, and he doesn't even notice me pull it open and leave.

Molly's waiting in the hall. "See? It wouldn't have made a difference if we told him you were here or not. We … didn't want you to see him like that."

"Like what?"

"Hyperfocused. He gets like that sometimes. We probably won't see him for a few days."

"A few *days*?"

Molly crosses his arms. "We only didn't stop you because Rush says you're a good guy. So you better not judge him."

I screw up my face. "Why would I judge him? I want to understand."

"It's him. Most of the time, his attention is clouded because of his sparkly brain. But sometimes, it gets super focused on things and literally cannot let them go. Like, if we made him come out of there, he'd be physically here but mentally back in there. And it would make him hella anxious to not be doing the thing he feels like he has to do. Understand now?"

"Not even a little bit." I turn my frown back to the door. "Can I help him somehow?"

"Help? He doesn't need help. He's not in danger. Just give him space, and in a few days, he'll pull through."

No matter what Molly says, his complete disconnect is a worry. "Will he remember to eat?"

"Nope. We take it in turns bringing up food and something to drink. This isn't our first rodeo, cowboy. And once Madden's home, he'll sit up here with him. Try to get him to sleep."

"He won't sleep?"

"Nope. He's been up here since he got home last night."

Okay, so he might not be hurt, but that's *definitely* not healthy. I don't like it. But according to Molly, there's no way to help.

"Does … did something happen? Why now?"

"He's escaping," Seven says, joining us. "The world is too much, so he's hiding in his head."

"Neither of you are doing much to reassure me," I point out.

Seven nudges Molly. "Imagine being this mentally well-adjusted?"

"Excuse me, I am too mentally well-adjusted." Molly plants his hands on his hips.

"Uh-huh. Tell me about your mommy issues?"

Molly flips him off. "It's Rush's choice to live his life this way. It's not up to us to tell him if it's right or wrong or healthy or not."

"But what the fuck is he hiding from?"

Seven's face tightens, turning all hard edges and even scarier than usual. "He saw that scum last night. The chapjockey thought he had the right to put his hands on Rush."

My brain short-circuits. "He … what?"

"Felt him up. Rush thinks it's his fault because he didn't tell him to stop."

My blood pressure shoots off. Roars in my ears. "What. Exactly. Happened?"

Seven huffs, looking like he's about to punch a wall. I'm feeling the urge too. "He was trying to win Rush back. Kept moving closer even though Rush told him he wasn't sure. He was scared of *you*. Then foul-fingered frogface slipped his hand between Rush's legs and told him he missed his dick. Rush took off after that and was pretty upset when he got home. It was a real effort to get that much out of him."

Anger burns in my gut, overriding all my common sense, and turning my vision red. My fists curl tight. "I'm going to kill him."

I don't give them any more than that before I head for the stairs and thunder down them. My anger is a storm in my ears, and I know I need to cool it, I know I need to calm things down, but then I remember he put his hands on *Rush*. He upset *Rush*. I'm seeing red.

It's not until I get to my car and the passenger door clicks open that I realize I'm not alone.

Seven tosses me a look, evil glint in his eyes. "I'm coming with you. I've been waiting for this moment for months."

There's no way in hell I'm arguing with having someone his size for backup.

I nod his way, and we both jump in the car. I'll wait outside his house all day for him to get home if I have to. I've got nowhere else to be today. Definitely nowhere more important.

And like the universe is solidly on my side, his car is in the driveway when I pull up. Seven and I don't say a word as we jump out and cross his lawn, and I almost put my fist through the front door when I knock.

There's scrambling inside. A thump followed by a curse,

and a moment later, Ian pulls open the door. The sight of him, pants unbuttoned, shirt open, another doe-eyed man gazing back at me from behind the couch is all the incentive I need.

My fist smacks into his cheek before he even sees it coming, and Ian hits the wall.

"What the fuck!" he explodes.

He starts for me, but before he can get hold, Seven cuts him off. His large fists grip the collar of Ian's shirt, and he lifts him until they're eye to eye and Ian's toes are scraping the ground.

"I don't believe in violence. I also don't believe in intimidating someone. But for someone as filthy-hearted and disgusting as you, that all went out the window when I watched you eat fist. I hope the rest of your life is as scummy as you are." Seven tosses him on the ground like he weighs nothing, then salutes Ian and pulls the door closed behind us.

Ian shouts something that I miss as Seven turns to me with a huge grin on his face.

"That felt great."

"Intimidating him?"

"Getting to say my piece. Screw him and people like him." He kicks the grass on the way back to the car. "Why do people have to go around hurting each other?"

"They're assholes?"

His jaw tics. "Yeah. Well, I wish they could just … not."

"Not?"

"Exactly. How hard is it to be a decent person?"

I sigh, running a hand through my hair. "If I had an answer to that, I might be a decent person myself."

Seven nudges me. "From where I'm standing, you're doing all right." He nods to my hand. "How does it feel?"

I flex my hand, easing the ache building across my knuckles. "Sore," I say. "And so, so sweet."

Chapter 20

Rush

It's not right. Isn't working. All messed up. Every new design, every new idea, every new stitch in fabric that isn't good enough drives me further and further into frustration. I broaden the lapels and add an extra button and bring in the waist and let out the waist, lengthen the front, then the back, but it's not working it's not working it's not working.

What am I missing?

I jump as hot liquid hits my shirt and quickly set the mug down to fan the mess off my skin. It's sticky, and when I glance down, I'm hit with the filthy stains decorating the front of my shirt. Do I have another one up here? I thought I did. I comb through fabric over my workstation, built up around my sewing machine, tossed over the chair in the corner.

A growl builds in my chest because *of course* the edge of my red velour is crushed under the chair leg. I can't take care of fucking anything. Once I'm done with this suit, I'll be able to take a moment to get a list together. To set up the atelier in a more streamlined way. Maybe shelves on the far wall and racks for my rolls of cotton, a nice big bench in the center of the room instead of the long one shoved up against the wall, some drawers for my buttons and needles and pins, and a whole wall of thread.

It will make everything so much more streamlined. I just need to finish this suit, and then I'll have time to get organized.

"You always say that."

I jump at the voice and spin to find Madden sitting by one of the large windows. "When did you get here?"

"Which time?"

"Time?" My brain almost short-circuits trying to keep up with the conversation. "I didn't know you were here."

"Figured, after you jumped a foot in the air. I'd offer you my shirt, but …" He waves a hand over his naked form. "I'm probably the wrong person for that."

"Why do I want your shirt?"

He laughs. "Because I'm irresistible. Everyone wants something from me."

I tap out a rhythm on my worktop, trying to figure out where the fuck that black silk went. Maybe I'm making this all too complicated. Trying to be different. But that was the point of staying off the meds, right? Not only did they make me feel shitty, they were a total block on my creativity. My work was more consistent, but god fucking damn the things I produced were boring as hell, and I couldn't get past it. Couldn't break through that creative wall where everything was dry and brittle, barren as the desert.

My creativity is free now, but I can't nail the ideas down. They're a hurricane of rapid-fire vibes. Feelings. An overall vision of what I want that I can't still for long enough to *see* it. I know it's there. The same way I know that everything I'm sketching out and trialing doesn't come close to the exquisiteness of the real thing.

"I know it's frustrating," Madden says from somewhere very far away. "But you ready to sleep and eat yet?"

"When I'm finished."

"When will you be finished?"

Why is he asking such arbitrary questions? "When I'm done. I'm trying to think."

"Maybe sleep will help with that."

"Maybe your face."

Madden laughs. "What?"

"What?"

"Just drink your coffee."

I glance immediately toward my sketch desk and the mug waiting for me. Thank fuck. Coffee. Caffeine. Braining.

"Think you'll go to work this week?" he asks.

"What are you talking about?" My eyes fall shut against the delicious hot liquid that will hopefully help me settle.

"You haven't been to work in three days. Better hope they don't fire your ass."

My eyes fly open. "What are you talking about? I've only been in here since last night."

"Yeah, sure, and out of the two of us, who is making the most sense?"

I huff. "Well, it certainly isn't you."

"Check your phone."

"My phone ..."

Madden jumps up, ducks under my sewing desk, then reappears with my phone in his hand.

"You hid that," I grumble.

"Did not."

"Did too."

"Did *not.*"

I grumble at his immaturity and check the display.

Saturday. I huff. "See, I don't even have to be at work because it's a weeken—" Wait. It can't be Saturday because it's Wednesday. I had dinner with Ian on Tuesday night. It's been a day. A day where I admittedly should have been at work, but …

Fuck.

It's *Saturday.*

I didn't miss one day of work—I missed three. Hunter said I didn't have to come in on time anymore, but he never said that I didn't have to come in *at all.* Madden's right. I'm going to be fired. The only job where I felt like I knew what I was doing and Ted loved me and I got to have plant custody battles with a guy who can jerk me off like no other.

That's life *basically* made. A dream scenario. Throw in my creative solutions to Autumn and her tea, and I really can't want anything else out of life. I need to fix this.

I pull out my phone and open my emails to Hunter before typing out the fastest message I can manage, and then I grab my coat from the floor and head for the door.

"Where are you going?" Madden asks, following me out of the room.

"To work."

"On a Saturday?"

"Yes."

"At ten at night?"

"Obviously." I don't have a minute to wait. If I want to keep my job and prove to Hunter that I'm not a total flake, I have to get my ass there, set up at my desk, and get all of my work done. I'll call clients and file my claims and follow up on quotes and make the most amount of money anyone's ever made for this place. Okay, that's a tad dramatic, but I'm going to do my goddamn job like I should have been doing all week.

I stuff my feet into the first shoes I see by the door and leave. I'm a man on a mission. A man set to prove himself. If this was a movie, it would be my montage moment. I'll take the place by storm and show Gates what exceptional numbers really look like.

Fuck. The next bus isn't for an hour.

An *hour*. It's not even midnight, for fuck's sake. They want me to sit on a bench for a whole goddamn hour when I could be getting through my work. My bank account is not going to thank me for it, but I pull out my phone and order a car. It reminds me of the night I met Hunter and how he made sure I got home safely. Such a gentleman.

Now it's my turn to be gentlemanly and make sure he doesn't get reamed hard for my shitty numbers. I'm romantic like that.

It's not until I've been dropped off and am standing outside the very large, very locked doors that I realize something.

I don't have my key.

Frustration bubbles to the surface, and I shake the doors, hoping for some miracle to let them open for me.

The only miracle I'm answered with is the very loud screech of the alarm.

I cry out and clamp my hands over my ears, sending a glare up toward the red flashing light. How is this fair? How is it possible that I'm thwarted by a simple electronic lock pad and an obnoxiously loud security system. Overachiever.

The itch to kick something is strong while I ignore the sound fucking my eardrums and wait for security to arrive. They're fast enough, and I recognize the cutie I flirt with some-times, but it takes for-freaking-ever for them to turn off the sound.

It cuts out, and I peel my hands from my ears.

"Is it over?"

Cutie Cameron chuckles. "Until the next time you attempt a break-in."

"In my defense, I didn't attempt a break-in this time. I just, uh, attempted to open the doors. Without a key."

"Hmm … yeah, that's a real distinction."

"Thank you."

The other security guard gestures toward me. "You know this man?"

"Yeah, he's fine," Cameron says. "He works late a lot."

The other guard casts a curious glance over me. "*This* guy?"

I huff and fix him with my most unimpressed look. "I'm the only guy here besides the two of you."

"That you are."

"And I work here."

"So you say."

Cutie nudges the other guard. "Stop messing with him. Go on up, and, oh—" He reaches into his pocket and pulls out his business card. "Call me if you ever get stuck again. Instead of making a nuisance of yourself."

I look from the card and back up to him again. "There's a number of the security office on the front door."

"Don't make me spell it out."

"Spell what out?"

"He's giving you his number," the other guard says. "To get together later."

"Oh." I look at the card for a minute longer, trying to work out if I am actually going to call him. The flirting is a cute little confidence boost, but I'd always known it wasn't going anywhere. "No, thank you."

Cutie's face falls.

"This isn't a personal decision. I just don't know when I'd ever use it."

"I was kinda hoping to ask you out."

"I don't think I'm interested in anything like that."

Cutie nods. "Fair enough. Let us know if you have any trouble getting out." He winks. "The number's on the door."

They leave, and I head toward the elevators, wondering how anyone could possibly *miss* the number on the door. Was he actually telling me despite me already pointing it out to him? Or was the wink supposed to indicate teasing?

My brain is too busy mushing through a potato strainer to follow.

The coffee has relaxed me fractionally like I thought it might, and the whole way up to our floor, my arms get heavier and heavier. It's okay, though, because I have a bunch of Twizzlers in my desk drawer, and Gates is bound to have some diet soda in the fridge, so I'll balance out the fatigue.

My work isn't hard. I'll be able to scale the mountain load tonight, and by Monday, I'll be back on track. Nothing for them to fire me for.

I grab a bottle of half-flat soda and my packet of Twizzlers before setting it all out on the desk. The soda lid will be my time marker—every fifteen minutes, I'll take a shot of soda—and the Twizzlers will be my reward for everything I get done. I scribble out a list of the most important things to get through, then switch my computer on. I'm here. I'm ready.

Time to blow these guys out of the water.

Chapter 21

Hunter

Hunter,

I swear I'm not as flaky as you've probably assumed I am, but it turns out it's Saturday and not Wednesday like I thought it was and that maybe I missed a lot of time? I'm sorry! It was an accident, do you believe me? Probably not, but that's okay because I'm going to head in there now and get all my work done and it'll be like I never took time off at all. I'll make it allll up to you and even bring you a coffee Monday when I pick up Ted's so long as you promise not to fire me. I did send you that very considerate list of reasons not to quit, after all. Maybe I should have focused on reasons not to fire me. One, you'll miss the ant puns. Two, you'll miss these inappropriate emails. Three, you'll possibly even miss me. Four, we definitely cannot kiss any more if I'm not always around to remind you of it. And five—this is probably most crucial—it's not fall yet. Autumn still has months to work out which flavors she's going with this year and I'm not above suggesting cilantro. Rip, your tastebuds (if you fire me. Which you definitely shouldn't).

Rush

. . .

Rush, the ridiculous,

I forbid you from stepping foot in that building. It's a fucking Saturday. Stay home, get some sleep, we can talk on Monday. And no, that's not code for fire you. You're not fired. I'm not at all mad. I might have told Ted that you called in sick so don't worry, you're covered.

Hunter

P.S. As for three, "possibly even" isn't in my vocabulary.

I WAIT for him to write back. It doesn't come, and while I really don't want to be *that* person, I also don't want Rush thinking that he has to go into work, so I pick up my phone and call him.

His phone rings out. Fucking hell.

On a whim, I scroll down to Seven's number and try him next.

"Yeah?" he answers, sounding croaky as hell.

"Hey, any chance Rush is home?"

"I dunno. Call him."

I sigh. "He's either not answering or can't find it."

"Kinda stalkerish of you to be doing the call-around for him."

"Can you shut up and go look?"

Seven chuckles and has some kind of murmured conversation on the other end. "He went to work."

"Of course he fucking did."

"Something about not wanting to be fired."

"Yes, I picked up on that, thanks."

He snorts. "Don't get snappy with me. I'm not the one who interrupted sex." After that delightful overshare, he hangs up before I can even say, "Have fun."

Rush is on the way to the office. Rush also doesn't drive. I'm also pretty sure he hasn't slept for days.

Sorry, Seven. Stalkerish or not, I have to go find him. It

takes me half an hour to get there. I ride the elevator up to our floor, and while the front of our offices is dark, I can make out a soft glow coming from around the side where our bank of desks is.

I let myself in and make my way to our section, but as I get closer, I don't see him. The office is sort of creepy at night, which isn't something I noticed, given that I thought Rush would be here.

A soft moan interrupts my musing, and when I step around the next bank of desks, I find him, arms splayed over his desk, cheek on his keyboard, wearing the same T-shirt, sweats, and socks he was in the other day, under a heavy coat. There's Coke spilled beside him, along with Post-it notes, Twizzlers, a busted-open packet of pens, and zero concern for possibly attracting ants.

But he's sleeping. Face relaxed and half-smooshed on one side. Cute, thin nose, smooth forehead, curls still a wild mess.

Something in my chest pinches as I crouch down beside him.

"Rush ..."

He doesn't stir. Guilt trickles through me at trying to wake him, but he can't stay here. The problem is, though, if he wakes up, will he want to keep working, or will he let me take him home? I scruff my hand through my hair, wishing I was big enough to carry him. Or had a fucking cart to put him on or something. Even a pull-out bed in my office would be preferable to the line of "cbfvcbfv" across his screen. I give his desk a quick clean, then put some actual effort into waking him.

Really hating myself for having to do this, I take his shoulder and give him a firm shake. "Rush."

"*Hersomeofer,*" he mutters, shifting and filling his screen with more letters. "What ... what's going ..."

"That's right, wake up."

He groans and turns toward me again, blinking open sleepy eyes. "Whadryadoin?"

I laugh as I try and translate. "Waking you up. Home time. Come on."

"But—"

"No."

He pulls himself upright, swaying a little under the effort. "But—"

"I said no."

A frown mars his smooth forehead, impressions from the keyboard decorating his cheek. "Not the boss o' me."

"Actually, I am." I smile as I grip him under the arm and tug him up beside me. His weight leans into my side, so I loop my arm around his waist and keep him upright. "You good?"

Rush tilts his face up toward me, squinting against the light. "What are you doing here?"

"Saving you."

"Why?"

"Because we all need to be saved sometimes."

His pink tongue darts across his lips. "You're really sweet."

"Uh-huh. Tell me that Monday when you're piled under your workload and I'm on your ass that it isn't done."

He pouts. "I can do it now."

"Try it and I'll call security."

"I'm going to hate you on Monday."

"Thanks for the heads-up."

We make our way out, Rush's arm around my back, but he's not leaning against me anymore.

"You know, I think you can probably walk on your own now."

"Can but won't."

I hate how much I like that answer. "If I didn't know better, I'd say you were trying to feel me up."

"Smell you, actually. Big difference."

"Agreed. I'd much rather feel you up right now than smell you. When was the last time you showered?"

Rush cringes and tries to pull away, but I wrap both arms around him and yank him back against me. "Stop, I stink."

"You do." Feeling bold, I burrow my nose in his hair. "I don't fucking care."

Rush whines. "That's not fair."

"What's not fair?"

"Your super-sexy, growly tone."

That's news to me. "I have one of those?"

"You do with me." He spins in my arms so we're chest to chest. "And it always makes my dick hard."

Rush with a hard dick is a fucking dangerous combination.

"No."

"No, what?"

I pinch his side. "Don't be cute with me."

"Nothing cute about things my mouth could do to you."

I choke on my laugh. Not because I think this is funny because I never, not in a million years, would have believed that man I found shivering in the cold could be so confident about what he wants.

"I really don't know how to take you."

His lips tremble, and I pick what he's about to say as he opens his mouth.

"And I'm *not* talking about which position."

"That's good because it would have been a long list."

"Rush ..." It's more of a plea than anything. My forehead kisses his, and I stand there holding him, trying to remind myself that we can't take that step again. "You've had a big couple of days."

"And I've got a big couple of other ones ahead. It's just us here. We could do it on your desk."

The imagery of him bent over my desk, being railed from behind, tests every little bit of my resolve.

Then he keeps talking.

"Wham, bam, thank you, ma'am. I'll even record it if you want me to."

"Record it?"

"Yeah. That'd be the ultimate revenge, huh?"

My good mood crashes. Burns. I grip his hair, forcing his head back and waiting until his eyes are on me. The second those clear hazel eyes are on mine, I'm fucked to try and pretend like this is anything casual. "I told you I won't fuck you for revenge. The day you take my cock is the day you forget his name. When we fuck, Rush, the only name you'll remember is mine. Because you'll be screaming it."

A shiver runs through him. "'When?'"

"Yeah, when. I want you too badly for it not to happen."

"Good thing I have a shitty memory, then. Ex-fiancé slash boyfriend who?"

I loosen my grip and kiss his nose. "Nice try. The only thing you're sleeping with tonight is your pillow."

"How can you get me all riled up and then leave me high and dry?"

"Use it when you jerk off in the shower you desperately need."

Because while I might think Rush is one of the most gorgeous men I've ever met—inside and out—right now, it's mostly on the *inside*. He both looks and smells like he hasn't showered in a month.

"Are you going to drive me home?"

"Of course."

He presses closer, pointer finger tracing a pattern into my chest. "It's very late, you know."

"I know. That's why I'm here collecting you."

"Probably shouldn't be driving around. In the dark. Lots of silly people on the roads after midnight."

"Silly people standing right in front of me as well."

"I have a very comfy bed."

"Is that why you haven't slept in it for most of the week?"

Rush's face falls. "That … I …"

"Seven told me."

"Told you what?" His breath catches. I feel it against my torso.

With a sigh, I turn my hand to show him where my knuckles are still a purplish red. "Let's just say it's one thing to touch you without my permission. It's a whole other ball game when he touches you without yours."

Rush's bloodshot eyes go shiny. The hand on my chest strays higher, surer, skimming my neck and brushing my jaw. "I think that's the sweetest thing anyone has ever said to me."

"That makes me furious. Consent shouldn't be the mark of a good person."

"No, but putting me first is." His soft lips brush a kiss across mine. "Stay tonight. Please."

He's already found my weakness. Needing me. "I'll stay." His face lights up, so I hurry to add, "But only so I can make sure you sleep. Actually sleep. Until at least lunchtime tomorrow, but preferably longer."

"I'll let you have your way. This once. But that's only because I'm really, really tired."

"Good boy."

Rush preens. "And there you go making me hard again."

"I like it way more than I probably should."

Chapter 22

Rush

I wake up with one leg thrown over a pair of thighs and one arm thrown over a very warm, very bare, very muscular chest.

My head is tight like I'm hungover, body wrung of energy, but I know that scent. Happiness washes through me before I even get my eyes open.

"This is one way to wake up."

"I'm glad my sacrifice made you happy."

"Sacrifice?" I look up at Hunter, who sends a devastating smile my way.

"I've been awake for hours and need to pee, but every time I try to get out of bed, you snuggle into me tighter."

"I make no apologies for the me I am when I'm asleep."

"Good. Make no apologies for when you're awake either."

"And that does it! I'm not letting you up for the rest of the day."

He pries my hands off him, and it's like taking candy from

a baby because that body is definitely my candy. Who the hell knew Hunter looked like that under his suits? Sure, I could tell he probably looked good, but like *that*? I need to feast on his muscles.

He leaves, keeping my door slightly ajar, and a moment later, Kismet, the squishy-face tabby, pokes his head inside my room.

"All good in here."

He just stares back.

"In fact, you might want to evacuate to the other side of the house because things are about to get *loud*."

"That so?" Hunter's deep voice has me thinking for one bizarre moment that Kismet is talking back until he steps into view.

Kismet's fur stands on end, and he lets out a feral hiss before bolting.

Hunter gapes after him in shock. "I know movies use animals as their way of showing who the good and bad people are, but I swear to fuck, that cat's got it wrong."

"Eh, it's bad Hunter I'm after anyway."

He kicks the door closed, then leans back against it, crossing those impressive arms over his mouthwatering chest. "How was your sleep?"

"Refreshing."

"And your shower last night?"

I can't help my smile. "Thorough."

Hunter's eyes dip to where the blanket is covering me. "How sure are you about that?"

"Totally positive."

"But *are* you?" He stalks closer. "Or do you need another opinion?"

My teeth sink into my bottom lip. "There are some places that are *really* hard for me to check myself. Almost impossible. Definite two-person job."

"And where are these places?" he asks, pulling back the covers.

I shiver as the warmth evacuates into the room, and all I'm left with to heat me is Hunter's intense focus. "Ah … my mouth is one of them. You should probably taste it. Make sure it's fresh."

"You've just woken up. I can guarantee it's not fresh."

"Morning breath connoisseur, are we?"

Hunter's chuckle is deep in his chest as he climbs onto the bed and sets his hands on my knees. He pushes them open. "Anywhere else you can think of?"

"My dick!" The words fly from me before I can stop them. "I spent a lot of time on it, but it only got messier after I cleaned it, and I can't get a good look. I bet you could. Really use all the senses. Touch, sight, taste …"

His lips hitch up on one side. "Sound?" He grips the band of my underwear and yanks it down under my ass.

"I can make as many of those as you like."

"I'd say your dirty talk needs work, but you don't need it with equipment like that."

"Thanks. Grew it myself." I'm trying to joke, but Hunter looking at my cock like that has my voice all breathy.

Apparently, he's having the same talking issues I am. "God-damn, Rush, that is one pretty dick."

I glance down at myself. I've never thought of my cock as pretty before, but I suppose I don't have any complaints about it. It gets horny and gets off as well as any other, and it's big compared to most of the guys I sleep with, not that it makes any difference to me. The only complaint I have is that it's a bitch to get in, which is why I prefer to bottom than top most of the time. "I think I'm going to need to see yours. You know. For comparison."

Hunter's lips hitch in the corner. "But you didn't say please."

"I don't remember you saying please when you took mine out."

"Why would I say please when I'm doing you a favor?" His fingertips run gently down my shaft, and it's the best kind of torture. "This is all for you, Rush."

"For me." My voice is heavy with cynicism. "Right." It's never for me. The number of times I've been left to finish things myself is well into the double digits.

Hunter grabs my pajama pants and rips them off in one movement before lying between my legs. "I don't like your tone."

"What are you going to do about it?"

He sinks his teeth into my thigh, and a sharp pain travels through my leg to my dick. "Try again."

"Want me to beg you for it?"

"Why don't you try it and see?"

In other words, yes, yes he does. And that knowledge is thrilling as hell. Not only is my dick achingly on board, giving Hunter all the power in this situation, having to trust that he's going to make it good … I want that. Fuck, I hope he actually follows through. Ian was always great in bed until he got off, and then everything would come to a fizzled-out end. I want more than that. I want to share. Give and take. To know that the man I'm with actually cares if I enjoy myself as well.

"I'm sorry I doubted your generosity." My voice is syrupy sweet as I widen my legs. "You're so kind to be helping me like this. To be inspecting every inch of me. I need you, Hunter. I need you to make sure I did such a good job."

His eyes darken as they drop to my dick. "Better put you out of your misery, then." He leans in, nose dragging over my sensitive sac, inhale rushing across my skin. "Smells so good. Sweet."

"It's apricots," I tell him.

"Mm, I can tell. But do you taste like apricots too?"

"You might need to test that theory." His eyes flick up toward me, and I add, "Pretty please."

"If you need me to."

"I really, really do."

"I guess it would be cruel to leave us both curious."

Then Hunter licks the flat of his tongue from my taint, over my balls, and all the way up my shaft. He dips into my slit, flicks his tongue around the top, and then his mouth comes down over my tip. The suction, the pressure, the glorious damp heat engulfs me little by little. His mouth is stretched wide, lips red and shiny, thick jaw spread open to take my girth, and fuck me, the man can suck a cock.

He swallows around me, letting my cock slip into his throat as he buries his nose in my pubes, and then he pulls off in one smooth move.

"Just like I thought." His big hand closes around me, and I thrust into his fist. "Fucking delicious."

"Does it taste like … like apricots?"

"Hmm …" The sound rumbles in his chest. "I think I'm going to need another taste. More thorough this time."

"Take as long as you need. We want to be accurate, after all."

He dives back onto me, not taking time to fuck around with our act, and there's something so hot about seeing Hunter greedy for me. About fucking into his mouth and having him want more. His blow job goes from controlled to unleashed in a second flat, and where he'd steadily taken me into his throat before, I'm pummeling it now.

It's fucking sloppy and unhinged, and even when he scrapes his teeth over my burningly tight shaft, it only makes my balls ache more.

Him between my legs is a brand-new sight that I want to revisit. Constantly. In the near future. Because oh, holy hell, the things he's doing with his tongue are criminal.

I grip his hair, loving the messy strands between my fingers, and when his intense gaze pings up to meet mine, it sets off a jolt deep in my gut. I want to beg him to look again. To reignite that spark and let me burn in the feeling.

His hand wraps around me, jerking me in firm, smooth strokes to the same rhythm as his mouth. I'm rapidly heading toward my orgasm, not wanting to stop it, hoping that it stays like this, this frenzied, this mind zapping, right until the end. But it doesn't feel … right. To be lying here. Doing nothing. Being rewarded with the best damn blow job I've maybe ever had.

I have no idea where the voice comes from, but I manage to gasp out, "Don't you want me to touch you? Shouldn't I … I … help you out? Make you feel good?"

Hunter pulls off, continuing to jerk me while his other hand wraps around my balls. "The only thing I want from you is more of those sexy fucking sounds you're making. Because they're making me feel very, *very* good. My cock can wait." He attacks the hinge of my hip with a messy kiss slash bite. "Yours can't. The desperate thing is begging me to finish the job, and I really can't wait to taste you."

"Oh, fuck." My free hand tangles in my own hair as the other grips Hunter's head like it's a lifeline. He takes me back in his mouth, bobbing up and down, sucking hard, licking and jerking until he takes me off this fucking earth.

I plant my heels on the bed, diving into this feeling, this high, as I fuck his face and wonder when the hell sex ever got this good. He's going to suck me dry. He's going to leave me desperate to have this again.

His hair is soft between my fingers, rapid breaths loud in the room, and the sight of my cock pistoning in between those plush lips has my balls pulling tighter.

I can't stop myself grunting. Over and over. High creeping up fast, getting ready, bringing me to the edge.

I hover there for a moment, desperate to fall over the side and not sure if I can do it. Not sure if I can trust this is about to happen and not be taken away from me, but Hunter only sucks harder, fingertips dancing over that spot behind my balls.

It's too much. The pressure in my cock builds and builds and explodes. I come into his mouth, feeling him swallow around me, legs twitching with each pulse in my balls. Hunter takes his time to lick me clean as the aftershocks die down and reality sneaks back in.

Hunter pulls off and licks his lips as he pushes to his knees. "Exactly like apricot."

My gaze catches on where his cock is eager and waiting in his sleep shorts. "Let me." I hold out my hand.

Hunter smiles. "What happened to the begging?"

Shivers. Actual shivers. His deep tone is too fucking much. "Please let me get you off. I'll be so good at it."

He pretends to think for a second, then pushes his shorts off in one go. "I'll be the judge of that." He moves until he's straddling my chest. "You're going to have to open that mouth good and wide."

My jaw drops, and I sneak my tongue out for good measure. I'm so fucking ready for this. And even though I'm not horny anymore, it doesn't matter. This is what I've been wanting to do to him, and I'm finally getting the chance.

Hunter slaps his fat cockhead against my tongue. "Is this where you want it?"

I let out a whine, not daring to close my mouth to speak.

"Good. This won't take long. Sucking your cock made me so fucking hard."

"Really?"

He laughs, this time running his cock slower across my tongue. "Why do you sound so surprised?"

I drop my gaze, focusing on his flexing ab muscles rather than his face.

Hunter pulls back, hand wrapping under my jaw and angling my face until I'm looking at him again. "Why is that a surprise?"

"No reason."

"There's a reason."

I huff, not wanting to bring this up now. "I don't want to talk about it."

He sighs but doesn't push, just leans down and brushes a kiss over my lips. "For the record, your cock is one of the sexiest things I've ever seen. I'm going to jerk off to the image of having it in my mouth for a very long time."

Want shivers on my exhale. "I want the same memories with yours."

"Better stop stalling, then." He straightens, shifting higher, and presses his tip to my lips.

I open for him eagerly, and he slides into my mouth on one long thrust. The angle is rough on my neck until he leans forward and grips the headboard with both hands.

"Ready?"

With a mouthful of dick, all I can do is nod.

I'm rewarded with that gorgeous hitch of his lips.

He's slow at first, a gentle roll, and I take him deeper and deeper until he slips back into my throat. His shaft is hot on my tongue, silky smooth, and girthy enough to make my jaw ache.

He has total control. I love it that way. Looking up and seeing a solid wall of muscle staring down at me. Watching the way his hips flex faster and less controlled the more turned on he gets. All I can do is lie there and take it, suck like my life depends on it as my cock rallies to get back in the game. And fuck, is it rallying. There's no way in hell I would have thought I could get hard again, but here I go anyway.

"Oh, damn, Rush," Hunter mutters. "Look at you. Your mouth is fucking sin … God, you look sexy. Like that pretty mouth has been begging to have me fill it."

My eyes flutter, and I grab his hips to coax him faster. His cockhead is hitting my throat, girth stretching my mouth wide, salty taste spilling onto my tongue.

He grunts in response, and it travels all the way to my balls.

I can't stop staring at the way his muscles move, at his lust-drunk stare, his ruffled eyebrows. His balls are hitting me in the chin with every thrust, and the stimulation is almost too much. Too good. It's making my head swim. My cock hurts.

I moan around him, and Hunter's thrusts snap off rhythm. Get faster. Harder. The bed knocks against the wall, building to a heavier beat, the space between the thumps rapidly decreasing as Hunter barrels toward his end.

"God, your *mouth*," he cries out before pushing into my throat and stilling. His cock jerks against my tongue as he empties his balls, and while I'm trying to breathe through my nose, I strangle my cock.

It doesn't take long. I'm so cum drunk and turned on, nursing on his softening cock as I jerk myself off roughly. A minute later, it's all over, and as I throb out the last of my cum, I finally let him go.

His smirk is cocky as fuck when I look up at him.

"Like that, did you?"

"Way, way too much."

Chapter 23

Hunter

"Interesting morning?" Seven asks, nursing his coffee mug.

I try not to let my expression show how interesting I found it. Sex with Rush wasn't like anything I was prepared for, and all I know is I want to do it again. And again.

I should probably stop and think it through, make sure I'm not jumping in too fast and too hard, but when my brain is still swimming in my orgasm, it's hard to think about little things like consequences.

"Just woke up," I lie. "Taking a coffee up for Rush."

Seven leans his heavy forearms onto the breakfast counter. "You know we could all hear you, right?"

Holy fuck. "What?"

"Downside of this house. Sexing is loud, and the walls don't hold it in. Don't stress about it. We've all heard each other going at it. Well, except Xander. Though I think you might have broken him with how loud you two were."

My eyes feel like they're bulging from my head. "You're shitting me."

"I'm definitely not. Just thought you should know before you head in for round two. Don't be self-conscious about it. We all have noise-canceling headphones if we need it."

Oh, fucking hell. "None of that is information I needed to know." I finish making our coffees. "And we're not going for round two. I don't know what this morning was, but we have a lot to talk about."

Seven draws a deep breath, and I know something's coming. "Look, Molly's all but married you two off. That's a lot of pressure, especially for something that's only new or casual or whatever, but he's a romantic at heart. It's disgusting. We'll probably get married one day, and it'll be all his fault. But I'm not a romantic, which is why it means a lot when I say I love Rush. I had a feeling something was up with that hermit he was dating before it was confirmed. I had bad feelings, man. Real bad ones. I don't get that with you. I don't give a frolic what you guys are up to. Serious or getting your rocks off means sweet all to me, but if you say you two need to talk, then do it. I hurt Molly by not talking to him, and I'll always regret it. Don't do that to Rush. My man has been through enough."

Seven and Molly's relationship isn't something I know a lot about, but I do know what he means about hurting someone. I don't want to hurt Rush. I want to protect him. Those feelings are a bit too much for me to deal with at the moment, but they're on me, not him.

Telling Rush that I'm falling for him when we've only known each other a few weeks isn't a comfortable-sounding conversation.

I manage a smile. "Ever think he'll be the one to hurt me?"

"No chance," Seven says. "That man thought you were the moon the night you both met."

And after dropping that little nugget, he gets up and leaves.

I climb the stairs and open Rush's bedroom door to find him sprawled naked on the bed. All that bronzed skin and muscle is spoiling me, and my gaze drops to the tattoo that goes from his shoulder to his bicep that I hadn't paid much attention to before.

"Still have a way to go before you catch up with Seven," I point out.

He laughs. "This one alone took me four sittings. I didn't like it."

"Too painful?"

"Too boring. He kept snapping at me for moving, and I'd end up all sore from trying to stay still for that long."

"Sounds horrifying."

"It really was." His face lights up when I hold the coffee out to him.

"Exactly what I need. Orgasms and coffee. Sure you don't want to move in?"

I climb onto the bed beside him. "I know you don't mean it, but I did appreciate your offer of a room here. It's still a no, but I appreciate it."

"When it comes down to it, we don't *actually* have a room. I would have made one for you. Eloise guilted me into it."

"Suddenly feeling a whole lot less appreciative," I tease. "But speaking of places to live … I take it the other night didn't go well?"

"Nope. It went terribly. But he probably thinks it went well, I'm not sure. Oh! Actually. Where's my phone? I have a feeling he sent me a message."

"A feeling?"

"I might have imagined it. We'll see."

Rush rifles through his bedsheets as I set my coffee down and reach over the side of the bed to where he tossed it last night.

"Here."

"There it is. Thank you."

I watch while he unlocks it, apprehension settling at what Ian could have to say. I'd be willing to bet a fucking shitload that it isn't an apology for what he did.

"Huh."

"What is it?"

"Just … it's a lot."

He hands over the phone, and Rush is right—it is a lot. Ten messages of Ian swinging between begging Rush to talk to him to snapping that he's being ignored. It's eye-opening reading these messages, seeing someone so emotionally unhinged, when the guy I knew was … not that. At least, not that he showed me. He'd always been charismatic. Friendly. Almost sweet. What a total mindfuck to see everything he was hiding.

"I'd really hoped he would try to tell me that we could be together because he was working on a plan to get you to leave Seattle." Rush's face falls. "I'd been *so* sure it would work."

"It's a big thing for him to admit. Don't feel bad. He would have been stupid to cough that info up, and given he hid us from each other for a year, he's no dummy."

I hate that he looks so defeated, staring at his phone like he's begging the universe to make the message come through.

The only time Rush should be using his begging is with me.

"I guess I'll have to think of something new for next time."

"Next time?"

He looks up, gorgeous face so sweet and sincere it makes me want to kiss him. "Well, it's not over yet."

"Yes. It is."

"I'm not letting him do this to you. We'll get it out of him. All I need is one confession. Oh—maybe I can record our whole next date or go back to his place with him and rifle through his office? There'd have to be evidence on his computer. Or his phone. I don't have the passwords to either of those things, but I'm sure if I pay attention, I could figure it out. Maybe even message it to you so you can remind me if I forget. It'll be like we're agents of espionage, some 007 type of—"

I grab his phone and tug it from his hands. "No."

"Excuse me?"

"It's over, Rush."

"It's barely started."

I have to bite my tongue to stop from going overboard. "After what he did to you, I never want you in the same room again."

"But that's not a call for you to make."

"When the only reason you're meeting with him is because of me, yes, it is."

His cute face pulls into a frown. "I have to do this."

"You don't have to do anything."

"No, you don't understand." He snarls. "I *have* to do this."

"And I've already said you're not." We glare at each other for a minute, but it's clear he isn't going to back down. He might let me be in control in the bedroom, but there's no way he's giving it up to me anywhere else.

As hard as it is, I need to give him the truth.

I reach out and untangle his hands, linking my fingers through his instead. "I'm asking, Rush. Please don't see him again. We'll figure something else out."

"Like what?"

"We don't need the answer to that to make this choice. I don't want him to get the chance to hurt you again."

"He didn't hurt me."

I pin Rush with a serious look. "We both know you don't believe that. It might not have been physical, but what he did wasn't okay."

"I know it wasn't okay. I'm not saying it was okay, but I can handle myself."

"I'm not arguing that you can't, but I ..." I swallow. "I care about you. A lot. Knowing that you were in that position because of me made me lose it. I can't go through that again."

His expression softens. "You care?"

"I know you're a bit oblivious sometimes, but you have to have picked up on that."

He shifts closer, hand tightening in mine. The way he's looking at me is making my heart beat faster, my mouth drier.

"What does that mean?"

I try for a smile. "Literally? Or moving forward?"

"Moving forward. Like, are we in a relationship now? Do I need to change my display picture to one of the two of us? Should we tell work? What will Ted think? Oh fuck, I'll have to be moved out of the team, or everyone will think we're fucking so I can get ahead. People will gossip about us for sure—though probably worth it for more of your blow jobs—"

"Rush?"

"Yeah, honey?"

I snort through my laugh. "I care about you. I'm not proposing. Take a breath."

"So then what does that *mean*?"

"You need guidelines?"

"If you don't want me obsessing over this and thinking about it for the next week until I spiral into a world of what-ifs, then that might be nice."

Apparently, a see-what-happens approach isn't going to work for Rush. Right. "Well, I think the first step is you telling me what you think?"

"About?"

"Me."

He thinks for a moment. "You're calm."

"Right. Well, don't rip my clothes off at once."

"I know you're being sarcastic, but it really doesn't seem fair that I've got my dick on display and I don't get to appreciate yours."

"Concentrate."

"But that part is really hard for me," he complains.

I flex my hand in his. "I know, but stay with me. You think I'm calm?"

He hurries to nod. "My entire life feels like chaos, and no matter what I do, everything is always in shambles." Rush casts his eyes over his bedroom. Clothes litter every surface, and there are four empty mugs on his side table. A heavy sigh falls from him. "I have *systems*. Places for everything. My wardrobe is set out with an exact spot for every item I have, but I'm always moving too fast, always out of time, always missing something, and no matter how hard I push, no matter how much I scramble to get it together, it's *never* together."

Even hearing him explain it is exhausting. "Is there anything you can do to help?"

"Yes. Medication. Apparently. But while that helps slow things enough for me to grasp, one lot I tried made me tired and hazy, and another lot made me feel empty. I hate the lack of control. I just want to be me."

An ache breaks out in my chest.

"When I tell you you're calm …" He glances up. "It's a good thing. The best thing. Like I can lean on you and disappear from it all."

Warmth prickles in my fingertips, spreading along my arm and into my chest. "I almost want to check that you're talking about the right person."

"No, it's definitely you."

"So judging by all that, it's probably a safe assumption that you have feelings for me too."

He nods, and even knowing that we're in this together has me nervous as fuck. Our relationship isn't exactly what I'd call high stakes, but the thought of losing Rush holds way more weight than the reality of losing Ian.

I hate that he's always going to be the hidden shadow

beside us, and it's going to take me time to work through that. Same with Rush. We're both bringing the same scars of our last relationship with us.

But it would kill me not to try.

"This is what I want," I tell him. "Keep hanging out, keep trading messages, maybe go on a few dates. Sexual and emotional exclusivity. Sharing is something I've done before, but it won't work with you. Maybe it's because of what happened, or it's a *you* thing, but the thought of another man touching you makes me want to stab something. Preferably him."

"Assault with a deadly weapon is at least a year in prison."

"At least I'd have a place to live," I joke.

All the relaxed happiness in his eyes vanishes.

"Hey, back on us."

"Okay," Rush says. "Those terms match with what I want as well. I've never been into sharing myself, unless it was something casual, so I would need that exclusive commitment from you. At least while we feel this thing out. It hasn't been that long."

"It hasn't." The thing is, the timeframe doesn't bother me. I've seen where five years can get you. I've seen that people can betray you at any point. A few weeks or not, I just can't see *Rush* betraying me. I can't claim to be a good judge of character, considering how easily I was fooled in the past, but something about Rush is unbelievably straightforward. Innocent. Kind.

I have to hope I'm not being fucked with again.

Chapter 24

Rush

Getting Hunter together with my friends is the best part of my day. Well, other than the sex. And the relationship talking. It's definitely better than the messages from Ian by a long shot and also Hunter asking me not to see him again.

I don't want to.

Ian would be better off left in my past, and I was getting a good move on doing just that. But now he's gone and pulled all that shit with Hunter, I can't let it go. I can't. I want to, but it's like this needle in the back of my brain prodding in brief pauses and pricking harder whenever I have something remind me of it.

Every time it pops up again, I tell myself to forget it. To let it go. The more I focus on moving on, the tighter my thoughts grasp.

"What are we trialing this week?" I ask Madden, standing outside of the junk room.

"The Easy Feet. Ah, shoes? Umm … those things we were watching the other night."

"You *bought* those?"

Madden's best friend, Penn, sniggers from beside him. "How do you still sound surprised?"

"The turbo mop, I could understand. The foot-scrubbing shoes thing? This is a new low."

Madden shrugs. "What can I say? They got me. They got me good. Now, who are my guinea pigs?"

I turn big eyes on Hunter. "I already lost a chunk of hair during the hair-drying incident of twenty-one. I'm not putting any other body parts on the line."

"And you want me to?"

"He's right," Penn adds. "You're the only one of us who hasn't supported Madden's shopping addiction. You've got some catching up to do."

Then Madden, the traitor, cups his hand by his mouth and stage-whispers to Hunter, "Trust me, you want to try these ones and not what I have coming next."

"Say what now?" Penn puts his hand up. "I've changed my mind. I'll do it."

"Too late," Hunter jumps in. "Easy is basically my middle name anyway. These things were made for me."

"That's the spirit!" Madden brings his hands together. "Question though. You two going steady?"

Hunter hesitates for a second. "We're, umm, seeing each other. If that's what you mean."

"Sure is! But if that's the case, it means you're no longer a visitor, and so visitor rules no longer apply."

"Nope. Stop." I point at Madden. "You don't get to strip off due to a loophole."

"What's going on?" Hunter asks.

"I can't change who I am!" Madden exclaims. "This is my home."

"You're *barely* wearing shorts, and it's not like Hunter is here all day, every day."

"Our rule is *guests*. You're dating, so he's no longer a guest."

Hunter waves his arm between us. "What the hell are you two talking about?"

"Madden's a nudist," I explain. "He wants to get naked."

Madden plants his hands on his hips. "I don't want to *get* naked."

"Then what do you want to do?"

"I want to take off my clothes."

I give him a blank look. "I know you think you're making a distinction, but you're not."

"You're making it sound perverted. There's nothing perverted about it. I like the breeze on my balls, exactly as Mother Nature intended."

Hunter chuckles. "Don't let me stand in the way, then."

Hmm … he doesn't appear at all worried about my friend and roommate getting naked in front of him. Madden's a hot guy. Nice muscles. Does he want to check him out?

"I object!"

The three of them turn to look at me.

"Maybe Mother Nature doesn't want to see you hanging brain every day. Ever think about that, huh?"

Madden eyes me with amusement while I try to do serious damage with the daggers I'm glaring at him.

"What's wrong with you?" Penn asks.

"Let's all not pretend like Madden isn't a super-attractive guy. He's very well proportioned and has a nice heart and a pretty face and washboard abs—"

"What the fuck?" Penn asks at the same time as Madden says, "Dude, have you seen yourself?"

I hold up my hand. "I'm very familiar with the fact he has an attractive package too, and while I personally have no sexual attraction toward Madden"—I turn to Hunter—"we promised sexual exclusivity. Only a few hours ago. That means you're not allowed to get hot and bothered over my roommate. I wanted to put that rule out there before he takes off all his clothes."

Hunter looks like he's trying not to laugh, and I'm not sure why, considering this is a serious matter. "Are you jealous?"

"Excuse me?"

"You." He steps closer and pulls me against him. It's not a bad place to be, honestly, and when he tilts my face up toward him, my thoughts scramble. "You're jealous."

"Am not."

"I should hope not. You have no reason to be. The only man who gets me hot and bothered is you."

There's that tone again. The one that makes me all shivery. "Okay. Good. Well. Madden, you can free the D."

"Fuck yes." He's pants down in seconds, and Hunter doesn't even glance his way. I'm not sure that choosing not to ogle my roommate's cock is strictly romantic, but I'm feeling the vibes anyway. Going from being the side piece to the only piece is going to take some mental readjusting.

"Right. What am I doing?" Hunter asks.

"Easy Feet. Shoes. Things!" Madden brandishes a box from the pile. "You'll never have to bend over to wash those puppies again! Revolutionary! Extraordinary!"

"I saw the infomercial," I point out. "Can we move on?"

Madden pouts. "Always ruining my fun."

"You actually looked at these and thought, hey, great idea?" Hunter asks.

"Because they *are* a great idea," Penn says. "If you don't want to try them, I will."

"Nice try. You get whatever freaky shit is next."

"I'm hurt right now that you're not taking this seriously," Madden says.

If I'm reading him right, that's a lie. "No, you're not."

"Okay, no I'm not. But come oooon, I'm excited. I want to see if they work."

Hunter, resigned to his fate, drops the box beside himself, then sits down to roll up the legs of the sweats he borrowed from me.

"You can just take them off," Madden suggests. "Balls weren't supposed to be shackled, dude."

"Mine are in time-out." Hunter winks my way. "Someone drained them this morning."

"Bragging about getting to have sex?" Penn turns to Madden. "I've decided I don't like this guy."

"Good," I say. "Then get your bestie to stop checking him out."

"What?" Madden gasps, trying to play innocent. "He's a good-looking guy. I'm appreciating the wonders of nature."

Penn scowls. "Stop checking him out, Madden."

Madden blows him a kiss, and I know from our late-night chats that it's getting harder and harder for Madden to joke around with Penn. I try to imagine what it would be like if I had these feelings for Hunter and he didn't feel the same way.

Pain tickles my heart. Nope. Don't like that.

"Just put the ugly flip-flops on," I say.

Hunter tears into the box, and Madden gets it all set up. And sure, I might be a tiny bit self-conscious when it comes to Hunter and other men being around, but seeing them joke and make fun of the foot cleaner things really does make me happy inside. My roommates are my family, that will never change, and even with Émile and Molly joining the group, it's only making my family get bigger. Will Hunter and I ever have that one day?

It's what I'd imagined with Ian. A natural progression. He'd meet them and love them and want to hang out here all the time. I'm glad that never happened, though, because the breakup was hard enough without any of them having to go through it with me.

That urge prickles my brain again. Ian. I have to do something about him. There's no way Hunter deserves half of the shit he's done to him, and Ian is carrying on with life like he isn't a total fuckface.

"In a hotel?" Madden scowls. "Dude, no. Not cool. Move in here."

Hunter chokes back a laugh. "Rush has offered, and it was a solid no. Nothing personal, but we work together and are trying out dating. Living together would be too much."

Madden tilts his head. "Seven's right. You *are* mentally stable. What's that like anyway?"

Hunter throws a look my way, just for us. "Calm."

"Sounds boring."

"Eh. It works for me."

Penn's looking between them both. "Why don't you find a place to live? Not here long?"

"His—our—" I correct, "Ex blacklisted him."

"No shit." Penn glances Madden's way again. "Guess you'll have to head back to … where was it again? Portsmouth."

"Portland."

"Eh, Portsmouth sounds better. And further."

"You sound annoyed," I say, eyeing Penn. "Are you annoyed?"

"What would I have to be annoyed about?"

"Well, *I* don't know. That's why I'm asking."

He crosses his arms. "Just wanted to be the one trying out those things, is all. The least they could do is remember we're in the room."

Madden lets out his booming laugh and slings one arm around Penn's shoulders before driving his knuckles into the top of his head. They both topple over, and while they roughhouse, Hunter and I exchange a look.

"Was I ignoring you?"

That's a ridiculous question. "I'm right here. You were trying the shoe things like we all agreed on."

"Well." His lips twitch. "Apparently, not *all* of us."

The laughter from Madden and Penn dies down as they separate. They're both sprawled on the ground, and Madden suddenly props himself up. "I've got it."

"Got what?"

"The solution."

"The solution to *what*?"

Madden rolls his hand in our direction. "The blacklisting thing. The guys who own Bertha have a few places, right? Maybe one of their other houses has a room Hunter can rent."

Hunter perks up from where he's rubbing his feet over the brushes on the flip-flops. "You think they might?"

It's actually a really good idea. "I can ask."

"I mean, a room isn't ideal, but it's got to be better than what I have now. Beggars can't be choosers and whatever."

He's right. But Hunter deserves more than to be a beggar.

That prickling starts up again.

Chapter 25

Hunter

I pick Rush up the following weekend, nerves battering my gut. I'm down to my one last hope for somewhere to live, and I have everything crossed these guys can help me out.

Apparently, Rylan and Kai, the men who own the house Rush lives in, have a few places they rent for cheap. Rush's place is full of people way more artistically inclined than me, but hopefully, they'll have somewhere I can fit.

"How cute. We could be landlord lovers."

I snort and glance over at him. "Landlord lovers?"

"Exactly."

"You don't hear it?"

"Hear what?"

I'm not about to explain it to him. I'm too nervous. "How did you end up moving in with the others? Were you all friends or …?"

"Gabe and Christian were. Molly and Madden knew each

other from college. Seven and Xander met in foster care. Aggy next door actually knew my gran, and after my parents died, Gran was my guardian. Only Gran couldn't really handle me and didn't understand why I kept getting into trouble in school. I didn't understand it either, actually, but I don't understand a lot of what other people are thinking. Anyway, Gran and I had a big fight, I tried to run away, Aggy picked me up and convinced me to stay with her for a few weeks until I found my feet. Gran didn't want anything to do with me after that. So Aggy stepped in in her place, and I visited every Sunday. Helped Ry and Kai with some of the renovations they did. When it was finished and they told me their idea, I was the first person they offered a room to, and Madden moved in that same weekend."

"Wow. And you're all super close."

"Sure are. Basically brothers."

That gives me more hope than I want it to. "Maybe I'll find somewhere like that."

"You have somewhere like that. With me."

I laugh and rest my hand on his thigh. "I know you don't understand my reasons, but I don't understand how you can find your phone under your roommate's mattress or your keys lopped over the pipe under the kitchen sink. It's one of those things we have to trust the other on that there's a reason."

"Oh, I know there's *a* reason. It just doesn't make any sense. At least looking for bedbugs makes *sense*."

"Uh-huh." It's cute he thinks so.

We get to the restaurant, and after finding a park, I jump out to open Rush's door for him. He frowns up at me, clearly thinking.

"Is chivalry another thing you don't understand?"

"I'm pondering that if it's long been traditional for men to open the door for women, does that mean I'm the woman in this scenario? And who opens the door for nonbinary people?

Do they all open their own doors? Or do they have some kind of mind-control door powers where the doors fly open and out of their way?"

I stare patiently down at him. "Get out of the car."

"That didn't answer my question," he says as he climbs out, but he doesn't bring it up again.

We walk into the restaurant, and my first thought is that they mustn't get many kids in here because everything is so *white*. The walls, the floorboards, the tables and chairs. I'm too scared to order something to eat in case I mess up the decor.

"There's Rylan," Rush says, waving to a good-looking man sitting at a four-seater by the window.

"Rush." He gets up to hug Rush before offering me a hand. "Thanks for meeting up with me."

"Yeah, of course. Is your partner coming?"

Rylan sighs, smile playing at the corners of his mouth. "No. My ridiculous partner is not coming."

"Did you tell him Hunter only has eyes for me?" Rush asks, and I glance between them, wondering, far from the first time, if I somehow missed a step in this conversation.

"I did, but he worked himself up so much that I snuck out without him."

"I'm sorry," I say, taking one of the seats. "What was he worked up over?"

"He didn't want you to fall in love with him."

"He ..." I shake my head because I can't have heard him right. "Is there a reason he thinks I'd fall in love with him?"

"Because men usually do, to be fair. Well, not *in love*, but he has a way of attracting people very quickly. I learned early on to get used to it."

That sounds like a goddamn headache. "Well, like Rush said, I only have eyes for him, so Kai doesn't have to worry."

"I'll be sure to let him know." Rylan barely manages to contain the amusement in his voice.

The waiter shows up, and we order, me getting more nervous by the minute. We all know what this meeting is about —Rush spoke with Rylan before setting the time—but he hasn't mentioned a room yet, which doesn't seem like a good sign.

Am I supposed to be the one who brings it up?

Fuck me, how awkward. Begging for a room and then having to talk them into it too. I'd channel Rush's begging skills, but then Kai probably *would* worry I was hitting on him.

"What do you think?" Rush bursts out, and I could kiss him, I swear.

Rylan's gaze moves from him to me and back again, and the serious expression doesn't fill me with hope.

"The thing is, we don't have anywhere available at the moment."

My expectation crashes to the ground. I'm so fucking deflated that I actually smother my face in my hands and groan into them. How is this happening? I'm so determined to stay in Seattle, but unless I move in with the fucking guy I've just started dating, it looks like I'm running out of options.

Ian is going to win.

"I have a few friends with their own rental properties, so I asked around to see if any of them have something available." Rylan turns sympathetic eyes on me. "All their property managers advised against it."

"Fuck." I drag my hand through my hair. "*Fuck.*"

"I know it's frustrating—"

Rush cuts him off. "Actually, you don't because you don't know the full conversation."

"Full conversation?" Our drinks are brought over, and Rylan ignores his. "Is there a story?"

"Yes there's a story," Rush snaps. "Our ex-boyfriend is a real estate agent, and somehow, he's had Hunter blocked from every possible house he's applied for."

"*Every* house?"

I don't want to get into it and sound petty to someone I've just met. "I don't know how, but I've had a run of bad luck, and he hinted that he's responsible."

"I'm sure blacklisting tenants is illegal in Washington."

"Tell that to Ian," I mutter. "There's nothing we can do, and we don't have any evidence."

"I'm sorry. I wish I had something; I really do."

"Well, I appreciate that you at least said all that to my face," I say.

"Wait." Rush turns to me. "You were renting in Portland, weren't you?"

"Yeah, why?"

"And you had good records?"

"Yeah. Paid on time each month, lived alone, no parties or pets."

Rush turns back to Rylan. "What if Hunter gives you the number for whoever managed his last rental? Could you go back to your friends and tell them it's all bullshit and pass along the number?"

"No." While I fucking love that he's suggesting it, I don't want to put Rylan in that kind of position. "I don't want to be pushy about this."

"Well, I don't think we have much choice here," Rush points out. "Ian is being pushy first, and since everyone is so intent on believing him—"

"It's not that," Rylan says. "There's an excess of tenants at the moment. Plenty of them with really good histories, and I'm sorry because I know it sucks to hear, but in a choice between someone squeaky-clean and someone rumored to have a bad rental history ... well, which would you choose?"

"I'd choose Hunter," Rush says. He's so fucking loyal.

I take his hand, not bothering to let it go when our food arrives. I know he wants to keep pushing, but Rylan and I steer the conversation into easier waters. I'm trying not to act as fucked as I am, but it's hit the point where I can't think of a way forward.

If I didn't have Rush so squarely on my side, I probably would have given up by now.

Do I put my common sense aside and move in with him? Head back to Portland and do the long-distance thing again? Neither of those options is great, especially after what happened the last time I left a man alone for too long.

God, I should have hit him twice.

Once for me and once for Rush. I don't understand how one person can be that morally bankrupt. He already fucked my life over once, and now that I'm not in his control anymore, he's getting to me another way.

I desperately don't want him to win, but he's fighting with an army from higher ground, and I'm standing here with a one-shot pistol.

It would be so easy to give in, but then I glance over at Rush, at his sweet, unassuming face, and I'm swallowed by a rightness I've never felt before.

Everything from his frantically bouncing knees to the way his eyes dart around the restaurant to his conversation tangents. He makes me want to be better. Stronger. To stand my fucking ground.

There has to be a way.

Chapter 26

Rush

P.L. Ant is taunting me. After Hunter's latest note, I need to think of something cute and witty and not totally unhinged. Telling him I'm a deviANT for his dick feels more like second-date territory, though given we've had sex twice now, does that put us at third-date level? Or more like fifth? Is there a special category for men who are your ex-boyfriend's ex-fiancé and now currently your boss, who you made out with for revenge and then accidentally fell into bed with?

Probably not.

This lack of social structure sucks.

I shift in my seat, reading my screen and reading it again. The words make sense, but it's the doing of the things that's the hard part. I know what I *have* to do. I just … can't.

I crack my knuckles, reveling in each pop, but it's not enough, not grounding enough.

Eloise's face suddenly appears over the partition. "I'm on a call."

"Okay. Then why are you talking to me?"

She gives me her most patient Mom-smile. "Think you could grab me a coffee? I'm out."

"Yeah, of course." I jump out of my seat, accidentally sending it flinging back, but it doesn't hit anyone, so I call that a win. Maybe once I've been to the kitchen, made us both a coffee, and then come back, I'll be able to get my head into it.

There are a few people in the kitchen, most I at least recognize, and I throw out some hellos while I wait for the coffee machine. The microwave next to it has been left open a crack, and when I move closer, I work out why. The smell of something burned is wafting out. If I had to make a guess on who's the culprit, my only one is Taylor, Ted's assistant. She's even more distracted than I am, but hers comes from having a billion and one things to do every day. I can't imagine having a workload like hers, and the least someone can do is clean up some of the hurricane she leaves behind.

I grab a cloth to do exactly that, spending time on seals and the buttons on the front as well. It's still a bit whiffy though.

Some kind of lemon cleaner will get rid of the smell. Or a bleach? I search the cupboard under the sink, then make my way through the drawers. Cutlery, utensils, dish towels, a brush and pan. Other than some multipurpose spray, there's nothing here that will mask that smell, so the cleaners probably have the good stuff.

Luckily, it's a day Mika works, and when I find her in the cleaning staff's office, I give her the widest smile I can.

"Morning, Mika!"

She crooks an eyebrow. "What have you broken now?"

"Why on earth would I have broken something?"

She doesn't answer me, just waits.

"Someone stank up the microwave, so I cleaned it and wanted to borrow some bleach to get rid of the smell."

"I'll do it."

"No, it's totally okay. I don't mind."

She chuckles, standing up from her desk and grabbing her keys. "It's my job. And there's no way in hell I'm letting you wander off with bleach."

"I'm capable of cleaning a kitchen appliance."

"You're also capable of ending up on the seventh floor, drenched in bleach and wearing someone else's clothes. Let's stick to our strengths, sweetie."

I'd argue, but … it's happened before. Ah, minus the bleach.

"I *told* you—"

"Yes, yes, there was a reason." She waits patiently as I pass her so she can lock up. "There's always a reason. Which is why I'll do my job, and you can go back to doing yours."

Gah, my job. My job that I was supposed to catch up on.

"Thanks, Mika."

I dart off, backtracking to my side of the office, determined to *sit* and *concentrate* and—

There's a line of M&Ms on my desk. I drop into my seat and stare at them. They're resting on a sheet of paper, three little legs drawn on either side of the candy with a task written neatly next to each one.

Across the top are the words, "For when you need assitANTs."

I glance over my shoulder towards Hunter's office, and as soon as we catch eyes, he points to his own before pointing at his computer screen.

Focus, he mouths.

I swoon instead.

Then, I pull my shit together and decide that if I can't do it for me, I'm going to do it for him. I'll impress him by turning my entire day around, and then who knows? Maybe he'll even reward me for how hard I worked later.

I turn to the list of ten things he's written. *Close off approved claims.* Nope, too much paperwork. *Call customers we need more information for.* Nope, too complex. I'm skimming, looking for something easy to cross off and start the momentum, but by the time I hit job number ten, it's obvious why I haven't made progress today.

It's all too hard.

Like, I know what to do for the majority on there. There's one where I'm going to have to get clarification and another that's going to be a horrible conversation, but it's not like I've never told someone *no* before.

The issue isn't the work itself.

The issue is that I've subconsciously decided I can't do it, and so I can't do it. I blow out a long breath, rocking on my chair and trying to decide on one already. Just *one* thing. But if I close off those claims and then get information on the others, and then that information leads to those claims needing to be closed off, then that job ends up back on my list. I'd be better off getting the information first, but if *one* person doesn't answer, that job will be outstanding too, and I know one of those clients won't be reachable until four, my time. Calling with bad news … I skip right over that one.

There's no pattern. No efficiency here.

I'm about to take the list to Hunter and ask him to rewrite it in order when Eloise pops up over our divide.

"Didn't get me a coffee?"

I frown. "I have a very long list and no time to be taking coffee orders."

"Uh-huh."

"Maybe tomorrow."

She leaves, and I almost ask her to grab *me* one, but that's asking for trouble. What if there's not enough sugar? Or she gets the wrong mug?

I glance down at the line of mugs on my desk, counting all five of the ones I keep here. So, apparently, she would have been guaranteed to get the wrong mug, considering none of mine are out there anyway.

I gather them up, long past needing to wash them out. Honestly, there's probably something growing in the bottom of the green one, but if I don't look too closely and scrub nice and hard, I'll never actually find out.

Seamless plan.

Only when I pass by Hunter's office, he jumps up and cuts off my path.

"No."

"It's okay. I have to—"

"No."

"But—"

Hunter takes the mugs I'm clutching one by one. "I've got these."

A sinking feeling settles in my gut. "But ..." But *what*, Rush?

Hunter's challenging gaze asks the same question.

"I'll ... go back to my desk."

"Great plan."

"And work."

"Even better."

"Right, then. Now. I'll see you ... at some point later when I'm very accomplished."

His lips twitch. "Can't wait."

Then the smart-ass leaves with my mugs, and I wonder if I should have warned him about the growth in old greeny.

Oh well.

The day runs on. Hunter plonks a coffee down on my desk

without a word. The coffee disappears. I listen to music. Gates and Autumn argue. There's something sharp in the carpet under my desk. Just a weird prickle someone walked in. One side of my nail is jagged. Then it isn't. I count birds as they fly past the window on the other side of the office. Eloise leaves early to pick up her kids, because she started early and she's allowed to, and Hunter really is a genius when it comes to making people happy.

"Boo."

I jump at his deep voice in my ear and spin to look at him. His expression is amused, even as his gaze moves from my face to my list on the desk. The list that currently doesn't have anything crossed off.

Regret fizzles through my veins.

"What have you been doing all day?" he asks.

I open my mouth to confidently tell him but then glimpse the time on my screen. Six. The office has almost cleared out. And I literally can't think of a single piece of work I've gotten done.

"I know I was very busy." I felt it. I'm lethargic as fuck now and want to go home for a very long sleep.

Hunter steals Gate's empty chair and drops down beside me. Then he snags an M&M.

"Hey, I've been very good with resisting those until I got the job done."

"I know, and I figured since I did that job instead that I'd get to have the reward."

"You ... you did my work?"

He pops another candy into his mouth. "Productivity tastes *so* good."

I screw up my face. "Shit. I'm sorry."

"Don't be. I'm winning today." He pops another M&M.

"You did *three* of my jobs?"

He glances around. "Shh ... people will think you're my favorite."

"Aren't I?"

"Definitely not. Autumn holds that spot." He laughs. "You're my least favorite employee by a long shot. But that's okay. Because you're my favorite human outside of here. Now, let's get moving on your list so we *can* get out of here."

"You don't have to help."

"But if I don't, then you'll be here late, and I won't be able to spend time with you. This is purely selfish. Nothing else."

I glance around to make sure all the pods near us are empty. Then I run my hand up his thigh. "What do I get if I'm a very good boy?"

He catches my hand before I can reach his dick, and when he speaks, it's in that tone that gets me all riled up. "Be a good boy and you'll find out."

Chapter 27

Hunter

"So …" Rush looks up at me with his devastatingly earnest expression. "I was good."

It takes real effort not to check whether he's serious. Good? He distracted me more than he helped, and while he definitely made a real fuss of doing *things* and being *busy*, none of it was productive. But it was also obvious how much he was trying and couldn't connect whichever dots there are in our brains that help us stay on task.

I have days where I'm unfocused. I've heard about people with ADHD having difficulty concentrating, but I've never seen it in action.

The organized, managerial side of me wanted to wring his neck.

The logical side of me debates whether I should bring up medication again. It's hard to know where the lines are between what's my business and what I'm allowed to be concerned about and what he needs to figure out on his own. Either way, none of it is something we should be talking about at work.

I press two fingers to my lips as I look him over. His hair is wild, his tie is undone and hanging on either side of his neck, there's a hopeful smile pulling at his mouth, and the way he's leaning toward me, whole body begging to be touched …

A groan vibrates across my chest. "You're going to get me into trouble."

"Not intentionally."

My laugh slips out at the way he's looking at me. "Sure, now you're focused."

"You have something I really want."

"Which is …" I know what it is. He knows I know what it is. Doesn't mean I don't want to hear him say it though.

"I think … because *all* my work is done, that I should be allowed to play with your cock."

I moan and press the heel of my palm between my legs. "Not very professional communication."

"When the fuck have I ever cared about sounding professional?"

He's got me there.

I glance around the bullpen, but we're the last two people left. The lights above us are on, but all the others stretching out to the windows on one side and the elevator banks on the other are dark.

I stand abruptly. "I need to see you in my office." Then I turn on my heel and cross the room. Another two lights come alive as I pass beneath them, and I can feel Rush hot on my heels. Anticipation is pumping through my veins, risk following it at being caught doing this at the office, but even with that warning, my dick is hardening, thickening into a steely length at the things I want to do to him.

I push down on the metal handle into my room, and as

soon as the door's open, Rush presses against my back, and we both tumble inside. It's darkish, invaded by the LEDs shining through my glass wall, but when Rush attacks my neck with kisses, tongue sliding over skin, my brain fizzles down into nothing but a puddle of want.

"What do you need?"

"To be fucked."

"Remember my rules?"

Rush shudders against my back, hand flexing tighter where it's wrapped around my bicep. "The only name I remember is Hunter."

The two syllables sound perfect on his tongue. I reach behind me and loop my arm around his waist, pulling him until he's trapped between me and the desk. The scent of apricots fills my nose, wraps me up in Rush and his warmth against me. My nose finds his nose, and I take a moment to hold him, to want, before I take every last delicious moment as mine.

I tug off his tie. "Love that you're already getting undressed for me."

"If I'd known it'd turn you on, I would have taken off my pants already too." Rush reaches for his belt, and I slap his hand away.

"Don't ruin all my fun."

"The fun hasn't even started yet."

I laugh, throaty and light. "I'm starting to work out that every moment with you is fun. Other than work, obviously. But we're ignoring that for right now." The leather of his belt slips easily through the buckle, exposing his top button and giving me access to his rigid cock under the cotton of his pants. I grip him, squeezing gently, loving how he fills my hand and then some. "Where do you want me? In your mouth ..." I run my fingertips gently over his full bottom lip.

Rush snorts, then spins in my arms. He pushes down his pants, leans over, forearms planted on my desk, and then the smart-ass shakes his delicious butt at me. "Here. Right here, thank you."

"You're ridiculous."

"I'm horny, and you're taking too long." He sends a cute pout back over his shoulder, but his eyes have darkened, and when they sweep over me, I feel his need slither down my spine.

"Be good or you get nothing."

He scoffs. "I've already been good. I'm tired of being good. Don't you know my attention span is limited? Why are you trying to torture me like this?"

"Someone's being dramatic."

He drops his face to the desk with a grunt. "My hole is right there. *Right there.* Just put your dick in it. I'll treat him real good."

While I love his begging, my cock is also getting impatient. His ass *is* right there, and it's one of the most glorious things I've ever seen. I step forward until I can run my hands over it, loving the feel of strong muscle under my palms and the way he presses back into my touch.

The way I want him is all-consuming, the thought of finally fucking him going to my head and making it hard to think.

But one point hits me. "Condom? Do you have one? I don't."

The grin turns smug as he reaches down into his pants pocket and fishes something out. "Swiped it from my wallet before coming in here." He holds up a condom.

"Thought you were getting lucky, huh?"

"I know you find it impossible to resist."

I run my hands up his back and then down again. He's right about that. If Rush wants me, I'm his. I take the condom, then drop to my knees behind him. With no lube, I'm going to have to soften him up another way, and eating Rush's ass is not going to be a hardship.

He squirms at the first flick of my tongue, wriggles his legs as wide as the pants around his ankles will allow. I keep my laugh to myself as I dive in again, focused on getting his hole nice and wet, on softening his opening, ready for me to press my tongue inside.

"Fuck, Hunter." He rolls his hips forward into nothing. "So good. So damn good."

The possessive need to pleasure him purrs in my chest. I spear my tongue forward, circling the rim before fucking it into him. Rush shudders, and it spurs me on.

I'm so achingly hard and trapped frustratingly inside my pants, but I don't move to pull myself out yet. I don't reach for Rush's dick either; instead, I slip my hand between his legs and roll his balls in my palm.

A sound hiccups from him, his ass tightening around my tongue for a second. "More. Need more."

I give it to him, get him softer, wetter, tongue teasing slow and shallow before pushing deeper. He pushes back against me, sexy noises filling my office as I eat him out, bent over my desk.

Anyone could walk in. Could see us like this. Hear him. I don't fucking care.

The whole bullpen is dark, lights off in here, just a soft glow from the security lights by an exit door and my computer screen, which Rush bumped in his enthusiasm.

He's whimpering and shaking; my dick is straining. I'll never be able to walk into my office and not picture exactly this.

Not able to take it anymore, I give him one last lick and stand, pulling my cock out through my fly.

"Finally," Rush complains, sagging against the desk as I tear open the condom and roll it down my shaft. I'm so ready for this. To feel him around me.

The connection I have to Rush goes beyond getting off, and

while that scares me, I'm also not about to fight it either. So much good has come out of a shitty situation, and it still blows my mind.

And as hot as it would be to fuck him bent over my desk, I'm burning for something else.

I spit on my cock, smearing the makeshift lube over my shaft, then reach for him.

Rush is compliant, gives himself over to what I want even as I turn him and lift him onto my desk. His pants go next, somewhere across the room, before I hook one of his legs over my shoulder and pull him to me. He's so close. Smells so good.

Rush grips my shoulders as I reach between us and press my cock to his hole.

"Ready?"

"*Please* fuck me already."

I hold Rush to me as I press forward, eyes locked the entire time. The feel of his hole splitting open, engulfing my cockhead in the heat of his body, spreads pressure over my length and fills my balls with a lusty ache.

I've never needed anything more.

A grunt builds in my chest as my hips meet his ass.

The leg he has wrapped around my waist squeezes me closer.

"I feel so full," he sighs.

"Good?"

"Very good. You know it's good. Now I'm going to need you to fuck me hard because I'm already so close to coming, and I don't know how much more torture my poor ass can take."

"Torture?"

He nods, pretty eyes shining up at me. "My balls hurt." Rush wriggles against me.

My first thrust is slow and deep, building gradually to something more powerful. We don't need to talk. Don't need to kiss. I exist in this space where Rush and I are gripping each other tightly, doing everything we can to make each other come.

For a quick and dirty fuck, there's too much emotion building inside me. My cock barrels in and out of him, knees thumping the side of the desk with each thrust, random grunts and growls taking the place of my words as I bury bruises into Rush's skin. I leave some where I'm gripping his hip and others where I'm holding the back of his neck.

I'd bet he's doing the same. The pain from his nails on my ass cheek bites through me, desire numbing the sting and redirecting it into my balls.

Our foreheads meet, and I pick up speed, bodies moving in frantic rhythm. I'm sweaty under my suit, heat building around my collar, room stifling with the smell of sex and the warmth of our heavy breaths.

I've lost track of everything except Rush, except this deep need traveling from my chest to my cock and back again. I wish I could pump his hole full of cum, then kneel on the floor and watch it run back out of him. Wish I could fuck him and fill him up and then leave my cock inside him until I'm hard again. Wish I could do so many delicious, claimy things to his body and then hold him. Kiss him. Tell him things that will make him smile and then help make the world as easy for him as it is for me.

"You're so beautiful," I whisper against his lips.

He shudders and nips at my jaw. "Your *cock* is so beautiful. It's hitting the spot. I'm so fucking close."

Knowing Rush is riding the edge kicks all the feelings flowing through me to a thousand. I want him to feel amazing. To let go.

I release his hip and wrap my hand around his thick cock.

"Y-you don't want to finish?"

"Oh, I will."

"I'm okay to do that, you know?"

I tighten my grip on him. "Why do you keep saying that? Do you not want me to?"

"What? No. I …"

"Rush?"

He buries his face into my neck. "I've gotten used to it, I guess. Finishing myself off once … *he* was done."

My jaw clenches at the reminder of Ian, but I did ask for it.

I stroke Rush's cock, hard and slow. "Look at me."

He does, but I can tell it's hard for him.

"From now on, when we're together, you get to come first. Every time." I start to fuck him again, hand moving in time with my cock. "The only thing I care about is making sure you get off. Making sure you feel good. Joke's on *that asshole* because seeing your face when you come is a fucking wet dream. I'm so honored you share that with me."

Rush gasps, rocking up into my hand. "You're only saying that because you're balls-deep inside me."

"Nope. And I'll prove it to you. Every drop of cum you spill from now on will be because of me."

"Let's get round number one over with, then."

I love how easily he believes me. My mouth crashes with his as I finally stop holding back. I fuck him hard and fast, strangling his cock in my grip, mouths fused together as we race toward the end. I catch every one of his moans with my mouth, feeding him back a mix of *fucks* and *oh gods*. Sex with Rush is indescribable.

He rips his mouth from mine as his whole body stiffens. "I'm gonna—" He doesn't even get the sentence out before he spills over onto my hand. Thick ropes of cum cover my fist and his torso, and I'm glad I opened his shirt before we started fucking.

He drops back against the desk, boneless and sated, and I pull out for a second to slick my cock up with his cum.

"Fuck," he rasps. "Why is that so hot?"

I don't answer, just shove my cock back inside. With Rush done, I can let myself finish. Let myself fall into the pleasure he gives me.

I grip either side of my desk as I rail him, Rush's hands joining mine to stop from slipping away. His hole is pliant, a sloppy mess from his cum, and it feels incredible wrapped around me. My gaze travels from his gorgeous face, to his mouthwatering body glistening in his release, to his spent cock, and my balls pull up tight.

He's a debauched, flush-cheeked, pornographically sexy sight. My hips snap forward out of my control, harder and faster, balls frustratingly trapped in my underwear. Still being dressed while he's almost naked is a fucking turn-on, even as sweat drips down my spine and gathers on my hairline.

Rush arches beneath me, squeezing his hole tight. "Come in me. Show me how good I make you feel."

His deep voice hits me right in the chest, and I let go, grunting out my release. Waves of pure bliss tingle from my balls to my toes, and I get lost in my orgasm, taking what feels like minutes to fill the condom.

Then I crash, a panting heap against him, cock softening for a few seconds before it slips out.

"You're going to be covered in my cum," he warns.

I don't even care.

"Will you come home with me tonight?" I ask.

He hugs me tight. "Only if I can take the left."

"After that, you can have any part of the bed you want."

Chapter 28

Rush

I'm convinced Hunter is the greatest guy in existence. I'm convinced Ian isn't. And while I told Hunter I'd forgotten all about him, I just can't. He's a needle needle needle poking at my brain. Every time I do something, the weight of revenge being unfinished bugs me. Irritates me. If I can clear up this problem, I can move on. Refocus. Steer my life back onto the bumpy tracks I've been traveling.

"Rush." Madden waves a giant hand in front of my face, blocking out my view of the Monopoly board. "It's your turn."

I scowl at the sight of my roommates watching me. "I know that."

"Did you though?"

"You think you're being cute, but you're really, really not." With a heavy sigh, I pick up the dice and roll. Two. A fucking two. I slam my car down on its space.

"Want to buy it?" Molly asks.

"No."

No one else reaches for the dice, and I have no clue who's up next, but it doesn't matter. Because Hunter is in a hotel, and Ian is in his bed, probably ruining more men's lives, and I'm sitting here playing a board game and trying not to kick the thing over. On purpose, not by accident like Christian.

Poke.

Poke.

Poke.

My face twitches with irritation.

"Want to talk about it?" Seven asks.

"Talk about what? What do you mean?"

"Whatever has gotten you all snizzly."

"I'm not *snizzly*."

"Pissy, then," Madden says.

"Not snizzly or pissy ..." I try to latch onto the emotion infecting me. "I'm ... *antsy*."

"Right. Totally different."

I barely have the mental capacity to glare his way. "I can't stop the itching in my brain."

"Could be a tumor," Xander helpfully suggests. "Want me to look it up?"

"Nope." Seven plucks his phone from his grip as Molly wraps his arms around Xander's waist. "There will be no WebMD for you."

I jump in before they can continue. "I'm ninety percent confident tumors don't itch. Ache, maybe. Probably a headache more than anything, whereas this itch is in my brain but ripping out everywhere."

"So what's causing this mental affliction?" Gabe asks from where he's squished in beside Christian.

"Ian."

"What?" Madden swings around to look at me. "I thought you were over him. This isn't some kind of STD, is it?"

"What? No. I'm antsy because Hunter is still in a hotel, and he doesn't want me to do anything about it, so now I'm stuck."

"Stuck?"

"Yes, it's horrible."

"Why are you stuck?" Christian asks, sounding like he doesn't follow the conversation, the poor lamb.

"Because Hunter told me to let it go."

"What's so confusing about that?"

Sometimes talking with them is exhausting. I love my roommates. My brothers. The men I'll always have in my life no matter where we all end up, but they really do struggle with communication sometimes. I remind myself to be gentle with them—they can't help it—and try to break it down simply. "It's confusing," I say softly, "because I can't let it go."

"Why?"

"Because I can't."

Molly nods. "Thank you for making that clearer."

"You're welcome." I slap my hands on my thighs. "Now, how do we fix this?"

Madden leans over to kiss my head. "The fact you think this conversation somehow makes sense and know we're auto-matically in this with you is one of the reasons I love you so much."

"That sounds more condescending than loving."

"Awww, look at you picking up on social cues."

"Fuck off."

Xander looks around the circle. "Wait, you guys *aren't* following?"

Seven laughs. "You are?"

"Rush is upset that Ian is getting away with blacklisting The Hunter from finding a place, and while he wants to respect his boyfriend's wishes, he literally can't. He won't be able to let go of the injustice until he does something about it, and he's worried about where that will put his relationship when he does and how to explain to The Hunter that it will be detrimental to his sparkly brain to fixate on this forever without coming across as sounding completely batshit crazy."

I lean back smugly and point at Xander. "Exactly."

"If anyone understands what it's like to have a brain that takes over control from your common sense, it's me."

Molly's face falls, and he pulls Xander in tighter before whispering something in his ear. It's rude to whisper, but I'm not going to point that out because Xander's on my side, and I like that.

"Now that we've got that cleared up, please help."

"Seems easy to me," Gabe says. "You need to explain to him how Xander explained to us."

"But that won't solve the problem. I need to figure out how to make it better so I can then go to Hunter and tell him how to make it better in order to convince him to let me make it better."

Seven turns to Xander. "Translate?"

"How do we expose Ian for the piece of shit he is?"

Seven's smile is evil. "There's a beware site for Seattle dating. People post about guys and girls who should be avoided and why. We can smear his ugly mug all over that."

"That's too temporary. And not everyone has access to that —I've never heard of it before, for example, and I've been in Seattle dating for years."

"You want bigger?" Madden asks in surprise.

"I want consequence. An actual one that will actually impact him."

They all fall silent when I need them to be their usual loud, overenthusiastic selves.

"Fine." I stand, midway through Monopoly Monday, and head for the front door. It's high time I paid Agatha a visit anyway, and hopefully, she'll be able to help with my wobbly thoughts.

I make my way to the house next door. It's bigger than ours, all original but kept in near perfect condition. Agatha is the queen of her little palace, but she's getting old, and I honestly don't know how much longer she'll be able to keep living here by herself. There are a lot of stairs, and statistically, she's at a higher risk of a fall by walking up and down them every day.

I knock on the door loud enough for her to hear me before letting myself inside. Warmth rushes through me. Familiarity and a sense of belonging aren't far behind it. There haven't been many places I fit in my life, but here is one of them.

"Is it someone come to murder me and steal all my things?" she shouts from a room down the hall.

"I could easily steal your things without having to murder you," I tell her as I reach the room she's sitting in reading.

"I'd put up a fight."

"It wouldn't be very effective."

Aggy tilts her head before dog-earing the book and tossing it aside. "What are you worried about?"

"Not so much worried as antsy."

She makes an understanding sound. "Is there anything you need my help with?"

"I'm still working that out." I climb onto the couch beside her and curl up at her side. "Can you hug me a bit?"

She laughs and wraps me into her boney arms. I frown at the prominence of her collarbone under my cheek.

"You're getting thin."

"No, I'm getting *old*."

"Not that old."

"I'm eighty next year, Rush. I never thought I'd make it that far, but because I have, I'd like a party. A big one. I've also already told the others, so if you forget, it's okay. We've got you covered."

Something heavy crosses my chest. "I don't forget important things."

"Of course you do, but that doesn't mean you don't love me." She pauses. "Have you reached out to your grandmother?"

"No."

"Do you want to?"

I bite the inside of my mouth. "She didn't want me when I was younger, and I haven't changed, but she's gotten older, so she definitely doesn't want me now." At one point, that made me sad. I felt alone for a very long time, but now I have a family and Aggy and Hunter.

Hunter.

"I think I'm in love."

"Well, that's nice."

I snigger quietly. "Don't you want to know about him?"

"I already know all about him. My lost boys are gossips, and I cook with Molly every week. I know the damn man's shoe size, for crying out loud."

"He's very special."

"I know."

"How?"

"Because he caught your interest."

If only she knew how wrong that was. "Ian caught my interest, and he was cheating on us both the whole time."

She squeezes me a little tighter, laugh full of the life it had when I first moved in here. "That man never had your interest. Got you into bed, sure. Strung you along, of course. But held your interest? Not even a tiny bit. You never once stopped by to tell me you were in love with him."

She's right about that, and I don't even know why exactly. I'd thought I was at the time. I'd thought Ian was amazing, and while we didn't talk or spend all our time together like Hunter and I do, I'd still thought I had it good.

No, you'd thought you finally found your match.

Like the thought has sucked the life out of me, I sit up, pulling away from her hold, trying to keep the tears back that are pushing at my eyes.

"I've never cared that I have ADHD," I tell her.

"I know." She eyes me. "But you do now?"

I go to shake my head and stop. "I think … I think that's what's getting to me. All this time, I've been focused on Hunter and how Ian screwed him over. But … he screwed me over too. And not about the cheating thing. He made me feel … he *lied* to me. Made me think I'd found someone who understood me because he was going through it too."

"He told you he had ADHD?"

Not in those exact words, but he knew what he was doing. "He made me trust him. He used it like it was a convenient excuse, and I didn't think I cared, but I do. He used who I am against me. That's not okay, Aggy. But he did it, and he gets to keep doing it. He gets to keep hurting people, and I hate it. He did it to me, and he's still doing it to Hunter, and he'll do it to other men who don't deserve it. I want to make it stop."

"You've always had a very strong moral compass."

"I don't like it."

She reaches over to squeeze my hand. "In a world where there is so much bad, it's one of the most valuable things to have."

"I want to be able to move on."

"Then work out how to do that."

I deflate, completely empty and powerless. "I don't know *how.*"

"Maybe not yet. But you will."

Chapter 29

Hunter

"Are you okay?"

Rush shifts again, looking even less put together than usual. His buttons aren't done up right, and when I tried to point it out to him, he popped the top one to fix them, got distracted by the elevator, and hasn't gone back to them again. His tie is crooked, his curls have a weird part going on, but more than his physical appearance, it's his eyes. Dazed. Unfocused. I want to take some of it away.

We reach our floor, and before Rush can break ahead to drop off Ted's coffee, I tug him around the corner into a nook out of sight of the main office. Then I unbutton his shirt quickly and match them up in order again.

When I'm done, I look up, hoping to find him watching me with that indulgent smile, but he's staring blankly into space instead. "There you go."

He smooths his free hand down the front of his shirt. "Right. Thank you."

Then he leaves me standing there as he makes his way across the office.

Even for Rush, that was weird.

It's not like I expected a kiss goodbye or anything like that, but one of his sweet looks wouldn't be too much to ask for, right?

I attack my thumbnail with my teeth the whole way to my office. If I'm going to be dating Rush, I need to understand that he might not always behave the way I want him to or how I'm used to. It's like any relationship, and we're still in the adjustment period. Still getting to know each other.

And this is a whole new side of him I get to learn about.

Except … all last night, and again this morning, the feeling that I'm missing something is sitting heavy over me. Rush said he needs guidelines, a set expectation so he knows how to behave, and I think I might need those as well. I don't just want to be dating him; I want to be his partner. I want to be able to rely on him when I need to and then return the support.

We never really talked about those days he spent in his atelier, if something triggered the reaction or how to handle it when it happens again. Because it will, if what his roommates had to say is any indication. That was definitely a situation where Rush needed something from me, but I have no idea what that something was.

It's not just those moments either.

It's days like today, where his mind is clearly elsewhere.

It's days like last week, where he can't physically make himself get through his work.

And he needs to know the same about me.

On days where I don't feel like enough, he needs to know how to handle me. How to calm those thoughts and bring me back to myself.

On days where I'm untethered and out of control—and those days are common at the moment—he needs to know how to ground me.

We have a lot of big conversations in our future.

The thing is, I'm confident we can tackle them.

All day, I'm treated to a view of Rush. It's different from what I'm used to. Less chaotic. He's at his desk for most of the day, sitting quietly, but I get the impression he's not actually working. He's too still. Too busy staring off across the bullpen or tapping his pen against his nose or completely engrossed in his phone.

He hasn't even *looked* at P.L. Ant, who I left on his desk this morning. Our poor baby is so neglected.

And my poor baby is struggling with something.

Throwing caution to the wind, once lunchtime rolls around, I leave my office and approach his desk.

"You free for lunch?"

He blinks at me for a moment, like he's struggling to work out what I said. "Ah, yeah." He chances a quick look at the others. "Do we have businessy things to discuss?"

"Sure." I make a mental note to invite the others for lunch at some point over the next week. "Let's go."

I'm hoping that leaving the office, at least for a short while, will get Rush back out of his head. There's a small sandwich shop across the street that we snag a table at before I go and order for us both. He's still quiet and vacant when I get back and sit across from him, but I get the feeling there's a lot going on in his head.

"Talk, Rush."

"What do you mean?"

I try to make my smile reassuring rather than sympathetic. "There's something bothering you."

"There's a lot of things bothering me. Like global warming. The water shortage. Whether I paid the gas bill on time—"

"Do those things usually make you distant?"

"Well, I'm never actually distant from me, so how would I know?"

I rub my temple, wondering how I get through to him. "How do I make what I'm saying clearer?"

Rush cocks his head. "Just say what you mean. It's very easy."

"Okay …" What do I mean? "You haven't been acting the way you usually do today, and that's okay, but it leaves me unsure about what my role is here."

"Your role?"

I nod. "Do I support you? Leave you alone? Push you to talk about it?"

Rush blinks a few times before focusing on my face. "You need guidelines."

"Usually when I'm in a relationship, these sorts of things feel intuitive. However, after what happened with Ian, I don't think I can trust those feelings anymore. I want to be your partner, and I want to make sure we're starting off right. If you can tell me what you need, I'll tell you what I need."

Instead of clearing up his expression, Rush's face pulls tight. I watch him pick at the edges of his sandwich, debating with himself over something. His lips twitch, but he still doesn't speak.

I reach across the table to wrap my hand around his. "We don't have to talk about it right now, but can you think about it? Maybe write a list so you don't forget?"

"Umm, yes. I think so."

"Good." But his words don't reassure me. Neither does the way he can't meet my eyes. Unease tries to creep over me as I consider the possibility I've been trying to ignore. That this caginess doesn't have anything to do with Rush and his thoughts … it's to do with me. Suddenly, the way we're holding hands feels stiff, so I pull away. "Is everything okay with us?" I force myself to ask.

"Yeah, totally, all fine. Everything is really, really so great."

The vague tone riding his words makes me question if he even heard me at all. Things have been going so well for us, and as far as I know, nothing has happened to change that.

But I guess it might be time to face the glaringly obvious.

I'm not a catch.

Rush has enough on his plate without worrying about me and my imploding life as well.

Things between us have been fun and fast, but it's a lot to expect him to stand by when we're so new. Is he over babying the man who can't find somewhere to live? Mad that he put himself in that terrible situation with Ian for me? Frustrated that between work and home, he can't escape me?

It would explain the feeling that he's pulling away. The lack of interest in our note passing.

A chill runs through me, and I wrap my sandwich back up, not able to stomach it. I don't want to get ahead of myself, but is this Seattle giving me another sign?

Because if I don't have Rush, what *do* I have?

I can't face the answer to that question.

Chapter 30

Rush

Lunch with Hunter is amazing, and the food tastes great, and I love his company, but I'm so in my thoughts that I don't get a second to really appreciate it. I wish this niggling would go away. Wish I could ignore the annoyance and focus on Hunter and how he makes me feel.

Which is perfect.

I'm not perfect—I don't think anyone is. I like me though, and I've never had an issue with who I am, but when I'm with Hunter, that feeling intensifies. I see me the way he sees me, and the way he sees me is pretty fucking great.

He's not turning everything into a way to get me into bed.

He's not trying to compete with my overactive brain for my attention.

Which is why I'm so, so boilingly indignant over the shit he's dealing with. My friends told me to tell him the truth, but scaring Hunter away isn't something I can do easily. He cares about me. I never knew how much I was missing that in a partner until I realized what it was really like.

Ian told me all the time that he cared.

Hunter shows me.

The difference between the two is glaringly obvious.

Hunter brought me out for lunch to show that he noticed I was off. That he *cared*.

My thoughts are still a storm cloud, nails digging into my fisted palms, when we step out of the elevator and back onto our floor, only to find Ted waiting for us.

"I'm sorry, I don't have a coffee for you today," I say, going to step around him. Ted smoothly moves to block our path.

"As much as I'd love a coffee, I was hoping to catch you two for a minute, if I could?"

"Of course," Hunter answers for us. "Everything okay?"

I glance up at him because why wouldn't it be? But his question and the slight hesitance in his tone … does he think everything is *not* okay?

Is this a situation where I should be worried but don't realize I should be?

"What's going on?" I ask, head swiveling from Hunter to Ted and back again.

"I just want a chat," Ted says.

I relax a little. We chat all the time.

Only when I fall into step beside Hunter, his usual easy conversation doesn't come. Neither do his smiles.

As soon as we step into Ted's office, I flop down into my usual chair and say, "I think Hunter's worried, so you should probably reassure him."

Ted's expression lightens slightly, but there's no reassurance as he sits.

I slowly straighten in the chair. "You said you wanted to chat."

"I do."

"Then why is there so much tension that even I can pick up on it?"

"This isn't an easy conversation—"

The blood drains from me. "Oh no. Am I fired? Is it because Hunter did all my work for me? Madden's truck won't make it across state lines …" Sweat is prickling under my arms as I consider how fast everything I love will unravel if I lose my job.

Ted holds up his hand. "You're not fired."

I relax for about a second before the implication hits me. "*Hunter* is? No way, man. He's the best boss we've ever had. If you fire him, I swear on my late-night infomercials that I'll never bring you another coffee again."

He almost rolls his eyes, but apparently, he's too professional to actually follow through. "Can I talk?"

"I don't think I'm going to like what comes out of your mouth."

Ted turns to Hunter as he pulls something out of his desk drawer. "I found this in your office."

The silk material is familiar. Too familiar. I recognize that tie because I made it. For me.

And left it in Hunter's office the night we fucked there.

I jump to my feet. "I object!"

Ted cocks an eyebrow. "Object to what?"

"You have no proof that's mine."

"Rush …" Hunter groans, and I swear Ted almost smiles.

"You wear this tie every week, and I'm guessing this is from the day you spilled my coffee on it because the mark is still there."

Okay, that makes it harder to argue with.

"What are you getting at?" Hunter asks as I sink back into my chair.

"I need hardly point out that an employee's tie left in your office is … not normal. Is there anything you want to tell me?"

I turn to Hunter with big eyes, begging him to think of a story. Any story. His dark eyes bore back, and I'm scared he's going to do something stupid like tell the truth. Us dating is iffy with work; fucking in his office is taking it to a whole new level.

"I'm very forgetful," I say before Hunter can reply. "I once left a sock in Hannah from accounting's drawer. You can't expect me to keep track of every item of clothing I have. It's not reasonable, Ted!"

His lips definitely twitch this time. "I want to help you, so let's cut the shit. What was your tie doing in his office on a night you both left very late? Yes, I have the logs for when you swiped out that night. I also have the ability to check your emails and interoffice messages. I don't want to do that. It might be in your contracts, but if there's anything personal in there, I don't want to know. I'd rather be able to trust my employees."

"We're dating," Hunter says like it's the most simple thing in the world. "Our next step was to bring it to you, honestly, but we weren't sure if things would work out. It's still very new, and we didn't want to cause headaches if it wasn't going to last."

I turn to Hunter with a frown. "You think we aren't going to last?"

He takes my hand. "We will if I have anything to say about it."

I'm not so sure I like that answer, but Ted smiles, so I guess he does.

"Thank you for telling me. In that case, we're going to have to work out what this looks like from a business perspective."

"How can you read my emails?" I ask.

Ted cuts off whatever he was saying. "Anything done through the company servers can be accessed if needed."

My heartbeat picks up at the thought of some of those emails. "Is that *legal?*"

"Yes. Like I said, it's in your contracts."

"That doesn't make it right!"

"Rush …" Hunter soothes, but I shake off his hand.

"Why does the company want to spy on us?"

Ted chuckles. "It's standard practice. In fact, I think you'd be hard-pressed to find a company these days that doesn't track their employees' communication. It means we can keep you all safe in case there's harassment going on, and it also keeps us on top of any potential illegal activities conducted at work. It's really good business sense."

Hunter says something I don't hear, and then they both fall into conversation that I want no part of. They track us. Our conversations. And it's all totally normal.

I think you'd be hard-pressed to find a company these days that doesn't track their employees' communication.

My gasp is so loud it fills the room. "You did it!" I jump to my feet, brain humming with satisfaction. "Ted, you clever, wonderful, smartastic man!" I half climb up onto his desk in order to lean over and smack a kiss on his forehead. "I love you!"

He chuckles. "What did I do?"

"You made everything make sense again. Oh my god, we need to go. Now. This is … this is …"

I feel like I'm floating on clouds as I leave the room, full of helium and hope.

If all businesses track communication, then wouldn't it make sense that the largest real estate agency in Seattle would as well? If Ian was stupid enough to blacklist Hunter with his own log-ins, surely his boss will be able to see that?

Blacklisting renters is illegal. E-fucking-legal.

I'm a few steps across the bullpen before I realize Hunter hasn't followed me. Doesn't he *know* how important this is? Why isn't he hurrying? We could have him in a home by tonight, goddammit.

Well, maybe not tonight, but we're on a mission.

I huff and retrace my steps to pop my head back into Ted's office.

They're both *sitting* there.

"Are you coming?" I ask Hunter.

He glances between me and Ted before a smile creeps over his handsome face.

He shrugs Ted's way. "Ah … I love you?"

"We can finish this conversation tomorrow," Ted says. Hunter's out of his seat in a flash, and Ted calls after us, "But I will expect an explanation."

"Where are we going?" Hunter asks, trailing me.

"To the future!" I throw my arm around his shoulders. "We're getting our revenge."

Chapter 31

Hunter

Savant Realty is on the corner, a large black and glass office that attempts to intimidate the street traffic below. They're the type of place that has billboards all over the city, Ian's face dominating a decent number of them, and at one point, I'd felt right at home attending their events with Ian.

Now, I wonder how many of his work friends knew about the other men as they smiled and shook my hand.

"I don't know what this is going to achieve," I say.

Rush's idea is a crapshoot at best. Yes, Ian had issues with his boss not wanting to promote him, but that doesn't mean anything.

"I struggled to get a promotion too," I mutter to Rush. "It doesn't mean it's anything personal. Sometimes there are just no positions."

A scowl crosses Rush's face. "He also told me he couldn't get a promotion because his boss hated how scattery he is. He made out like he was being left behind because he had ADHD. Sure, he never actually said the words, but it was always 'we're the same' and 'I know exactly how you feel' and 'you're so lucky to have a boss who understands.'"

"That does sound bad."

"He played me, and it sounds like he played you. He knew exactly what to say so we'd feel comfortable with him. Well, screw that. If his boss wouldn't promote him, there was a reason, and I doubt it's the same reason he gave either of us. Statistically, it's impossible. And besides, we have no other choice. So we might as well try this."

I let out a loud exhale and get the door for him. "After you."

And with all the confidence of a bull charging a red flag, Rush walks on in.

The foyer is large and glass, gleaming black desk bang in the middle, guarding the entrance to the halls behind. There are two receptionists: one woman on a Bluetooth headset and a man smiling toothily at us.

"Welcome to Savant Reality. What can I do for you?"

"We're here to see Davis Shore."

"Do you have an appointment?"

"No." Rush presses his palms to the desk. "But he'll meet with us if he knows what's good for him."

Yikes. I hurry to step in and pull Rush back. "If he can," I correct. "We appreciate he's a very busy man."

The guy drops his politeness. "He's booked out for weeks, sorry."

"It's five minutes."

"Sure. I can book you five minutes."

Rush perks up. "Really?"

"Three weeks from now, yeah."

I'm about to tell him not to worry about the receptionist on a power trip when Rush bursts out, "But then Ian will keep getting away with it! It's not fair it's not fair it's not fair."

The guy shushes Rush harshly before looking around. "What about Ian?"

"He's a cheating cheater who cheats, and he needs to get his comeuppance."

The guy leans in. "How do you know he's a cheater?"

"Because he was using *me* to cheat on *him*." Rush hooks his finger back over his shoulder toward me.

I wish I could evaporate from this situation.

Something in the man's face twitches. "I caught him with my best friend. After we'd been together a month."

"When was that?"

"Two weeks ago." The man types quickly on his computer. "I can get you five minutes, but I have to warn you: Shore won't care if you're here to rat him out for cheating. He brings a lot of money into this place."

"Good. We're not here about that."

"Best of luck, then." The man steps out from behind the desk. "Follow me."

We're led down a long, glossy hallway to an office right at the back. It has a shitty view over the street below, but everything inside, from the art to the desk to the plush carpet, looks expensive.

Shore is sitting behind his desk, clearly confused at us barging in here, but the moment he sees me, his expression clears up.

"Hunter, right?"

I hold out my hand. "That's me."

"Huh." His gaze strays to Rush. "I heard you and Ian parted ways."

"I bet you heard some not-so-nice things about me in the process."

Shore's lips tremble like he's trying not to laugh. "Didn't appear very upset about you cheating on him, I will say."

The noise that leaves Rush doesn't sound entirely human. "Hunter did *not* cheat on Ian. Ian cheated on *him*. And I know that for a fact because I'm the one he was using to do the cheating, only he was also cheating on me in the process."

I smile at Rush, even though we've obviously lost Shore. "Yes. All that. But also, you've seemed like a reasonable man the few times we met, and so I've come to you for help."

He waves toward his chairs across from his. "I have a meeting in a few minutes, so you'll need to make it fast."

I hurry to take the seat. "I've been in Seattle for a few months now, and I'm struggling to find a place to live."

He nods, eyes turning sympathetic. "Unfortunately, there's a housing shortage at the moment, but—"

"That's not it. Because we don't have much time, I'm going to lay it all out there. I called Ian for help—he at least owed me a favor—and not even to get a house, but to get my application in before it was already rented, and he all but admitted that he has me blacklisted."

Shore's attention sharpens. "What do you mean?"

"He wanted to make sure I couldn't stay in Seattle, and he's done a fantastic job of it."

"I tried to get him to admit it," Rush says. "But he wouldn't."

"So there's no proof?"

My gut sinks. "He basically confirmed it on a phone call."

"There's a difference between 'basically' and 'actually' though. I can't do anything about a hunch."

"Of course you can," Rush says, leaning forward. "It's enough of a reason to look into his emails and whatever else. Isn't that why companies track things like that? To make sure their employees aren't doing anything wrong?"

"And let's say I do that. What do you want?"

My shoulders sag. "The blacklisting removed. Talk to my previous real estate agent—there were no issues. I paid everything on time. I want to be able to find a place to live."

"And Ian?"

Rush goes to say something, but I cut him off. "I don't care about Ian. I don't care what happens to him. If it wasn't for him interfering with me finding a place to live, I'd be happy never thinking of him again."

"Well—"

The door to the office bangs open. "Make this fast, Davis. I have to …" Ian trails off when he glances up and sees me, and then his gaze shoots to Rush. The look that crosses his face is almost predatory. "What's going on here?"

"None of your business," I answer at the same time as Rush says, "I've always been so interested in meeting Shore, seeing as how he won't promote you because of the ADHD."

"ADHD?" Shore echoes.

"Yes." Rush turns big eyes on him. "It's one of the things Ian and I bonded over. And how you actively discriminate against him because of it."

"That's enough," Ian snaps.

Shore frowns. "Do you have ADHD? This is the first I'm hearing about this."

Ian's face twists. "I already warned you about Hunter. Now he's brought some random man with him as well. You need to call security."

"That didn't answer my question." Shore's voice has turned icy.

"Because it's not a question worth my time answering."

Rush's hand shoots into the air. "I have messages. Ian canceling on me because he needs to meet with Davis over his 'issues.'"

"Issues?" Shore repeats.

Rush nods fast. "And how he's sick of the harassment at work for being so forgetful."

"I'd like to see these messages."

Something on Rush's face twitches, which reminds me … Molly's been deleting his messages from Ian. He's bluffing.

I glance at Ian. "You sure you want that? Your employer seeing blatant proof of what a slimeball you are?"

Ian's face reddens. "You need to call security. Last time I saw him—" He points right at me. "He assaulted me."

"You assaulted Rush."

"How the fuck would you know?"

"Because he's my boyfriend, asshole."

"He's *what?*"

Before I can answer, Shore's voice cuts through the argument. "I've had enough. This is *my* business, and I will not allow it to fall into some *Days of Our Lives* melodrama."

"Understandable." Rush jumps to his feet. "We'll take our concerns higher."

"Stop." Shore turns to Ian. "Hunter claims you've blacklisted him. For no reason. Now, I'm going to be reaching out to some people to get to the bottom of this, and if I find you've used personal shit to ruin a man's life, you'll be out of here. This is my company, my brand, my name. You know my expectations. And as for this ADHD business—"

"He's lying."

"He better be. Because if you're going to bring me up on harassment, there had better be some goddamn evidence."

"I would never."

"Good."

"I'm the face of this company," Ian pushes. "I'd never do anything to hurt it, and the fact you're choosing to believe two … two … *burned exes* instead of one of the highest-ranked salesmen in your company is insulting."

"No, what's insulting is two of your *burned exes* barging into my office and making claims against you. I am *pissed*, Ian, that I'm having to deal with this today. So no, I won't be taking their word on it. I won't be taking yours either. I will be running checks on Hunter myself, and if they come back as anything other than squeaky-clean, I'll be making some calls. You better hope no one so much as utters your name."

"You can't …"

"Can and will. You can all see yourselves out. I now have a busy afternoon ahead of me."

I jump immediately out of the seat, and Rush follows me, hand slotting into mine on the way to the door. His expression is as conflicted as I feel because it's hard to know how that went. Shore seems like a good guy, the kind who wants things kept aboveboard, but how the hell would I know if he'll actually help or just cover up what Ian is doing?

I wish I could have pushed more, but—

I'm shoved so hard from behind I fly into the wall. My face smacks against plasterboard, and a thick arm presses against the back of my neck.

"How fucking dare you," Ian hisses. "Happy now? He's going to fire me. You know how hard I've worked for this job, how I've done everything I can to be the best. And then you come in here making up lies—"

I try to throw him off me. "If it's a lie, he won't find a reason to fire you, will he?"

"Fuck you." He shoves me again. "All you've done is ruin my goddamn life. I hope you're happy when I'm homeless. When I have no job. Nothing. All because of you."

At one point, maybe I would have believed him. Thought that in some way it was my fault, but now? All I want to do is laugh in his face. He'll never see himself as the problem. He'll never take accountability. And *damn* do I thank the universe that Rush showed up that night because not only did it bring us together, but it also got me far, far away from Ian.

"…thought you might be interested in seeing this," comes Rush's voice.

Ian immediately drops his grip, and when I glance back, Shore is in the hallway, jaw somewhere around his ankles.

"Home. Now."

"But—"

"No. You're suspended until further notice. *Assaulting* someone in *my* office?" Shore looks like he's about to breathe steam. "Get out."

Ian shoves me one last time before leaving. The three of us stand there watching him go.

"Are you okay?" Shore asks.

"I'm …"

"No." Rush whirls to face Shore. "He's not okay. He's emotionally and physically wounded. Without a home to return to, I don't see him being able to recover."

Shore eyes Rush for a moment, then glances back at me. "Excellent rental history, you say?"

"Perfect. No missed payments, everything maintained and looked after."

"Do you have the number for the last people you rented through?"

"I do."

"Right." Shore heads to reception and talks to the man who showed us to his office. "Make a meeting for Hunter to see Jodie, please."

"No problem."

Shore nods at us. "She'll sort you out." Then he heads back to his office, and the receptionist looks our way. "I take it things went well?"

"Other than being attacked, I think it might have," I say. "From the looks of things, you might not have to deal with Ian for long yourself."

The guy grins. "I was hoping he'd show his ass if he saw you both. It's why I told him Shore wanted to see him."

"Wait. He wasn't Shore's next meeting?"

"Nope." The guy sighs happily. "Revenge sure is sweet."

"It will be when I have a place to live."

"Oh, look at that. Something with Jodie magically opened up. Follow meeee."

I glance over at Rush, and he glances at me. Is this really fucking happening?

He reaches over to squeeze my hand. "Let's go."

We go, and I try like hell not to get my hopes up.

Chapter 32

Rush

Hunter grips my face, walking me backward into his room, punctuating every word with a kiss. "You are—" Kiss. "The most incredible—" Bite. "Man I've ever—" Suck. "Met."

I lean in, seeking his mouth with my own. His big hands warm my cheeks and send my brain fizzy. "Show me how incredible you think I am."

Today went better than I ever would have thought it could. Jodie was amazing and has a list of houses lined up for Hunter to see already, along with her assurance that if his history is as squeaky-clean as he says, he'll get first pick of the bunch.

My heart couldn't be happier. And neither could my brain now that prodding and poking has stopped.

Hunter groans right as my legs hit the side of his mattress. "The things I want, Rush."

A tremble washes through my limbs. "Like?"

"Like … getting to know you inside and out. Discovering what makes you happy and protecting you from what makes you sad. Proving to you every day how amazed I am that I met you, let alone get to spend this time together."

"Not the dirty talk I was expecting, but carry on."

Hunter's body shakes with laughter beside mine. "Fuck, you make me happy."

"Really?"

"Yeah. Every day."

"I know that most people don't value happiness all that highly, but for me, it's everything. Thank you for saying that."

"Thank you for making me be able to. You know, for a second, during lunch, I thought maybe you were getting sick of me."

"Why the heck would you think that?"

"You just didn't seem to want to be around me."

I'm quick to shake my head. "I was distracted. Annoyed. For you, not at you."

"I know." He squeezes me. "And I'm glad that's a new thing I got to learn about you."

I drop my forehead to his temple, grinning against his jaw. "You're very sweet and romantic, but can we get onto the dirty talk now?"

His deep growl fills my ears. "Fine. We're getting naked and getting off. My cock is going in your pretty hole, but before I do that, tell me something."

I hum as I pull back and Hunter brushes my hair off my forehead.

"Do you ever want to top me?"

I check his face, trying to read it for signs of what he wants, but there are none. I don't think. "That's a tough question."

"Why?"

"Because it's not straightforward. Do I *want* to? Sure. I

want everything with you. But, well, I'm a big guy. Sometimes after all the stretching, it still hurts, and when I know the guy I'm with isn't enjoying it, it's a buzzkill. Topping feels good, but I've sort of grown to hate it."

His brown eyes soften. "We can work on that. If you want to."

"I'm not sure yet. Do I need to give you an answer right now?"

"Nope." Hunter wraps his hands around my thighs and hefts me off my feet. I scramble to grab hold of his wide shoulders while I wrap my legs around his waist. "Right now, I'm going to fuck you. Probably tomorrow too. And maybe the next day and the next, right up until you don't want me to anymore. And if you ever want to switch things around, you'll let me know, okay?"

"Of course."

"Good." His kiss is firm. "There are no rules, baby. We make our own."

"I like the sound of that."

"Me too."

Hunter lays me back on the bed before crawling up to blanket me. We touch from hips to chest, a delicious warmth burning between us as Hunter slowly writhes his body against mine. His hard body is such a turn-on, his control of his movements, his rigid cock meeting mine with every measured rut of his hips. He's breathing deeply into my mouth, and I'm catching every exhale, swallowing the sound and the building desire taking over us both.

"Need you naked," he complains.

I'm with him there. While this is great, it'd be way better to have all bare skin around me.

I growl in frustration as I work to unbutton his shirt, then move on to mine. Hunter helps, shoving it off my shoulders and down my arms before flinging it somewhere across the room.

The hotel sheets are stiff under my back, impossible to get a good grip on as Hunter plunges a hand into my pants. I arch up into his touch, rubbing my cock into his palm, panting over how good it feels and how it's not enough.

"You know," he says, kissing a brain-tingly line along my jaw, "I've been all in with you since the start. Felt in my bones how right this was. Trusted you before I knew I trusted you. But this is the first time I've let myself actually believe things will work out."

I frown, pulling back far enough to meet his eyes. "What do you mean?"

"In the back of my head, I've always had that doubt that I'm going to make it here. That lingering idea that I'm going to have to run home defeated, and no matter how I feel about you, long distance wouldn't work. Not after what happened. But now … I have a place. Somewhere I can belong, at least for now. Which means I can give our relationship everything, without holding back."

Holding back? This man already gives me everything. "I never doubted you." His hand tightens around my length, making my body fizz. "Not ever. You're the type of person who wants something done, and you do it. It's so confusing and amazing to me. I'll never fully understand you, but I don't have to to know that …" My throat gets all sticky.

"Rush?"

"I might be falling for you a little bit. Or a lot. It's hard for me because my other relationships have all been a steamy pile of turd turkeys—"

"Turd turkeys?" His eyes crease with amusement.

"Seven."

"Of course."

"My point is that I've thought I felt things before, but now that I know what a real partner is, what it really feels like to be cared about, I'm scared of how deep this feeling is going to go. I'm scared of what happens if you get sick of me. If I'm too much, or—"

His lips press hard and claiming to mine. "You will never, ever be too much."

"Yeah, I'm sure my grandma felt the same, and yet, I was."

His smile curls out against my mouth. "Let me be clearer. All those things about you that you think are too much are the things I love most. I'm sure we'll get frustrated with each other because it's what all couples do, but one of the most refreshing things about you is that you talk about things. You don't play games. And you expect the same from me. There's still a lot we both have to learn about each other, but goddammit, Rush, I'm excited to learn those things. Nothing in my life has ever felt this right."

My heart feels so big that it's competing for attention with my cock.

"Love?"

Hunter exhales steadily, eyes soft. "Maybe. It's soon, I know, but I think I'm headed that way. Fast."

My hands shake as I cup his face. "I think I'm headed that way fast as well."

His mouth comes down on mine, lips soft, tongue hard and desperate as he kisses me so deep that my toes curl. I never want this to stop, but also, I really, really need to get off.

My heart is as horny as the rest of me.

"I need you," I rasp, reaching for his belt.

He waits while I undo it and then pushes his pants and underwear down and off. His red, swollen cock points right at me, the sight making mine throb.

Hunter leans in to run his mouth up my length. His warm

breath is caught by the cotton of my pants, wrapping around my heated skin and making me crave more.

"Pants off, please."

The smile he gives me is sinful. But he does as I asked and *slowly* opens my fly and drags my pants down. Then he holds my gaze as he sucks the crown of my cock into his mouth through my underwear.

It feels good but nowhere near what I need. "Why do you hate me?" I complain.

And when Hunter does nothing to fix the problem, I take matters into my own hands.

"Nope. Nuh-uh. I know how you work." I push him off me and onto his back before I straddle his hips. Then I hook my underwear under my balls and give my cock a good stroke. Hunter looks up at me, clearly amused, but I don't care.

He likes things slow.

Today, I'm too impatient for slow.

I spit into my hand and jerk off over the top of him.

"I thought I told you that's my job?" he asks.

"I can touch my own dick if I want to."

"As long as you're only doing it because you *want* to." He glances down at my hand working over my cock and licks his lips. "If you really, really want to be touching yourself instead of fucking my mouth, that's totally your choice."

Oh. Damn.

I scramble out of my underwear so I can straddle his chest and then press my leaking tip to his lips. "Open sesame?"

He laughs, and I sink inside. Hunter's mouth closes around me, sucking hard, licking wet stripes over my sensitive tip. I push inside until my balls hit his chin, and seeing his lips stretched obscenely around me does something deep in my gut.

I pull out, and he sucks in a deep breath.

"Fuck, you're big," he gasps.

"If your mouth can't even take me, how do you expect your ass to?"

"I'd make it work."

Pure sweet floods through me. "You would, wouldn't you?"

"Yup. Now I'm interested to see what you think is going to happen now you're up there."

"Sex." That's about as far as I've gotten. Crazy, wild sex. Sex that will leave me bowlegged for days.

I lean over to his nightstand and grab the lube and some condoms, then pour out a generous amount on my hand. I reach back to work myself open, then slide my cock back into his mouth again. This time, I don't try to go deep, just lazily press the tip in over and over, trying not to come at the way his tongue teases my slit.

When I'm ready, I pull my fingers out and slide back down the bed while Hunter rolls on a condom. Then he grabs my ass cheeks, the grip firm and possessive and fucking delightful.

"You good there?" I ask.

"Just helping." He flexes his hips so his cock nudges my hole.

"You're almost as impatient as I am."

"No one is as impatient as you are."

"True. I want to keep teasing you, but there's no physical way that's possible." I need to be filled, and I need it now. I grab his cock, holding it in place, as I lower slowly down onto it. The fat head splits me open as I sink down further and further until Hunter is completely inside me.

There's no greater feeling than being stuffed full of his cock. To be able to clench down around him, have him pressing that amazing spot deep in my ass, and know that I get to come this way. Sure, topping feels good, but it doesn't have the same satisfaction of being stimulated from both sides, and even if I could top easily, I still don't think that would be my preference.

My hips rock forward an inch, and a little *"oh"* falls from my lips.

It's like he was made for me, every part of his body perfectly fitting every part of mine.

I build up the pace, bouncing up and down on his cock, drowning in the sparks setting off all the way through my limbs. My brain is swimming in lust, drowning in horniness, cock bobbing with every movement, begging to be touched. The more I move, the more I become a disjointed puddle of pleasure.

I'm about to reach down and give my dick some relief when Hunter's big hand wraps around me. His palm is full of his spit, leaving his fist a perfect tunnel for me to fuck into. Between his cock pummeling my ass and his hand tightening around my cock, I'm in heaven.

Limb-buzzing heaven.

"Now, this is a view," he rasps.

Hunter's dark eyes burn out at me from under heavy lids. The intense stare makes me feel so wanted, so claimed. I push myself faster, ride him harder, and as I do, Hunter moves to meet me. The sound of skin slapping against skin fills his little hotel room.

It's intense and fast and sweaty and consuming. The way I need him inside of me. The way even fucking doesn't feel like close enough sometimes. My head and my heart are fuzzy and full, whole body tuned into Hunter.

The way he grunts through clenched teeth. The way his fingers crush my ass cheeks. How his other hand slides over my tip, driving me so out of my mind that my balls are tight and painful. I'm torn between whether I want more pressure on my prostate or to fuck his fist harder, and I alternate between the two, sluttily taking everything I can from him.

"You've gotta come, Rush. Come on, baby, put me out of

my misery." It's nice to hear him beg for a change. For him to be the desperate one.

I grind down onto him as hard as I can, taking his cock deeper than ever, sinking into the feel of him jerking me off.

Every nerve ending is singing, alive, begging for more. I bite my fist, so fucking close, grinding my hips over and over and over.

"*Fuck.*"

My cock throbs, release bursting from me as my balls pulse in time with each shot. I'm a sizzling, bubbling mess when Hunter pulls out, flips us so I'm on my back, and pushes back inside me again.

He fucks me hard and fast, like a man possessed. Knowing he can't help himself makes my cock try to perk up again, but I need at least a couple of minutes. Hunter doesn't have that long left in him. Every muscle strains as he holds himself up over me, sending my ass higher with the force of his thrusts, and then I watch as his gorgeous shoulders tighten and he growls through his release.

Hunter collapses on top of me, all sweat-slick skin and heated muscle covering me from neck to ankle. My arms twist around his back, holding him tight, pressing us closer until we're molded together as one.

"You sure know how to fuck a guy," I murmur into his neck.

"Just you. Fucking you is my favorite thing."

"Good, because you're going to be doing it a lot, just a heads-up."

"Thanks for the warning." I can hear his smile in his words. Feel it in my gut. I try to remember a time when I've ever been this happy and come up empty. When I was a kid, probably, but those memories with my parents are hazy. Moving in with Aggy was heavy with the anxiety that I was going to annoy her too, and while I love my roommates, my brothers, it's nothing like this.

I have a person.

A person who's all mine.

Who doesn't play games and make me second-guess. I never knew how much I needed Hunter, but I do now.

And if he maybe loves me too, I'm not ever letting him go.

Chapter 33

Hunter

Eight months later

"It's not right," Rush squeaks, tugging at the sleeve of the ugly Christmas sweater I'm wearing. I glance down at our matching outfits, trying to pin what it is he's stressing about. My sweater is red and knitted, with a silky red strip running down both arms. It has ridiculous reindeer with bells on the front that, when next to Rush's midnight-blue sweater, are positioned to look like they're pulling the sleigh Rush has on his.

He's been working all week on these and the ones he gave his roommates, and while I always worry for him when he gets so hyperfixated that he forgets the rest of the world, it was also nice to be the one to look after him.

The last year has been a real adjustment period for us both, but with Ian fired from the real estate job and hiding out nursing his wounds, we've finally just been able to focus on each other. Nothing else.

Before Rush can get too in his head again about details, I loop my arm around his waist and crush him against me.

"I know what you're forgetting."

"You do?"

I watch the way his eyes finally focus and hold up a sprig of mistletoe.

Rush melts against me. "Sorry. I was fussing."

"I love your fussing," I assure him, leaning in to kiss him. Rush immediately tries to deepen things, but I cut it off. "My parents will be here any minute."

His face falls. "Are you sure you want them to meet me?"

"We've been over this."

"No, I know …" His gaze drops as he absentmindedly plays with the bells on my chest. "I'm just saying that if you need me to hide out up here, I'll understand."

"Are you embarrassed?"

"No! I mean, yes, the last time I saw them, I *was* dressed like a slutty little elf, and they've probably seen more of me than I've ever wanted my potential future in-laws to see, but that's not it. It's not *ideal*, but …"

"Talk to me."

He sighs, clinging to me tighter. "I've never met someone's parents before. I'm scared. We both know I don't make the best first impression, and you love them, and what if they think I'm not good enough for you? What if they hate me because of what happened? I want to make you happy, and if they don't like me, it's not going to make you happy, is it?"

My heart breaks for him. I hate that Rush hasn't had the most supportive family structure and that even now, years later, he still feels like a burden on people.

I've told my family all about him, and while, yeah, they were hesitant about the whole situation initially, they promised to keep an open mind. The more they've gotten to know him through me, the more they've warmed to him, and I know that they're as excited to meet him as I am for them to.

Sure, there's still a smidge of wariness with them when it comes to me being in *any* relationship after what happened, but I know them. I know Rush. One meeting is all it'll take for them to love him completely.

Audrey already does.

"I'm not worried at all. There isn't a single thing about you that they won't like."

"You're … you're sure?"

"More than sure. I'm so damn excited that I get to introduce you to them as mine. I'm not sure what I did to deserve you, but it still hits me sometimes. This deep gratefulness that I get to call you mine."

"Thank you."

"For what?"

"Loving me as I am."

I drop a kiss on his forehead. "It's the exact same way you love me."

There's a knock from downstairs, and a moment later, heavy footsteps jog down to get it. From being in this house so much, I can pick them as Seven's, and while we've become really close friends, I also don't want him giving my straitlaced parents a heart attack before they get a chance to meet Rush.

"We better go down."

"Yes. Down. Right." He pulls away from me, eyes zeroing in on my sleeve, and before he can doubt and second-guess and work himself into anxiety, I grab his hand and tug him from the room.

"The sweater is fine."

"*Fine?*" His face falls, and I almost laugh.

"It's amazing. I just mean there's nothing wrong with it."

"What if they don't like that?"

My parents? Oh, they'll hate them. Ugly Christmas sweaters aren't something they've ever been interested in, but I know they'll be polite, and when it comes down to it, they'll appreciate that Rush took his time to make them.

There's no one in the hall downstairs, so we follow it through the house to the backyard, where the party is being held. It's a rare cloudless day, still cold as balls with a weak sun, but we got lucky after the rain that's been falling all week.

Rush grips my hand, and I turn to him. "I can't believe how many people are here."

"What do you mean?"

"Well, for so long, there was only us Bertha Boys and Aggy. Penn, mostly. But that was it. Now ..."

I glance around at the full backyard. All of Rush's roommates are here, along with their partners. Aggy, of course, and then ... "Who *are* all these people?"

"You've met Gabe but not his boyfriend. Aleks plays hockey, so he doesn't get around a lot. The two men with them are partners and work with Gabe. Then Elle is Émile's sister, and the man with her is Darcy Ritcherson." He points to an older man with long dark hair. "That's Molly's dad and Molly's best friend, who is also dating his dad—"

"Wow."

"Yep, and—*oh*." Rush's voice goes up a notch. "Those two people heading our way must be your parents."

I tighten my hand in his. "All I need you to focus on is breathing."

"Right."

"Properly."

"Okay."

My parents reach us, and I let Rush go for a moment to pull them into a hug. Mom squeezes the life out of me, and Dad isn't much better, but almost as soon as we part, their curious attention moves to Rush.

My gut is swimming with nerves and happiness as I set a hand on his back. "This is—"

"Rush! It's about time we got to meet you," Mom says. "Do you like hugs?"

"Well, that really all depends on the hug. Some are very awkward and lifeless."

She blinks at him for a second, and I almost laugh.

"Better make sure it's not awkward and lifeless, Mom."

Mom scowls my way before pulling Rush in for a hug like her life depends on it. She whispers something to him that I miss, but whatever it is makes him smile, so I'm okay with letting them have that moment.

When they pull away, Rush nods. "Your hugs are good."

"I passed." She pretends to flick her hair back.

"I'm just going to shake your hand instead," Dad says, reaching out.

"Better not make it awkward," Mom teases.

I steer them away from the back door. "There are plenty of other people for you to meet. No need to crowd my boyfriend."

"Yeah, if you think you're getting away from the embarrassing stories that easily, you're mistaken."

Ehh. She can bring out all the embarrassing stories she likes. I *want* Rush to know them all.

As soon as they're gone, I turn to check in with him.

"How are you feeling?"

"Great. Amazing. That was good, right?"

"That was very good."

I watch as relief floods over him. "I've been so anxious."

"I know." I pluck at the front of my sweater. "But we got through it."

"Think I should grab my presents for them now?"

"Whenever you're ready. Don't feel like you have to babysit them all day though, okay?"

He sends me a cheeky grin. "Are you kidding? They have *embarrassing stories*. They're not leaving until I hear them all."

He ducks back inside to grab the presents, and I look out across the yard. From what Rush has said, the group is twice the size as it used to be, and I'm honestly not surprised. From the first moment I stepped into Big-Boned Bertha, I felt at home, welcome, comfortable. Rush and his brothers might have had a hard time of it growing up, but it's shaped who they are now. And who they are now is pretty incredible.

I've gotten close with them all over the last year, and if the newcomers are anything like me, we're happy to be included. To be welcome in this bubble where judgment doesn't exist. Just support. Respect. Understanding.

My place right here is what I was fighting for all along.

Seven appears at my side and holds out a beer. "It's cold as balls out here."

"It's December. We're just lucky it didn't rain."

"True. Even Madden's wearing a sweater."

"Yeah, but is it because he's cold or because Rush gave it to him?"

"Either way, no one is in danger of being poked in the eye by his nipples."

"I … umm. I'm thinking of asking Rush to move in with me." I can't look at Seven after getting the words out. The guys are close; I'd never want to get between them, but after renting a place I wasn't feeling for six months, last month, I moved into a place that I can see myself staying in long term.

And I can see Rush there with me.

"Wow," he mutters.

"I know. I don't know what he's going to say, and I'm worried about him feeling torn about whether he wants to stay here or—"

"Nah, I don't think you need to worry about any of that." Seven smiles wide. "You ask, he'll be there in a flash. He'll always have his atelier here, even if he moves out. Once a Bertha Boy, always a Bertha Boy." Seven nods toward Gabe. "No matter where we live, we're family. You too."

"Me?"

"We ganged up on your ex together. We're bonded for life, my friend."

I knock my beer against his. "I did *not* see my life ending up here."

"None of us did. But the good news is we're just getting started. Ask him. Rush deserves it."

And those three words magically take the worry away. They reframe my worry about stealing Rush from his friends to comfort that Seven thinks I'm the best thing for Rush. And with how protective Seven is of people, it makes me believe it.

"I'll do it tonight."

Seven grabs me in a side hug. "In that case, pre-congratulations. And also, pre-warning. I will *not* be helping move. I love you both, but moving can go to hell."

"Uh-huh, we'll see."

"I swear, man. Not happening."

I hug him back. "Let's see what Molly has to say about that."

Seven groans, and I know I've got him. No way in hell will Molly not want to help, and if he's helping, so will Seven.

"Mols doesn't control me."

"Sure. Not intentionally."

The big man scowls and walks away, all but confirming my point. He can pretend to hate it all he likes; I know him better than that.

Our early Christmas is amazing. I meet extended friends, catch up with my parents and Audrey, suck up to Aggy over her Christmas pudding, and even manage to get Kismet to stop hissing at me long enough to feed him treats.

And that night, when everyone leaves and it's just Rush and me, lying in his bed, room awash with moonlight, I ask him.

His eyes shine up at me as he answers with the most perfect word I've ever heard.

"Yes."

Epilogue

Hunter

"Goddammit, Rush. You didn't tell me what a bathroom hog you were before you moved in," I call through the locked door.

The shower is running, and he's got a podcast playing over the sound of the water. He said he'd stop locking the door. He always forgets.

The water cuts off, and the podcast follows it.

"Sorry! I'm coming!"

His panicked tone instantly makes me warm. It's frustrating that I can never stay mad at him, but it makes things so much easier. We'll have a little bicker, and then he gives me that sweet smile of his that's my weakness, and we move on. Usually to fucking.

And that one argument helps us learn another piece about each other.

He appears, surrounded by steam, towel gripped at his

waist, looking guilty as hell. "In my defense, if I didn't lock the door at home, someone would always walk in. You try jerking off while your roommate is brushing his teeth right beside you."

I cock my eyebrow. "You jerked off?"

"No, I don't need to do that *now*. I'm saying I do it without thinking, and to stop doing it, I have to actively think about not doing it. Do you know how impossible that is?"

I kiss him, hook a finger in the front of his towel, and flick it open. The material drops to the floor.

"From now on, you can apologize by opening the door naked."

"Noted."

I pass him into the bathroom and pluck my toothbrush out of the cup sitting next to P.L. Ant, but my gaze catches on Rush in the mirror. He leans against the doorframe, gorgeous golden body on display. But it doesn't hold my attention. Not when his face looks like that.

I spit my toothpaste into the sink. "You need to tell me something."

"Yes."

"Shoot." Where I used to feel nervous or on edge when I'd see that expression, I've learned. It doesn't mean Rush is having second thoughts about us. His hesitation to tell me things doesn't come from not knowing how I'll react or it being bad news; it comes from him not knowing how to phrase things.

"I don't like forgetting things."

"Okay."

"I don't like being behind all the time."

"Is there anything I can do to help?"

He quickly shakes his head. "I think it's something I need to do."

I set my toothbrush aside and turn to him so he knows he has my full attention. This overthinking explains the longer-than-normal shower this morning. "What is it?"

"I think I want to try meds again."

"Really?" It's something we've talked about a few times, and I'd had the feeling we might be heading in that direction, but I've been clear that I'll support him in whatever he decides.

Rush sighs. "I really hated it last time, and I'm scared of the side effects like losing my creativity again, but I've been talking to some people online who said it makes a huge difference once they find the right balance. A lot of people didn't have any issues with their creativity at all. Maybe I gave up too fast last time."

I close the distance between us and draw him into a hug. I recognize that tone. His need for support. "Just tell me what you need from me. Maybe you try again and hit the right balance. Maybe you don't."

"And if I don't?"

"Then we continue exactly as we always have."

"What if we do and you don't like me anymore?"

My laugh is so loud it bounces off the tile. "And what if a meteor hits me on the way to work today? We've faced so many things together worse than a bit of drug experimenting. Let's take it as it comes, okay? Talk to your doctor. That's the first step. I'm not going anywhere. Meds or no meds, our life together is fucking perfect, Rush. That's the one thing I don't want you to ever forget."

His smile is so pure it lights up the room. "With you, I never, ever could."

THANK YOU SO MUCH FOR READING!

Too impatient to wait for what's next? I have early chapters, character art, and bonus content here: https://geni.us/saxonpatreon

Look out for Madden's book, coming late 2024.

Author's Note

Thanks so much for reading these gorgeous guys!

The fact you keep showing up for me, release after release, means the absolute world! My dream has always been to have a career as an author and it's mind-blowing to me that I get to live it.

If you're a lover of signed paperbacks, special editions, audiobooks or merch, don't forget to check out my store.

You can find it through the link or QR code: www.saxon-jamesauthor.com

My Freebies

Do you love friends to lovers?
Second chances or fake relationships?
I have two bonus freebies available!

Friends with Benefits
Total Fabrication
Making Him Mine

This short story is only available to my reader list so follow the
below and join the gang!

https://www.subscribepage.com/saxonjames

Other Books By Saxon James

ACCIDENTAL LOVE SERIES:

The Husband Hoax

Not Dating Material

The Revenge Agenda

FRAT WARS SERIES:

Frat Wars: King of Thieves

Frat Wars: Master of Mayhem

Frat Wars: Presidential Chaos

DIVORCED MEN'S CLUB SERIES:

Roommate Arrangement

Platonic Rulebook

Budding Attraction

Employing Patience

System Overload

NEVER JUST FRIENDS SERIES:

Just Friends

Fake Friends

Getting Friendly

Friendly Fire

Bonus Short: Friends with Benefits

RECKLESS LOVE SERIES:

Denial

Risky

Tempting

CU HOCKEY SERIES WITH EDEN FINLEY:

Power Plays & Straight A's

Face Offs & Cheap Shots

Goal Lines & First Times

Line Mates & Study Dates

Puck Drills & Quick Thrills

PUCKBOYS SERIES WITH EDEN FINLEY:

Egotistical Puckboy

Irresponsible Puckboy

Shameless Puckboy

Foolish Puckboy

Clueless Puckboy

STAND ALONES WITH EDEN FINLEY:

Up in Flames

The Bastard and The Heir

FRANKLIN U SERIES (VARIOUS AUTHORS):

The Dating Disaster

And if you're after something a little sweeter, don't forget my YA pen name

S. M. James.

These books are chock full of adorable, flawed characters with big hearts.

https://geni.us/smjames

Acknowledgments

As with any book, this one took a hell of a lot of people to make happen.

The cover was created by the talented Rebecca at Story Styling Cover Designs with a gorgeous image by Michelle Lancaster, and edits were done by Sandra Dee at One Love Editing, with Lori Parks proofreading the bejeebus out of it.

Thanks to @capt.christine and @lis_photoart on IG for creating amazing artworks for my website editions.

Charity VanHuss you're the most amazing PA I could have ever dreamed up. Without you I'd be even more of a chaotic disaster and there isn't enough space to list the many hats you wear for me. Paige Treff and Lara Janz, you round out my team in the most incredible way and I'm always excited to see what fun ideas you both have next.

Eden Finley, thank you for being there for all the doubt spirals and hand-holding. Whether you wanted to be or not.
AM Johnson, Becca Jackson, Louisa Masters and Riley Hart thank you so much for taking the time to read. Your support is incredible and I really appreciate it!

Along with my beta readers who looked out for Rush's ADHD accuracy, I also want to thank Kitt Dobry, Rebecca Appleton and Willow Thomas for their sensitivity read as well. Your insight was invaluable.

And of course, thanks to my fam bam. To my husband who constantly frees up time for me to write, and to my kids whose neediness reminds me the real word exists.